SPLINTERED LIGHT

Other titles by Cate Sampson

CARNABY

SPLINTERED LIGHT

CATE SAMPSON

SIMON AND SCHUSTER

First published in Great Britain in 2014 by Simon and Schuster UK Ltd
A CBS COMPANY

1 3 5 7 9 10 8 6 4 2

Simon & Schuster UK Ltd
1st Floor, 222 Gray's Inn Road
London
WC1X 8HB

Simon & Schuster Australia, Sydney
Simon & Schuster India, New Delhi

A CIP catalogue record for this book is available from the British Library.

PB ISBN: 978-1-4711-1583-7
EBook ISBN: 978-1-4711-1584-4

Printed and bound by CPI Group (UK) Ltd, Croydon, CR0 4YY

www.simonandschuster.co.uk
www.simonandschuster.com.au

For James, Alistair, Rachel, Kirsty, Pete and Tom at the end of our Beijing era and the beginning of the new.

For dear Beijing friends, especially Annabelle, Antonia, Carrie (again!), Helen, Jen, Jo, Kathy, Laura, Lucy, Patty and Pia. And for Prudence and Danna, who are – and always will be – like family.

PROLOGUE

The girl lies fast asleep on her back with her arms flung above her head as though she's been surprised. She hasn't pulled the curtains, and light from the street falls upon her face. If someone were to stand in her room and look down on that face, they would see her eyelids flickering with the rapid eye movement of deep, dreaming sleep. They would notice, even in this weak light, that one of those eyelids is dissected by a faded scar that runs from her forehead through the eyelid, and then to the cheek below. It's a miracle that the slicing blade left the eyeball intact.

Shrunk to child-size, deep in her dream, the girl's tiny hand is clasped inside her dream-mother's and she's dragged along the green path.

'Hurry up! It's teatime. Hurry up! Hurry up!'

The girl digs her tiny toes into the gravel path, and in the same instant her sixteen-year-old toes twitch against the sheets.

'I don't want to go home!'

Gargantuan oak trees form a green-spangled corridor overhead. Leafy shadows dance in shafts of golden light around her angry little feet.

A red lady, as blonde and as beautiful as her dream-mother, is sliding along the path towards them.

'*I hate you*,' the dream-child screams at her dream-mother, so that the beautiful ghost will notice her.

The woman floats past. Her clothing is already stained with blood.

A teddy bear is stuffed in the top of the bag that hangs from the lady ghost's shoulder, half in, half out. The little girl twists, straining against her mother, watching.

The bear tumbles slowly to the ground, where it lies, beady eyes staring up into foliage and fragments of clear blue sky.

The girl yanks her hand from her mother's grip, freeing herself, and races back towards the bear. She squats down to pick it up. She runs after the lady, little feet pounding heavily on the gravel.

The woman floats too fast. The girl can't catch up. She stops and yells.

'*It fell out!*'

The red lady swivels around. She sees the bear.

She glides towards the girl, through the corridor of trees. She's smiling in gratitude, holding her arms out. The girl slows right down, ready to turn around and run the other way if this levitating, bloodstained woman attempts to hug her.

When the lady stops, hovering in front of her, the girl thrusts the bear towards her. She wants to turn and run. But behind the red lady, a man emerges from the greenery. The girl sees the knife in his hand. Its blade is long and keen.

Dream darkens into nightmare.

The girl must run or fight, but her feet are sunk into the sludge of dream-sinking gravel. She cannot move. Her muscles will not respond. She cannot breathe . . .

In front of her eyes, the knife plunges into the red lady, again and again, as though the man can't control it. The red lady stretches out her hands towards the girl, entreating her to help, but the girl can't move. She knows what she should do. She should fight the bad man, but she can't. Her dream holds her in a straitjacket.

Suddenly, arms surround her, plucking her from the sticky ground, raising and embracing her, racing away . . . over her mother's shoulder, the girl watches the dead lady drain, shuddering in a pool of red. She watches the man lift his pale face from the body at his feet to the girl and the woman who are fleeing . . . He begins to run after them, knife dripping and twitching hungrily in his hand.

'*He's coming*,' the girl cries in her mother's ear. Sixteen years on, her terrified voice reverberates around the girl's dreaming head. She can feel even now how her mother flags and staggers beneath her daughter's weight, lunges desperately towards the road . . . towards the stream of cars whose drivers do not, cannot, understand why a woman with a child in her arms might throw herself into their path; drivers who have no time to stop . . .

The girl looks over her mother's shoulder, and sees that he has caught up with them . . . He lunges, knife in his hand . . . His face is frozen, just inches from hers . . .

The sleeping girl cries out in fear. She knows the rest.

Deep in her dreaming mind, alarms sound. Her muscles twitch, struggling to emerge from sleep, to flee what is about to unfold in her head.

Desperately her brain starts flicking neuronal switches, fusing the memory that feeds the dream. Just in time, the face of the killer disintegrates, splintering into a thousand pieces of light.

All that remains is a blur of green and blue and red.

CHARLIE

1

Charlie's eyes pop open on the stroke of seven, and immediately he remembers what day it is. First he feels a bolt of elation: he's not going to school today. Then a tidal wave of emotion crashes over him. He closes his eyes again and buries his head in the pillow. He's never felt like this before; it's like a storm of wind and rain and snow and hail stones, everything happening together: fear and excitement and shame and anger all at once, not making any sense.

He lies there, not moving. Wishing he didn't have to move all day.

His auntie knocks on his door.

'Time to get up, Charlie,' she calls through the door. Usually she'd say, 'Time to rise and shine,' but there's no rising and shining today. Her voice sounds strained, as if she's speaking through gritted teeth, and he can imagine her face, her jaw clenched, skin stretched and grey. What had she said to him about today? 'I'm not looking forward to it any more than you are. But it's our duty to your mum, Charlie, we can't pretend it's not happening. We've got to see justice done. Erica's got to look down from where she is and see that we're doing the right thing and we haven't forgotten her.'

'It won't make any difference whether we're there or not,' Charlie had argued, desperate not to go.

'It might,' his auntie had said. 'If they see her son there watching, and her sister, it'll remind the judge what Cheever did to Erica and to us and why he should stay in prison.'

Twelve years in prison for the murder of two women and the attempted murder of a child, and now Cheever's appealing. He's always insisted he was innocent, and now he says he's got the evidence to prove it. 'Don't you believe that lying bastard,' his aunty had said, 'he's staying where he is.'

'I'm not going,' Charlie had roared, stomping out of the room. Usually his aunty gave up at that point. But this time she had been relentless.

'You owe it to your mum,' she'd yelled after him, and Charlie had felt the words cut through him, to his heart. Truth be told, he couldn't remember his mum at all, only the photos he'd seen and the nice things people said about her. So it confused him, owing this duty to a woman who's like a ghost to him. Like an angel ghost.

It was all his auntie had said after that, whenever the subject came up – 'You owe it to your mum,' as though she knew it was all she needed to say.

So when she says, 'Time to get up, Charlie,' he gets up. He puts on his uniform, like she's told him to: navy trousers, white shirt, navy jumper. He brushes his teeth, gazing in the mirror as his blue eyes gaze uneasily back at him. He dribbles toothpaste on his jumper by mistake, tries to rub it off with toilet paper. The toothpaste doesn't budge, it just sinks further into the wool, and now it's flecked with toilet paper.

'It won't take long, they'll soon see they can't let him out. So when it's over you go straight into school,' she'd instructed. Just like she'd promised her boss she'd be at work for a late shift.

He wishes it was over now.

He hates the idea of going anywhere with his auntie. He devotes a lot of his fourteen-year-old life to avoiding being seen with her. She looks older than she should look, older than his friends' mums. She looks like life has beaten her up, which it has, and he's sorry about that, but he still doesn't want to be seen with her. If his mum was still alive, he would walk beside her without feeling embarrassed. He knows he would, because he's seen photographs, and she was really pretty. But his auntie's not his mum. She never has been, and she never can be, not however hard she tries. Actually, he's not even sure she's tried that hard since a policeman arrived at her door with Charlie on the thirtieth of May twelve years ago. Charlie knows she's never really wanted him. Young and freshly divorced, trying to make a go of her job and find a new man, and suddenly a man in uniform tells her her sister's been murdered in the park and hands her a screaming two-year-old to bring up. Charlie knows her story. He's overheard her tell it often enough.

Charlie wishes with all his heart that today could be like any other day. Like a day he gets up thinking, shall I go to school or shall I not go to school? Like a day he puts on his uniform and puts his school bag over his shoulder, walks to the end of the street, where his aunty can see him, and then turns in the other direction, away from school, towards the river or the town – just about anywhere, actually, it doesn't much matter where as long as he's not supposed to be there. Sometimes he goes with friends, but they're not as good at truanting as him, they haven't got the skills. And you've got to have the skills. Anyway, he doesn't care whether he's with his friends or on his own, actually he'd rather be on his own, except that way you've got to buy your own cigarettes instead of cadging them off someone like Chris, who doesn't know how many he's got anyway. It's a beautiful thing, Chris-piss and his vanishing cigarettes. He hasn't got a clue. When he runs out you can even tell him to go and buy more, and then nick those off him too.

Right now, at twenty minutes past seven, Charlie could do with a cigarette. Instead, downstairs in the kitchen, he pours pink and yellow cereal into his bowl and lifts the heaped spoon to his mouth, but he can't eat, he's lost his appetite. It's not often that happens. Usually he'll scoff anything put in front of him, but today Charlie's heart is beating so fast he can't count it, and his blood's gushing through his veins. If he eats, he thinks his stomach will convulse and chuck it all up again.

'You all right there, Charlie?' his aunty asks, tight-lipped. He thinks she suspects he's pretending to feel sick so he doesn't have to go with her. She always thinks he's lying. The thing is, he's been caught out a lot recently – well, for a long time really. Lying, or not lying, but not quite saying it like it is. So now, everything he says, she doesn't really believe it. His aunty's even taken to sniffing his clothes for the smell of cigarette smoke, like a police dog sniffing for drugs. It makes him think she doesn't trust him. Which drives him up the wall when you think how many true things he says to her. Like that the toilet's not flushing again, or that he doesn't like beetroot, or that he thinks their neigbour's pregnant. All true. Actually, the neighbour wasn't pregnant, she was fat, but he *thought* she was pregnant, so what he said was still true. And then of course there's all the truanting, which is lying in a way, but mostly he's managed to keep her in the dark about that.

Luckily Charlie's a good mimic, and he put his own mobile phone number down on all the school forms when they asked for parent/guardian contact details. So if the school rings to find out where he is on a day he's skipped going in, he answers in the voice of his aunty: 'Oh, Charlie's not too well today' or 'Oh, Charlie has a dental appointment today' or – and this is his favourite – 'Charlie's at his grandmother's funeral'. No one ever seems to know how many grandmothers you have. He's given his auntie a soft Irish accent, because it's the accent he can do best. And because his voice is breaking he has to do her voice all breathy and high, like she's got a cold and can't breathe properly. He suspects that some of his teachers don't believe in his Irish auntie, but it takes a brave teacher to say to any parent/guardian, even a fake one on the other end of the phone, 'I don't believe you're actually Charlie's auntie, you sound like a bad drag act.'

Anyway, even if the teachers do suspect, Charlie gets cut a bit of slack at school because of what happened to his mother.

'He's a troubled boy,' his form teacher said to his auntie the one time she found out about a parents' evening. He couldn't stop her going, once she knew. He planned all sorts of ruses to distract her and delay her, but somehow she still got there.

'He's troubled, or he's trouble, did you say?' his auntie had asked the teacher, who was surprised that Charlie's aunt didn't have an Irish accent but didn't like to mention it. 'Because at home, he's just plain trouble.'

'Well, we all need a little TLC, don't we?' another teacher chimed in. 'After all he's been through, he needs a lot of support.'

'TLC?' his auntie muttered. 'I'd say he needs a kick up the backside.'

The teacher laughed nervously. But really no one ever challenges Charlie at school. One teacher, Mrs Tepnall thinks Charlie's problems with reading and writing have a different name, a name that Charlie can't spell, and that begins with a 'b' or possibly with a 'd'.

But it's the past that hangs about Charlie like scent.

When your mother gets murdered, no one forgets about it.

'Ready?' his auntie says at last, glancing at him to make sure he looks half decent. 'Did you wash your face?'

He nods, lying. He tries to dredge up some words from the dread that consumes him. 'Did you?' he asks.

She stares at him, deciding whether to take offence, then half smiles, which is more smiling than she's done so far today.

'Cheeky monkey,' she says, clipping him gently round the face. 'Come on, we'll get through this. It'll be over soon.'

She walks toward the front door and opens it, waiting for him to go first. Charlie gazes at the door as though it's the door to hell itself, and then he walks through.

*   *   *

An hour later, they've arrived and he gazes up at the building that looms over him. It makes him feel small and scared, which usually only happens when he comes face to face with someone bigger than him. And actually that is what is about to happen, he's about to come face to face with someone much bigger than him. Someone he's terrified even of seeing. He doesn't know how he's going to hold it together. He wonders if anyone has ever just fallen to pieces, all the bits of them just coming loose and falling to the ground in a heap of arms and legs and nose and ears . . . because that's how this feels.

His auntie turns to him, and her face suddenly looks much younger, almost like she's a scared kid herself, like a person Charlie's never seen before.

'I appreciate this Charlie, I know you don't want to be here, but it means a lot to me to have you here with me. We're family, we've got to stick together, right?'

Then she puts her hand on his arm, like she thinks he can support her, and he looks at her in alarm and pulls his arm away, and she averts her face and says brusquely, 'Come on, let's get this over with.' She steps through the doorway, and he follows her.

Inside, a dour woman in a dark uniform stops him. For what is perhaps the first time in his life, Charlie does exactly what he's told. His auntie shows his passport to show he's fourteen years old. The woman looks doubtfully at his scrawny frame, but a passport is a passport, and a date of birth is a date of birth, even if his fourteenth birthday was only last week, so she frowns and lets him through. He turns out his pockets, he surrenders his Coke bottle. They climb a flight of stairs, and at the top his auntie asks a grim man wearing the same uniform as the woman downstairs where to go, and the man treats her like a criminal. It's crazy, Charlie thinks, like everyone's infected by all the evil of all the crimes they try here, like the place is dirty. Don't they realize that no one wants to be here, they just don't have a choice. Everyone's miserable, because it's a miserable place. The man says they've got to do whatever the judge tells them, and sometimes they'll have to come out while the judge and the lawyers do private things, and Charlie doesn't even think about disobeying.

And then he's there, in the public gallery, with the court below, with men and women in wigs, with piles of papers and laptops, and the judge is there too, a tiny man sitting on a chair like a throne, and you can hardly see him for the papers. Charlie's heart is pumping so hard he can hear it booming in his ears, but he's trying really hard to be quiet, because if he's not, he knows he'll get thrown out. He tries to hold his breath, because he thinks he may be panting, he's so scared. But that only seems to make his heart beat louder. So he allows himself some shallow breaths and looks around him. The clerk is standing at the end of his row of seats, giving him a death glare, and Charlie thinks maybe he's escaped from a cell and he's not a clerk at all. His auntie is sitting next to him, completely silent, with her head bowed, like she's praying.

To his right, a row in front, there's a teenage girl who looks older than him. She's grasping the edge of her seat tightly. So tightly that her fingers are white, and she's staring down at the courtroom so intently that Charlie thinks she must be mad. Maybe she's going to throw herself over the edge, so she lands on the lawyers and the piles of paper, or maybe she's going to sit there and explode. She could do that. It looks as though there's enough energy in her. Like a volcano. And her hair so long and dark and curly, as though it's electrified.

She turns, glancing towards him. Can she feel his eyes on her? He looks quickly away, but he's caught sight now of her full face. The pale skin, the jagged scar. And her eyes, which are wide and angry.

Charlie stares at his shoes. Is she angry because she thinks he's flirting with her? Actually, he'd fancy her if it wasn't for the scar . . . The scar . . . His brain starts to chunter, and then it starts to race. In an instant, he's put two and two together. Two mothers killed that day, two children left motherless, Charlie yelling in his pushchair and the other one, a girl, her face slashed. In Charlie's mind, she's still four, which is stupid, because he knows he's not two any more, so obviously she would grow up too.

He glances up again; he can't take his eyes off her. She's like him, then, she's the same as him. She's here to see justice done. She's here because she owes her mother. She's not allowed to forget, just like him. They have to be paying attention in case their mothers look down from heaven.

Suddenly he realizes that the court has fallen silent, and he wrenches his eyes away from the girl and looks down into the court.

Charlie feels as though a hand has grasped his heart and is squeezing tight. Deryk Cheever is walking into the dock. He's tall and lean, with dark hair turning to grey and he wears rimless glasses on his blue eyes. He looks more like a teacher or a doctor than a convicted murderer.

He's not what Charlie expected at all. He stares, holding his breath.

Charlie thinks the man looks like him, like Charlie.

For a moment, Charlie feels as though he's going to burst, and then his lungs remember to breathe, gulping in air with a noise that makes his auntie glance in his direction.

He leans forward as far as he can to get a better look.

It's like looking into a mirror, like seeing a reflection of his past and his future.

He hasn't seen his father since he was two.

LINDEN

2

Feltham Young Offenders Institution

Linden knows that Victor will be there waiting for him. Victor's always there, half past one on a Saturday afternoon in the Visits Hall, regular as clockwork. Like everything about this place. Like the rap on the door in the morning, and the breakfast package shoved through the door. Cereal, UHT milk, butter and jam. Every frigging day. Cereal, UHT milk, butter and jam. And bread from dinnertime the night before, stale by the time it gets to the morning. Dry, even with the butter and the jam, sticking to the roof of his mouth like toffee. What kind of breakfast is that? It's rubbish. One day he'd asked one of the officers what he'd had for breakfast, and he said bacon and eggs! Bacon and eggs – even the thought of it makes Linden salivate. Sometimes he lies on his bed and fantasises about bacon and eggs, the fat of the meat crispy and brown, and the egg yolk bursting under his fork.

In the Visits Hall, Linden can see Victor waiting for him, a big grin lighting up Victor's face as soon as he sees his little brother, and Linden can't help grinning too. Victor stands there waiting, and Linden thinks again how cool his big brother looks. Rock-star cool, dark glasses so the daylight doesn't hurt his eyes after a late night, and jeans that sit just right on his skinny hips. Linden feels like a slob by comparison. There's no such thing as prison chic. Victor takes off his sunglasses as Linden approaches and folds them into his jacket pocket, and Linden can see his smiling brown eyes, the scar under the left eye. Victor greets Linden with a hug. It's not a girly hug. It's a bear-man hug, the kind that almost breaks your ribs. Victor is the one who decides how long the hug lasts, and he always signals that it's over with a smart thwack on the back for Linden. So even while Linden's waiting for the hug to end, he's getting ready for the thwack.

They're not on their own. Around them, everyone is hugging, or kissing, or shaking hands. There's a television secured firmly high on one wall. Someone's turned it on to a twenty-four-hour news channel, so if you run out of conversation with your loved ones – or your not-so-loved ones – you can always sit and watch what's going on in the world outside.

Victor pulls up a chair and they both sit down.

'Are you counting the days, then?' Victor asks Linden.

'I'm counting hours now,' Linden says. 'There's only 48 of them. You didn't have to come today, I'll see you soon enough.'

Victor shrugs.

'Never mind,' he says, 'I've got nothing better to do than come and see my little brother.'

There's fifteen years between the two of them, but you'd never know it. Victor's hair, at thirty-two, is as black as Linden's at seventeen, and he's lean too, not an ounce of fat on him. Not an ounce of muscle either. Unlike his little brother,

Victor hasn't been working out in the Feltham gym for the last three years. Still, the smaller, slighter older brother is like a father to Linden. Linden hardly knew his dad, who died slowly of cancer when he was two and Victor was seventeen. He didn't see a lot more of their mother, who died five years later after a massive heart attack, leaving seven year-old Linden in the care of his big brother.

'What's the first thing you're going to do when you get out?' Victor wants to know.

'I don't know . . .' Linden thinks. He casts around for something Victor will approve of. 'We'll have some drinks, yeah?'

'We'll have some drinks,' Victor agrees, laughing. 'We'll have whatever makes you feel good – you'll be flying high and free as a bird.'

Linden nods, but he doesn't associate birds with freedom, not any more. Every wing at Feltham is named after a bird, and on the other side of the barred windows there are peacocks that squawk around the grounds and puff out their chests as if they're on patrol.

'Free as a bird,' He echoes his big brother. 'That's good.'

Free sounds good, but that's as far as he's got. He hasn't got a plan beyond Free, except to walk out of Feltham and never come back.

'Tony's got some work lined up,' Victor says, not even bothering to lower his voice, like he's talking about secretarial work, or some business project.

Again Linden nods slowly. He doesn't know what to think about Tony and his work, but he knows he should be grateful, he's got to find something to bring in some cash, or how's he going to eat? That's what scares him.

When he got here, aged fourteen, he was already used to scavenging for food. Now, seventeen years old, and hungrier than ever, he can't rely on Victor to put food in his mouth. Victor doesn't really eat, so he doesn't understand. He lives on adrenaline, not calories. Stand Victor sideways, and you can hardly see him, there's so little of him. Victor can blend into shadows and shrink into the smallest spaces. You'll never find him if he doesn't want to be found.

Linden glances around. He's not going to tell Victor that there are faces here that he will miss. Not the place, don't get him wrong. Not the eighteen hours shut in his cell, not the stinking toilet or the slimy, grubby showers, or the plastic mattress that some previous resident covered in graffiti. Not the food. Not in a million years, the food. And he won't miss most of the faces. He made one good friend inside. That was Marky, and Marky's already on the outside doing God knows what. Linden's big, and he can look after himself. But sometimes he doesn't feel safe here. Sometimes he thinks he'd be safer out on the street. But there are people he gets along with. He sees them in the gym, plays football with them. He knows this place now, after three years. He doesn't know outside at all.

'I heard them talking about a fight,' Victor says, nodding his head towards a couple of the guards, who're chatting by a window.

Linden nods. He doesn't want to think about it, but he can't shake it. It's not the first fight that's happened. There are fights all the time. There are bullies and there are victims. This one went too far.

'What happened?' Victor is persistent. It's one of the

hallmarks of his success. He never gives up, just keeps going at it 'til it works. Whatever it is.

'*Never walk away with a job half done*,' he always told Linden. '*Do it properly. Be thorough.*'

Which, Linden thinks, if it had been applied to school instead of housebreaking might have been a good lesson. But it wasn't. It's got Victor where he is today, which is a wardrobe full of fancy labels, an expensive watch, money to buy anything he wants. And it's got Linden where he is today, which is inside, detained at Her Majesty's pleasure for three years. Although Linden thinks if Her Majesty's really getting any pleasure out of his detention, then he's not a big fan of Her Majesty. What does it matter to her if Linden is locked up? He never did anything to her.

'Did you see it, then, the fight?' Victor's digging for a story. He loves a story. Linden nods. Nervously, he moistens his lips with the tip of his tongue.

'A new kid,' Linden says shortly. 'He was sitting watching TV on his own. They went for him out of nowhere.'

'What did they do to him?' Victor presses.

'Bad stuff,' Linden shakes his head. 'They jumped on him, kicked him in the face. He was screaming . . . Afterwards he wasn't moving. I heard them saying he's broken his back, so he's paralyzed . . . They said he's on life support and his family might switch it off.'

Victor raises his eyebrows. He's heard a lot of stuff from Linden's time inside, but this is extreme.

'Were you . . . ?' He lets his question trail off. He wants to know if Linden was involved, whether this could jeopardise his little brother's release. Perhaps he wants to know what his brother has become.

Linden shrugs. He runs his hand over his face. He doesn't want to talk about it, but he's under no illusion. Once Victor wants to know something, he doesn't let it go, he's going to have to tell him. So when he raises his eyes and glances at his brother's face, he's surprised to see that Victor's not paying him any attention at all, not any more. Victor's got one of those faces that tells you what he wants to tell you and no more. It's not often he lets you see into his head. But right now, Linden thinks that Victor's been distracted by a sudden, unpleasant thought. Linden follows his brother's eyes to the TV screen in the corner of the room. It's not long until Christmas and some joker's hung a sprig of mistletoe from it, attached to a dusty string of tinsel. Either the volume on the TV is turned down, or you can't hear the audio for the noise in the room. It's showing the street outside the Old Bailey and a man talking into a microphone outside, and a caption on the screen.

Deryk Cheever appeals conviction for park murders after twelve years . . .

Victor's gazing at the screen.

'What's that got to do with you?' Linden asks.

'I want to see if they show the girl,' Victor says. But he says it like he didn't even hear the question, like he's thinking out loud.

'What girl?' Linden asks.

This time, Victor glances at his brother, but still he doesn't really see him. It's as though his mind is somewhere else, miles away.

'No girl,' he says, shaking his head as if he's trying to get rid of whatever is going through his mind. 'Nothing you need to know about.'

CHARLIE

3

All these years, Charlie's known his father's a monster. He's known that he, Charlie, is the son of a monster, and he's guessed, from the way people treat him, that nothing much is going to come of the son of a monster. Charlie thinks it probably means that he has the native talent to be a monster too, if he wants to be, but so far he's never wanted to pursue that talent, even if it might be the only one he has. So when Deryk Cheever appears in court, and he looks like any other ordinary human being – two legs, two arms, two eyes, no horns – Charlie feels like his brain is exploding. He gulps. He glances at his auntie, expecting to see her jaw drop. Surely this wasn't what she expected. She's looking sad and grey, and her eyes are fixed on Charlie's father, but she's not looking surprised. Charlie frowns. If his auntie knew Charlie's father wasn't a monster, why did she say that he was?

His eyes go to the volcano-haired girl in front of him. He can see her fingers curl and tighten as her hands turn into fists on her lap. Charlie doesn't like looking at the girl. If the court was right twelve years ago, then Charlie's father killed the girl's mother, as well as Charlie's. Charlie knows it's not his fault, but he feels embarrassed about that. He thinks she must be surprised too, to see this ordinary man in the dock. Someone you'd never think had killed anyone.

Deryk Cheever's sitting down now, leaning forward, with a guard at his shoulder. Charlie stares at the seated man as though his life depends on it. He's thinking that any moment now this ordinary-looking man is going to cackle maniacally, or he's going to raise his eyes and they're going to glow red and Charlie's going to know his auntie was right all along. But none of this happens. Instead, Deryk Cheever nods to his lawyer, who gives him a small, restrained, smile of encouragement. Charlie sneaks a look at his auntie. She glances at him, but there's nothing on her face, no 'Sorry for misleading you'. He gives her a cold look. She's been lying to him about his own father. She should at least have told him, made it clear to him, so he knew what to expect. She should have said, 'He's a monster, but he doesn't look like one, he looks normal.' Then he wouldn't feel like this, like he's getting all torn up.

'He bullied her and then he butchered her,' that's what his auntie's always said about his father.

Charlie hasn't got his father's surname, and he's always been glad he hasn't, because that would be like advertising that he's the flesh and blood of a murderer. Charlie's a Brigson like his mother and his auntie. That's because Cheever and Charlie's mum were never married, so she never took his name. And that's because Cheever was married to someone else, although Charlie's mum didn't know that at the start. Still, even if Charlie didn't have the name, all these years he's known he has murderer's genes.

He's tried his murderer's glare in the bathroom mirror and scared himself. He's speculated that the teachers at school must be scared of him, even the men. Because won't he turn on them one day with a knife? Knowing what his father is, Charlie doesn't completely trust himself. He knows what he's made of.

There's a lot of talking going on, with the lawyers and the judge, but Charlie doesn't hear any of it, he just watches the man in the dock. His heart is pounding with secret excitement. He's desperate for this man to look up and see him and smile at him.

Then a lawyer says, 'New evidence has come to our attention, my lord . . .' and that gets even Charlie's attention.

Beside him, his auntie takes a sharp breath. But Charlie just feels as though he's floating through time and space, in limbo, as anything could be about to happen. As though his life could be about to change forever.

'We call Beth Cheever . . .' the lawyer says, and a gasp goes around the court, because it's the same surname as the convicted murderer who's sitting in the dock, his face raised, pale, expectant.

Charlie's eyes dart around the court, and a woman appears, walking to the witness box. She's got blonde hair put up on top of her head, and glasses, and a tight dress. She's pretty, but old – in her thirties Charlie guesses. When she opens her mouth to speak, to confirm her name and where she's from, she has an Australian accent but she gives an address in Brixton.

'Can you tell the court where you were on the afternoon of the thirtieth of May at half-past-four in the afternoon?' the lawyer asks, and Charlie leans so far forward that he nearly falls off his seat.

'I was working in the Green Shoots café by the tennis courts,' she says. 'I was doing that Monday to Saturday every day that month, I only had Sundays off.'

'Why do you remember the thirtieth of May as opposed to any other day you worked there?'

'It was my last day,' Beth Cheever says. 'It was a holiday job, and I was going back to Australia the next day. I remember looking at the clock to see if my shift was over. The shift finished at five, but it was still only half-past-four. I was a bit impatient to leave. And I remember, as I looked at the clock, hearing sirens and thinking they were close by, and wondering why. At five, when I left, the girl who came in to take over from me told me about the two women getting killed – she said the park was crawling with police at the north end, so if I didn't want to get mixed up in it all I should go the other way. I asked her what time the women had been killed, and she said just before half-past-four, so then I remembered looking at the clock and hearing the sirens, and I realized what I'd heard must have been the police and ambulance.'

The lawyer nods, and Charlie realizes the lawyers know already what the woman was going to say. So they must know the answer to the next question, too.

'Was there anyone in the café when you heard the sirens?' the lawyer asks.

'Yes,' she says, pointing at Charlie's father. 'Him, Deryk Cheever.'

Charlie stares. He thinks he might burst into tears. Next to him, his auntie is shaking her head as though she's disgusted. But if this is the truth, she's got no right to be disgusted. In fact, he, Charlie, should be disgusted at her for not believing it.

'How can you be sure after all this time?' the lawyer says. 'Can you remember his face after twelve years?'

'As it happens, I do,' she says. 'But what I really remember is his name. Just before I heard the sirens he was going to pay his bill, and he got out his wallet and it dropped on the floor, and his credit cards fell out. I helped him pick them up and I noticed the name on them. Deryk Cheever – it's my uncle's name, except that my uncle spells Deryk with an *e* instead of a *y*. That's the only difference.'

Charlie can hardly contain himself. He wants to leap up and punch the air. Instead he swallows his excitement and sits there while all the lawyers carry on talking. And the lawyer who wants to keep his father in prison tries really hard to make Beth Cheever say something different, or take it back, but she won't do either.

'We know that a driver, Mr Welsh, made the first call to the emergency services after Mrs Martens ran into the road with her daughter Leah and was hit by the car in front of the one Mr Welsh was driving. And we have the time of that emergency call as twenty-three minutes past four, which means the attack on the women must have happened in the few minutes before that. The police estimate that from the first attack on Miss Brigson to the death of Mrs Martens in the road, we are looking very roughly at a time scale from ten minutes past four to twenty minutes past four. You have told us that Deryk Cheever was in the Green Shoots café at half-past-four. Can you tell us at what time he arrived?'

'I'd say he'd have been there more than half an hour

when I looked at the clock at half-past-four,' Beth Cheever says. 'Maybe he arrived at about four? He ordered a sandwich and he had a cup of tea, he was there for quite a long time. Most of the time, he was reading a newspaper that another customer had left.'

The lawyer sighs. He's thinking it's a pity about the sandwich. Everyone knows you can't eat a sandwich in three minutes.

'Why has it taken you twelve years to remember this?' the lawyer asks.

'Like I said, I avoided the police that day, I didn't think I had anything to tell them, and I flew to Melbourne the next day. I've been in Australia ever since – until I came back to London a few months ago. I never knew the police had arrested a Deryk Cheever, I didn't know I could get him off.'

'Why come forward now?' the lawyer presses on. 'Did someone approach you?'

'Approach me?' she asks. 'No one approached me. When I came back to England last year, I saw an article about the park murders, and I read it because I'd been there that day – and it said someone called Deryk Cheever was arrested, and I thought no, that's not possible. I looked into it a bit more, and I realized I had information that could save him after all this time. I'd never forgotten him. I always remembered how sad he looked that afternoon. I told him he'd got the same surname as me, and he said he was sure I wasn't a loser like him. He said he'd screwed up, that he'd argued with his girlfriend and she wouldn't let him see his son any more, and his heart was broken.'

The words whisk Charlie into space.

His heart was broken! Broken! His father's heart was broken because he could not see Charlie.

Charlie sees his father incline his head towards the waitress, and Charlie thinks his father is trying to say thank you. *Thank you for telling them I'm not a monster.*

Silently, inside his head, Charlie adds his own voice to his father's. *Thank you,* he can hear himself whisper. *Thank you for saving my dad.*

And Charlie sits back in his chair, and he's trying not to grin, so his auntie doesn't see. He feels as light as a feather, like he might float out of his seat and hover over the court below.

His father isn't a murderer after all, and Charlie isn't murderer's stock.

Afterwards, when it's all over and the judge says his father can go free, Charlie hides his face from his auntie, but she's too distraught even to notice what's going on with Charlie's face. They make their way out onto the street, and she's still shaking her head and sobbing, and muttering that Cheever is lying, and that he paid the girl to lie, and she's got her face buried in her hanky, and her eyes are red and swollen.

'I've got to go to work,' she sniffs. 'Not that I'm any good to anyone like this, but I gave my word . . .'

'Okay,' Charlie says. He'll agree to anything if only she'll stop sniffling. It's too late for school now, but he says he'll see her at home later, which means they have to go in different directions. They walk together to the corner of the street and then she hurries off towards the tube, and he turns the other way to get a bus. But after walking a few yards Charlie turns around. He can't see his auntie any more, she's already disappeared in the sea of pedestrians.

He stands there, and he feels as though he's standing there all on his own, although there are people hurrying past him on the pavement. With his auntie gone, his freedom is complete. He stands there for a moment as though he's making up his mind. But just for a moment. He's already made his decision. He made it the moment the judge told his dad that he was free to go.

He turns, hurrying back towards the court.

He wants to be the first thing his dad sees when he gets out.

He imagines his dad saying, 'I can't believe it, Charlie! We're together at last.' Then his father hugs him.

Charlie's shaking with excitement, but there's a great big crowd gathering, and Charlie's afraid his father won't even see him there, let alone hug him.

Charlie looks around the crowd. He can tell which ones are the journalists easily enough, with their microphones or cameras. Suddenly, they get all excited, pushing and pressing forward, and Charlie realizes his father's about to appear. He tries to elbow his way through the pack but he gets stuck in the middle, surrounded by journalists' elbows and bits of equipment. One of them swears at him for getting in the way but Charlie ignores him because his father's coming out of the entrance with his lawyer. He pushes forward again but his way is blocked by journalists with microphones held in front of his father's face.

'How do you feel, Deryk?' one of them shouts.

Cheever lowers his head for a moment and closes his

eyes, like he's praying, or thinking what to say. Then he lifts his face to the cameras, and he's crying, and Charlie wants to cry too.

'I've had twelve years stolen from me,' his father says gruffly. 'I've been locked in a cell, with shit for food and called a murderer. I gave the police information at the time of my girlfriend's murder that they've never followed up. Now they're going to pay attention, and they're going to pay me compensation too.'

As Charlie's father starts to push his way through the crowds, a single furious voice yells.

'You're lying!'

Charlie swings around, with all the journalists and the cameras and the microphones, looking to see where the voice is coming from. It's the girl from the courtroom. The one who was sitting in front of him, with the scar and the volcano-hair. She looks furious. Livid with rage.

'You did this to me,' she yells, pulling back her hair and pointing at the scar. Then she points at him. 'I saw you. You're lying and you're the one who's going to pay!'

Charlie glances nervously at his father, who's standing staring at the girl.

'He's lying,' the girl shouts again. 'He should never be let out.'

A police officer approaches the girl, speaking to her, saying something that Charlie can't hear. The girl looks at the officer with contempt and for a moment Charlie thinks she's going to hit him, but instead she turns on her heel and walks quickly away.

One journalist, a middle-aged woman in a sheepskin jacket, pursues the girl down the street. The rest turn back towards Cheever but he's taking advantage of the diversion the girl provided to head off down the street, ignoring the taxi that's pulled up by the kerb. Charlie and the journalists set off as one, in pursuit. They have to break into a jog to catch up with Cheever, and Charlie's trying hard not to get trampled. When they reach Cheever, they surround him and he's got no choice but to stop walking.

'What do you say to Leah Martens who just accused you of lying?' A journalist shouts, above the hubbub.

'She should be begging my forgiveness for twelve years of my life lost, not peddling more lies,' Cheever says angrily. 'I'm innocent, and she'll shut up when the police arrest the right man. Now leave me alone.'

He stands like a statue, mouth shut tight even when they shout questions at him, so the press pack begins to disintegrate as journalists hurry away.

And then Charlie and his father are the only ones left.

LINDEN

4

At six, in his cell, Linden turns on the TV and picks up the chocolate bar that constitutes his evening snack. He had his evening meal in his cell at 4.45 in the afternoon, like he does every day, and he's already hungry. He's forgotten what it's like to feel full.

When Linden set foot in Feltham he could hardly read, but he learned quickly and they made him take exams. He got a GCSE in English and one in Maths, which is the best thing that happened inside. He likes to read, because books take him drifting outside the locked door of his room and the bars on the windows. But he likes TV too, for the same reason. He especially likes the news. Inside Feltham, everything's static, nothing ever changes, only who's fighting who. He saw a film once where time got stuck and the hero lived the same day over and over again, and he thinks his life is like that. But he's not a hero and he's not becoming a better person every day like the man in the film. He's stuck still. So the news gives him the feeling that things are on the move outside these four walls, that things are changing and happening, like there's some kind of flow for him to join out there. But it makes him nervous too, because where's he going to flow to?

Most of the places the books take him to are in a different world. A different universe. Sometimes, even a different time. Nowhere he can go to on a bus. He likes to forget about his life as he reads, but as the day of his release approaches, Linden's finding himself less interested in escaping into something that's not true, and more concerned about reality.

And the reality is, he's here locked in a cell, and when he walks out the door, he feels like the cell's going to come with him. '*Free as a bird*,' Victor said, but Linden thinks he'll only be as free as a bird in a cage. Because sometimes you can't see the cages around people, but they're there all the same. Invisible.

He turns on the TV, for a look at the world outside.

There's news of the court case again, the one Victor was staring at the day before in the Visits Hall. A man called Deryk Cheever, who's spent twelve years in prison for murder and attempted murder, has been freed by the judge because of new evidence. The news says that after all these years a witness has come forward to give him an alibi. A woman who was working in a café in the park at the time of the murder now says Cheever was having a coffee at the time of the murder, not cutting a woman's throat and stabbing a little girl.

The news presenter says they have 'dramatic footage from outside the court', and Linden watches as Cheever emerges from the court, makes his statement. '*Now they're going to pay attention, and they're going to pay me compensation too.*'

Then there's the girl's shout, '*You're lying!*' And the cameras go crazy, jigging around trying to find her, and then they've got her and they're zooming in just in time for her to lift up her hair and jab her finger at the scar, which hardly shows on the TV. Then she points at Cheever. '*I saw you. You're lying, and you're the one who's going to pay!*'

Linden stares at her. He wishes he could freeze the frame, and keep her there, so he could inspect her more closely. He's seen a lot of angry people inside Feltham. He's seen people burning up inside like her. He's heard more screaming and shouting than he cares to think about. He's done some burning up himself. One thing he knows is, either you control it, and you put out your own fires, or you explode.

Who is she?

Why does this case matter to Victor?

Suddenly, Linden is terrified of the world outside the walls of Feltham. How's he going to make sense of it? Inside Feltham is dangerous, but outside is dangerous too, and he doesn't know what he's going to do out there. He doesn't know what's been going on since he's been inside. Like, what's going on with Victor and the girl? The look in Victor's eyes as he watched the TV screen can only mean one thing. Trouble. But why? Why would a stabbing from twelve years ago interest Victor?

At least sitting on his bed in Feltham, with distant voices muffled by the prison door, nibbling at his chocolate bar to make it last, Linden knows where he is. He even knows what he is. He's a criminal, doing his time. When he walks out that door, what will he be then?

He lies back on his bed, not bothering with the TV any more. He thinks about the fight, the one where the new boy nearly got killed. He remembers standing there watching as David went up to the boy and dragged him off his chair and threw him to the ground. Watching as David started to kick him. Watching as David's gang waded in, kicking and punching until you couldn't see the boy on the floor and he wasn't screaming any more. Watching as David stepped back for a minute, his face glowing from the pleasure of the fight, and he saw Linden, and beckoned him to join in, to share in delivery of the death blow . . . if you're not with us, you're against us . . .

Linden closes his eyes.

Which way's he going to flow when he gets out of here? Who is he going to be?

As he falls asleep, the girl's scarred face fills his head again and he dreams that she will be part of his answer.

CHARLIE

5

It's early evening by the time Charlie heads back to his auntie's house, already dark and cold, but Charlie feels as though he's swooping through the winter sky like a bird. Charlie is the kind of boy teachers roll their eyes about. Every piece of written work that he touches turns to alphabet confetti. His grades are a stuttering *F*. He doesn't see the point, and he'll tell any teacher that. Every activity he takes part in is disrupted (by Charlie) and when he has a bright idea, the entire staffroom dives for cover. Like the Biology project in which he planned to demonstrate the dangers of smoking. His experiment involved handing cigarettes out to a group of boys in Year Seven, having them smoke for fifteen minutes, then seeing how far they could run. When a pile of smouldering cigarette butts were found ground into the turf after the boys had set off around the field, all hell broke loose.

The head teacher yelled at Charlie and suspended him for giving cigarettes to eleven-year-olds and ordering them to smoke in the interests of science. The Biology teacher yelled at Charlie because he hadn't measured how far the Year Seven boys could run before the smoking session.

'What kind of science is that?' the teacher shouted. 'If there's no control group, there's no conclusion.'

Finally, the head teacher yelled at the Biology teacher for giving the distinct impression to parents that he cared more about science than about the health of the Year Seven boys.

So the fact that Charlie's succeeded for once, and succeeded at something huge, is making him feel like a king. Or like a prince. It's his dad that's the king. His dad's the one who showed them all. He was tortured in jail for all those years and he didn't let it destroy him. He's showed them all, especially Charlie's auntie. He said all along he was innocent and now the judge said it too.

When Charlie found himself on his own with his father in the street, when all the journalists peeled off, he was speechless with the brilliance of it.

'What's your problem?' his father snapped at him.

'I haven't got a problem,' Charlie said. 'You're my dad.'

His father stared at him, and then he swore at him and turned and walked away, yelling over his shoulder, 'Tell whoever put you up to this to go fuck themselves.'

For a moment, Charlie stood there, staring. This wasn't what was supposed to happen. He ran after his dad.

'No one put me up to this,' he gabbled, as he caught up, slowing to a fast walk beside his dad. 'It's true, I'm Charlie, I'm your son. I was in court today, my auntie made me come, and I heard what that waitress said, and what the judge said, that you're innocent . . .' He paused for breath, and his dad's pace slowed then stopped. He turned and looked at Charlie, scrutinizing him from head to toe.

'I'm Charlie,' Charlie said desperately, thinking how hard it was to prove the one thing he knows to be true. 'I haven't got any birthmarks or anything to show you, so I don't know how to . . .'

His dad just stared at him. His jaw was set and his blue eyes were angry, like he could have done without this right now, like his life was complicated enough. Still, he put his hands on the boy's shoulder to stand him straight in front of him, and then he put a hand on the right hand side of Charlie's face, and turned his head. Charlie went along with it, because as long as his dad's hands were touching him like that, he was really happy.

'What are you looking at?' Charlie asked.

'I want to look at your ear,' Cheever said, with a new note in his voice. 'This one always had a kink in the ear-lobe.'

'It still does,' Charlie said helpfully, pushing his hair away from his ear so his dad could see more clearly.

'Yes,' his dad said slowly, 'I can see that.'

Charlie turned his head. 'You see?' he said. 'I'm Charlie.'

'Why are you here, Charlie?' his dad said, suspiciously, like he still thought Charlie was part of a conspiracy.

'Why shouldn't I be here?' Charlie said, shrugging. 'That day, in the park, you and Mum argued in the playground because you wanted to see me and she wouldn't let you. So here I am.'

Cheever's eyes glistened at that, like he might be about to cry. But his voice was gruff. 'A lot's happened since then . . .' he said. 'I don't know you any more, you're all grown up.'

'I'm fourteen,' Charlie clarified, 'and I don't know you, but I don't care because you're my dad.'

Cheever gazed at him, and then he looked around him, as though he was searching for something.

'Over there,' he said finally. 'There's a café. Let's have a coffee or something, yeah?'

Charlie turned and looked in the direction his dad had pointed and nodded. 'Good idea,' he said. 'Can I have a Coke?'

So they walked into the café. Or rather, Charlie floated, because this was a dream come true. And they ordered a coffee and a Coke, and they sat down.

'Charlie, listen to me.' His dad hunched forward and spoke as though his life depended on it. Charlie saw the lines around his eyes and the shadow of acne scars along his jaw. 'I didn't kill your mother. I loved her. Don't listen to anyone who says different. I loved you. I wouldn't hurt you. I loved you to bits. I wouldn't hurt a flea. The judge made a mistake all those years ago.'

'I know,' Charlie said. And he did know, because that's what the judge had said. 'They made a mistake. They thought it must be you who killed her because you were arguing with Mum in the playground.'

Cheever nodded. 'I'm not proud of it,' he said. 'And I'm not proud of the way I treated your mother, I know she was upset because of, well – because . . .'

'Because you were married, and you didn't tell her,' Charlie supplied. He's heard this endlessly from his auntie. Again and again. If only her sister Erica had never met the two-faced cheat, if only she hadn't believed his lies, she wouldn't be dead. His auntie never stops to think that if her sister had never met Cheever then Charlie wouldn't have been born. But Charlie doesn't like to press that point, because he's afraid his auntie thinks that might have been for the best too and she wouldn't be able to lie about that.

His dad nodded slowly, staring at Charlie's face. 'That's true,' he said. 'But it was complicated, your mother didn't want to understand. She was in the wrong that day to try and stop me seeing you, you've got to understand that. You can't treat your kid's father like that, it's not right.'

Charlie didn't like the way this conversation was turning out. He didn't like the way his dad kept referring to his mum as 'your mother'. He didn't like his dead mum being blamed for anything. It almost sounded like his dad was blaming her for getting killed and him going to prison, and Charlie couldn't see how either of those things were her fault.

'What are you going to do now?' he asked his dad in a small voice.

'I've got some scores to settle,' his dad said. 'I'm going to clear my name properly, so there's no doubting it. I'm going to shut that little bitch up.'

Charlie nodded, but he was scared by his dad's anger. He could understand it, of course he could. He'd be angry too if he'd been locked up for twelve years and then a judge said he was innocent but a sixteen-year-old girl kept telling everyone you were guilty. It was only natural.

'What happened to me – it shouldn't happen to anyone.'

Charlie nodded again.

'But who *did* kill my mum if you didn't?' he found himself saying.

His dad slumped back in his seat and closed his eyes, and Charlie felt his heart plummet. That question had been hanging around at the back of his head. But he didn't know it was going to leap out of his mouth like that. It should've stayed where it was, unspoken. Now his dad didn't think he was so special any more. He didn't think Charlie really believed that he was innocent after all.

But then his dad opened his eyes and looked straight at Charlie with such intensity it was like he was looking into his brain, and through his brain, and out the other side. Then his dad smiled. It was like the sun coming out, and a warm breeze and the first gulp of chilled Coke all rolled into one. Charlie smiled back, and his dad's smile got even bigger and Charlie tried to imprint the smile into his memory.

'I saw who killed your mother, didn't I?' he said. 'You and me, we can track him down. That'll shut her up.'

'When did you see him?' Charlie asked.

Cheever glanced around, like he was worried someone might overhear.

'I went to the café in the park, didn't I?' Cheever said quietly, leaning towards Charlie. 'Like the waitress said. She saw me there, she saw my name on the credit card.'

Charlie nodded. He'd been paying attention in court. He thought his dad was very lucky to have dropped his credit card in the café.

'On the way there, a man passed me, walking towards the woods where your mother was killed. It must have been him.'

'Who was it?' Charlie asked. 'What did he look like?'

His dad hushed him, his blue eyes darting around the half-empty café.

'I can't tell you that right this minute,' his dad said quietly. 'All you need to know is, when I find him, I'll be vindicated.'

'For Mum's sake,' said Charlie.

A frown of irritation passed across Cheever's face and then he said, 'For my sake, Charlie, for *my* sake. Your mum's dead, no one can help her. It's the living that need to protect their names against the likes of the Martens girl. So, Charlie, are you going to help me?'

Cheever grinned at Charlie, and suddenly Charlie felt a bit wobbly. He wasn't sure that cadging smokes off Chrispiss or feeling up Tiffany on a bench in the park were good enough training for tracking down a murderer. He didn't really know what his dad was talking about, because he realized he didn't know his dad. It was like suddenly being best friends with a total stranger. One minute his dad seemed friendly, the next he acted cold and distant. But Charlie forgave him. He'd been in jail for twelve years. An innocent man imprisoned. It was no wonder he was a little bit strange. And a little bit bitter.

One thing Charlie did know was that he really wanted to please his dad, even though he didn't know how. Charlie opened his mouth to speak before he knew what would come out of it.

'We should shut that girl up,' he said. 'Otherwise she'll keep lying about you.'

His dad gazed at him and then he said, 'Charlie, son, that's a very good idea. We should shut her up. Are you good at shutting people up?'

Again Charlie felt that flutter of fear in his stomach. Was he any good at shutting people up? There was a question. He hadn't had any success keeping the Year Seven boys quiet about the smoking experiment. Interrogated by the Biology teacher they'd cracked immediately. In fact, one of the reasons he liked to skip school was because usually it worked the other way. Usually, other people shut *him* up.

'Yeah,' he said. 'Yeah . . . I know how to shut people up.'

'Good, because that girl is a troublemaker. You'd think, if she knew what was good for her, she'd keep quiet, but instead she's yelling lies all over the shop and some people will believe her. She's got to be stopped.'

Charlie nodded. 'I agree,' he said, 'she's got to be stopped.'

Charlie's dad grinned at him. 'You know I'm really proud of you. We're going to make a good team you and me . . . I bet you've got a phone? Write your number down for me—' his dad broke off, looking embarrassed, pulling out a scrap of paper and a pen from his pocket. 'I've got to get myself sorted with a phone and then I'll text you my number.'

Swallowing hard and with a shaking hand, Charlie wrote his number on the scrap of paper and gave it to his dad.

'Like I said,' his dad said, tucking the piece of paper in his pocket, 'I'll get you my number and then you can call me any time. Night or day.' Then his dad laughed and said, 'I don't mean that, Charlie, don't call me at night.'

Charlie nodded, hardly believing what was happening. 'We can talk about how to stop her,' he said.

'Yes,' his dad said, 'that's exactly what we can talk about. The lying little bitch.'

And he gazed at Charlie with those blue eyes that made Charlie feel like he was looking in the mirror.

LINDEN

6

Linden's free at last. At least, he's out of the gate of Feltham and he's in Victor's car, and they're speeding away from Feltham like it's a getaway in a film. Linden doesn't quite feel free, but he does feel different. He feels lighter, like a great big weight is off his back so he can walk upright again. And he feels brighter because the sun's shining and inside a cell the sun doesn't make much difference, but outside it changes everything. He feels hopeful because out here there are things that are possible. But still he doesn't feel entirely free.

He tries to think what he'd need to feel really free, and he thinks it probably boils down to about ten thousand pounds. Ten thousand pounds doesn't sound too greedy, like you're only interested in loads of money, but it would pay the rent for a while, and for food and drink and some new clothes. He hasn't got a coat, and he's already feeling cold, but he'll have to put up with it because he's got no cash. If he had ten thousand pounds he could buy himself a nice coat and he wouldn't have to think right away about what he's going to do, how he's going to earn money, and who he's going to be. Victor has told him he'll look after him, but Linden knows that means Victor must have a plan for him and that means he's not really free at all. So unless ten thousand pounds falls from the sky, or he finds a job in the next two days, then either he's going to be as hungry as he was in Feltham, or his stomach will decide who he is going to be now he's out. And he's not sure it's a decision his stomach should take. Not on its own. He thinks he knows which way his stomach would vote.

Linden looks out the car window, his eyes running over the streets, and the pavements, and the shops and the buildings as they stream past. He can't believe any of it has anything to do with him. Most of the journey, while Linden's been thinking, Victor's been whooping like they've broken Linden out of jail, when actually all that's happened is that Linden's done his time.

'I think I smell a cel-e-bration,' Victor says, hitting the brakes and pointing to a McDonald's.

'Yeah,' Linden says, grinning, 'that's a good place to start.'

At the counter, Linden can't control himself. He keeps on ordering, first a cheeseburger and fries and then, going red under the gaze of the waitress, he orders chicken nuggets and onion rings, all as big as they get, and a cup of Coke that could fuel a rocket. Victor orders a black coffee.

'Really?' Linden says. 'A coffee? That's it?'

Victor shrugs. 'I'm not hungry. But you eat, little bro', you enjoy it, it's all on me.'

When they've found a table, Victor sits sipping his coffee, watching amused as Linden eats, leaning over his food protectively, as though he thinks someone might nick it off the tray, stuffing his mouth with food as fast as he can.

Eventually, when every carton and bag is empty, he stops eating. He groans and rubs his tummy.

'That was so good,' he says.

Victor shakes his head. 'That was not a pretty sight,' he tells his younger brother. 'Come on, let's get going.'

Later that night, they've had some beers in Victor's flat and they're stretched across black leather sofas, with thin cushions stuck under their heads, watching TV. The empty cans are stacked beside them on the wooden floor. Nothing much has changed since Linden left. The flat is tidy because Victor doesn't buy stuff. He's got the necessities: sofas, glass coffee table, TV and that's it really. Plain walls, no pictures, no photographs of family or friends. Nothing fancy or pretty, nothing soft. Linden looks around for a sign of a girlfriend but there's nothing. There never was. All the time Linden was here, from eight years old until he went to Feltham, Victor's girls came and went, but mostly they went, leaving nothing behind them, like they never intended coming back. They'd arrive at night, giggling, all over Victor, and then in the morning they'd go, looking miserable, sometimes in tears. When he was a kid, it never crossed his mind to think about Victor picking just one girl and settling down. Victor was too cool for that, too young. But now Linden wonders about things like that. He notices there's a few pairs of brand-name sneakers by the door, and a couple of designer jackets. Things Victor buys for himself – his watch, his phone, his sunglasses – are expensive. But Victor's flat has less stuff in it than most cells at Feltham. Inside, kids had stuck photos all over their walls, and their tables were covered in packets of biscuits and food they'd bought from the shop to supplement their miserable meals. Here, though, where Victor could have loads of things, there's nothing . . .

They've been channel-surfing, flicking from reality show to reality show, spending longer on the ones with women in bikinis and not so much time on stately homes. In breaks, the screen is filled with reindeer and bells and trailers for funny Christmas programmes with loud laugh tracks. They land randomly on a news channel and there's the girl again, shouting outside the court. *'I saw you. You're lying, and you're the one who's going to pay!'*

Linden glances at his brother's face. Victor is watching the girl intently. What is it about this girl, the one he said didn't exist when Linden pressed him in the Visits Hall? Why is his brother so interested in her?

The news presenter talks over the pictures.

'Newspapers are quoting police sources who took part in the investigation twelve years ago, saying Leah Martens never did identify Deryk Cheever as her attacker. The girl, who was four at the time of the attack, was questioned by police. She was the only witness after her mother was killed, hit by a car as she ran with her daughter from the park. But sources say that in the hours and days following the attack, Leah Martens's description of the attacker did not fit the appearance of Deryk Cheever. Following Cheever's release, the disclosure has raised further questions about why Cheever was arrested and why other avenues of investigation were not pursued.'

When the report is over Linden mutes the volume. He's

remembering the girl's fury. He remembers her pointing at her scar and screaming, *'you did this!'*

Was she making it up, then? Was she lying? Or was her memory playing tricks on her?

Linden glances at Victor again. He can't help it. He can't leave it alone. There's something about the girl, something about Victor's interest in her that won't let him leave it alone.

'Do you think she remembers a face from when she was four?' he asks.

Victor looks at him blankly.

'The girl who was attacked, I mean,' Linden says, 'I couldn't remember a face from when I was four years old, could you?'

Victor blinks, still saying nothing.

'So is she lying?' Linden persists.

'I don't know,' Victor says. 'Why don't you ask her if you're that bothered?'

Linden doesn't know what to say, doesn't know whether Victor's joking or . . . he must be joking. This is a common problem. Another thing he'd forgotten about. Trying to know when Victor's being serious and when he's joking.

'What does that mean? How am I going to ask her?' he says.

Victor grins.

'Who knows?' he says, standing up. 'Soon, she could be sitting on that sofa and you can ask her anything you like. No girl can resist my charms for long. But, come on, I've got some stuff to deal with, so we should get going.'

Linden runs the tip of his tongue over his lips. He has

no idea what Victor means about the girl being here, why would she come to this flat? But right now he's more worried by the last thing Victor said. The choices are coming sooner than he expected. Sooner than he wanted. He's not prepared.

'What stuff?' he asks, meaning, *Is this the kind of stuff that will put me back inside?*

Victor gives him a quick, hard look.

'What do you mean?' he says.

'What kind of stuff?' Linden repeats.

Victor shrugs.

'The usual kind of stuff,' he says. 'We're going to do a little creepin' and get ourselves some keys.'

Linden nods but he doesn't move from where he's stretched out. With a few beers inside him, he's beginning to see how this could go. Victor's the one person in the world who's family, who knows him through and through. Victor will do anything for him and he'll do anything for Victor. That's the way it is with brothers. Linden doesn't know why he's even fighting it. Linden knows he should go along with it; he can't understand why he's digging his heels in. It's not like he's got options.

'Come on, little brother.' Victor tries to jolly him along. 'You want to start slow, that's all right, you don't have to do anything. I'll hold your hand . . .' he holds his hand out, and Linden has a sudden flash of memory of Victor holding out his hand to him when he was a little kid and him grabbing it. Wherever Victor went Linden was sure to go. So now when Victor holds his hand out to him like he's still a little kid, it's half a joke and it's half Victor reminding him, *This is the way it is, your hand in mine.*

Linden stretches out a leg and kicks Victor's hand away none too gently.

'Nah, man,' he says. 'My belly's hurting, I think it was that burger.'

'Yeah?' Victor says. 'You can always use their toilets you know, you don't just have to lift their keys.'

Linden grins and rubs his tummy.

'Nah, I don't want to sit in a car tonight. You go,' he says generously. 'Keep all the goodies for yourself.'

'Yeah?' Victor looks doubtful. 'You're going to need to earn your keep, you know that, right? I can't keep you, you know, in the manner to which you've become accustomed.'

'I know that,' Linden says, rubbing his tummy again. 'My belly's hurting, that's all. It's my first night out. I'll come next time.'

Victor shrugs and says, 'I'll give the boys your love.'

And Linden says, grinning, 'You do that. Big fat kisses all round.'

When Victor's gone, Linden carries on gazing at the television, but he's not watching what's on the screen. He's thinking about the girl. *'No girl can resist my charms'* . . . Because Victor's face gave it away, and Linden doesn't know why but he thinks that Victor is going after that girl. *'Soon, she could be sitting on that sofa'* . . . And if Victor goes after her, he'll find her.

The question is, why does Victor care?

CHARLIE

7

Charlie has discovered the student in him. It's been hiding for fourteen years and his teachers have always doubted that this mysterious creature exists at all. Charlie, in their view, is a boy made for a vocational school. And by 'vocation', they mean chimney sweeping or digging ditches. He's made for any school, actually, that they're not teaching in. He's not clever, his teachers say. They showed him the graphs, the lines that curve and swoop, at the one and only parents' evening his auntie came to and when the teacher pointed at the dot that represented him, he was in the pits, the lowest of the low.

'That's me?' he asked, frowning at the dot.

'Not only you,' his teacher replied patiently. 'People like you – an average . . .' She struggled. 'An average of people like you . . .'

'An average of people like me . . .' Charlie was baffled. How did the man who drew the graph know what he was like? And if he didn't know what Charlie was like, how did he know what people like Charlie were like? And then how did he make an average out of all those different boys?

'So what you're saying is, I'm stupid.' Because what else could the dot mean?

'No,' she said cheerily, eyeing Charlie's auntie, 'we don't use words like that. It's all about potential, not just ability.'

'And I don't have any?'

'What, you don't have any ability?' she said, beginning to sound anxious

'No, you said potential. That's what counts.'

'Yes, you're right. Potential.' She tried to sound upbeat. 'Absolutely, that's what counts.'

'So I haven't got any of that either then?' he tried to clarify. Because if she was showing him the dot it must mean something.

She gazed at the graph, and at the minute dot that was Charlie. *Not a lot of potential, no,* is what she wanted to say. This was scientific, after all, and you couldn't mess with science, so she was pretty sure of herself. But to be on the safe side, she tried to be diplomatic. 'You're not much below the average, see?' she told him. 'That gives you something to strive for.' But if a dot was plotted on a graph, and the line was going down, he couldn't see what good striving's going to do. It was the first time he'd realised his life was already decided. He couldn't really think why he'd bothered with anything.

Anyway, the long and short of it was, they didn't expect anything of him. Never had, never would. And really why bother to try and change their minds? It was his ability that was stuck. His dot. They couldn't do anything about that.

But give Charlie an internet browser and he's as clever as anyone else. It's just, it takes him a long time to read.

He's online now looking for the girl. Leah Martens.

He finds her on Facebook. From this, he learns that

she's not in a relationship. He also learns her favourite colour, her favourite female singer, her favourite band and her favourite sport (kickboxing). What he doesn't find is the thing he wants to know, which is her address. Most of her friends on Facebook are probably at her school, but who wants to talk about school on Facebook? No one even posts a photograph of anyone in school uniform. It's all selfies dressed up for a night out, or hanging off each other's shoulders in parks and cafés. Except for Leah Martens, who posts a picture of herself in kickboxing kit taking part in a competition. Charlie thinks she looks ridiculous. He thinks kickboxing is not a sport for girls.

He knows roughly where she lives because of the park where she was attacked, which he assumes was close to her home, but he can't find an address for her, not even a street name. And who knows if she still lives in the same place anyway? The press must have protected her family, kept it private. Still, he thinks, he doesn't need to know where she lives. If he can work out where she goes to school he can find her. So he maps all the schools within three kilometres of the park and then he visits their websites, and although he knows it's a long shot, he trawls through photo galleries of plays and concerts and fashion shows. Mostly they make him want to go to sleep, these pictures of chemistry experiments and sporting events and performances of *Oliver*.

But then he finds her.

Oldbridge School. Not even that far away.

She's in the background of a photograph of a school fête. No one would take a picture of just her, because everyone would look at the scar. She must have got into the photograph by accident, Charlie thinks, or the photographer would have told her to get out of the frame. Anyway, it's not important what she's doing. What's important is, he knows where to find her.

Charlie waits outside the gates of Oldbridge School. Not right outside, where everyone will see him and think he's up to no good, but on the other side of the road, where there are some bushes and a patch of scrubland called the recreation ground. He thinks it's funny that he's bunking off school so he can hang around outside someone else's school. What's not so funny is that it's cold and he didn't put his coat on like his auntie told him to. He's wearing jeans and a hoody, because hoodies are the best disguise known to man, or at least known to Charlie. His school uniform, which he was wearing when he left the house that morning, is scrunched up in his bag next to a couple of textbooks he packed for the sake of his auntie. He's not going to approach Leah Martens, because if he goes up to her and says, 'Oi, my dad's going to get even with you!' he's betting she's going to run the other way. Or hit him. Or her friends are going to beat him up. Or call the police on him. So his plan – well, basically, his plan is that he's going to stalk her.

The afternoon sky is dull and darkening prematurely. But Leah Martens is one of the first out. She's not difficult to spot. It's the scar that Charlie sees first. Then, after that, he recognises the rest of her from the courtroom. If you didn't see the scar, if you just saw the hair and the face, he'd quite fancy the Martens girl. But she'd have to get rid of the scar first. Perhaps she could have plastic surgery.

She's wearing a dark green school skirt over black tights and she's got a thick winter jacket on, and a scarf wrapped around her neck. Her dark hair is tied up and twisted on top of her head and she hasn't covered the scar up with makeup. She strides out of the gate and Charlie doesn't know how anyone gets to be so confident. Teachers tell him he's perfected the art of the slouch, but Charlie doesn't think it's an art at all, it's just that slouching makes you feel better because you feel like nobody can see you and laugh at you. Like now, if he slouches while he's following her, she won't notice him.

She's with one other girl. Charlie can't hear what they're saying but he's pleased to see that Leah Martens looks miserable. He heard the radio say Leah Martens didn't even identify his dad after she was attacked twelve years ago, so now he's angrier than ever with her, because she's been lying all along, even screaming lies outside the court. Ruining his dad's life. Messing up Charlie's. Stopping his mum's real murderer from being caught. He despises her for what she's done.

He waits for the girls to turn when they're out of the school gates and then he begins to follow on, about twenty metres behind. Other students have emerged behind the girls and they give him some cover.

The walk takes twenty-three minutes and he's memorising the route all the way so he can repeat it at will. He thinks he's going to be paying Leah Martens more than one visit. The further they get from the school, the fewer people there are around. When her friend peels off down a side-street, it's just Charlie and the Martens girl and he drops way back. She speeds up, but that's because she's on her own, not because she's spotted him. Charlie's beginning to feel good about this. He can see a career as a private detective stretching ahead of him. In his imaginary career, he only follows beautiful women and some of them fall in love with him and start following him. Quite a lot of them actually. They say things like, 'We don't care that your dot is headed downwards on the school charts, we only want you for your body and for your remarkable prowess as a private detective.' His dad is really proud of him and tells a TV programme that Charlie's possibly the best private detective the country's ever had.

By the time Charlie steps back into the real world, Leah Martens is walking through the gate of a shabby old Victorian house – cracked plasterwork and peeling paint and rotting window frames. She goes up to the front door and takes a key out of her pocket, opening the door and stepping inside.

Charlie watches from the other side of the street. He notes that there are three doorbells, so this building houses a collection of flats. Then he sees her at the window on the ground floor. She's looking out on to the street.

She's looking right at him.

She frowns. She points at her eyes and then she points at him. Even Charlie can understand that message. She's seen him.

Charlie thinks she might come out after him. She might yell at him, like she yelled outside the court at his dad. He's got to get out of here.

How did the bitch see him? Has she got eyes in the back of her head?

He jabs his middle finger in the air.

Then he turns away sharply. He's never done that to a girl before. He's never thought that 'b' word, either, and he knows he only even thought it because his dad used it. He feels a bit sick. Rapidly, he starts to walk away. He lowers his eyes to the ground. He can't bear to look up in case someone has witnessed his humiliation.

LINDEN

8

Linden pushes open the door of the newsagent's. By his reckoning, this is his ninth shop of the day. It's his second day of job hunting, his third day out of Feltham. He's targeting the small shops, newsagents and convenience stores, hoping for somewhere tiny enough that the manager might like the look of his face and offer him a job on the strength of that. He tried to find out about work in Tesco's, but all the talk of applications and a CV scared him back out the door. Who's going to hire him to work on the tills if his most recent educational establishment is Feltham Young Offenders Institute?

Inside, the newsagents is tiny, and filled from floor to ceiling with tins and packages and packets. A boy is browsing the sweet display and an elderly woman is standing with an empty basket looking at an array of chocolate biscuits.

'Hi.' He approaches the man at the till. He's been trying to polish his introduction, so this time he holds out his hand and says, 'My name is Linden James and I'm looking for employment.'

The man looks him up and down, staring at his extended hand. Linden drops his hand to his side. He knows what the man sees: a tall guy, big shoulders, dark cropped hair. The kind of young man who could make some people nervous.

'I'm looking for a job.' He repeats himself, more simply this time.

The man inspects him for another long moment.

'Do you have experience of working in a shop?' He asks.

'Yeah,' Linden says eagerly. This is the furthest he's got anywhere. Most places it's a simple shake of the head. 'I used to work in a newsagent in New Cross when I was a kid. On Saturdays.'

Linden reddens. Age thirteen, he'd persuaded a newsagent to let him work one Saturday, and then Linden had nicked cigarettes to sell to his friends. The job hadn't lasted.

'Anything more recent?' the man asks. 'How old are you anyway? Eighteen?'

'I'm seventeen,' Linden says, but he doesn't answer the man's question about recent work.

'Linden James,' the man declares suddenly, excited by his discovery. 'I know you, you're Victor's brother. You've been in prison, haven't you?'

Linden nods mutely. There's no point in correcting him. *Not prison exactly* . . . But who cares? He should have known. He should have stayed further from home. This was a mistake.

'And you think I will give you a job here in my shop?' the man asks angrily. He slams his palm against the till. 'You think I'll let you near my money? You're mad.'

The boy and the old woman both look up, startled by the storekeeper's outburst. From the corner of his eye, Linden sees the kid pocket a packet of Skittles.

That kid's a natural, he finds himself noting. *Victor could turn him into a fine criminal.*

He wonders whether the granny's as quick off the mark with the chocolate biscuits.

'No one will give you a job, no one!' the storekeeper says, his voice cracking with excitement. 'Everyone round here knows all about you – and your brother.'

'All right.' Linden raises his hands as if he's surrendering and backs out of the shop. 'All right, I get the message.'

Outside on the street, his palms are sweating and he's feeling shaky. There's a cute girl outside the shop. He hopes she didn't hear what happened in there. He walks down the street with as much dignity as he can muster, which isn't much.

He's so hungry. Ever since he got out of Feltham, he hasn't been able to stop eating. It's as if he's making up for two years of starvation. Victor thinks it's funny, but it doesn't feel funny to Linden.

Now he can almost hear his belly. *Fill me up!* It screams. *Rob the shop! Steal a car! I don't care how you do it, just fill me up!*

It's getting harder to ignore that voice.

In the evening, Linden's slumped on the couch watching television. Victor's in his armchair and his friends Tony and Sameer are lying on the floor, half propped up with cushions. There are empty bottles all around and the smoke that's in the air is sweet and intoxicating.

'My little brother saw you askin' for a job,' Sameer says slowly, thinking his way to each word.

Linden frowns, then remembers the little boy pocketing

the sweets. No wonder, then, the boy's got thieving genes.

'Why are you bothering with that?' Victor sounds offended. 'We've got jobs for you.'

Linden shrugs. 'I don't want to go back to Feltham, do I?' He catches his brother's eye and Victor looks away.

'Then just get some benefits,' Tony says. 'There's no need to get a job.'

'Yeah, I'll do that then,' Linden says shortly, hoping they'll get bored and move on. He's thought about benefits. He's thought about signing on, about all the paperwork, and writing the word Feltham on a form, and some sneery woman looking him up and down like he's no good for anything and he's thought about getting up every morning and having nothing to do. Day after day. Like Feltham but worse because now it could be forever. There's no release date when you're free already. Time standing still, going nowhere. He'd rather do anything than that. Almost anything.

'You don't need to do any of that,' Victor says again. 'We'll look after you, we've got work for you. Proper work, that means proper money. No more crap trainers, no more rubbish clothes.'

Linden looks at Victor's Nikes and his designer watch. His brother has an eye for quality, always did.

'I don't want to go back there,' Linden says again. Sometimes he thinks he's convincing himself. It would be good to have a watch like Victor's on his wrist, a pair of trainers like Victor's on his feet.

'We'll look after you,' Tony says again, echoing Victor.

'Like we did last time, you mean?' Sameer says and laughs. He's slurring his words and Linden's not sure he heard right, but Tony and Victor do a double take. Victor reaches out a foot and kicks Sameer in the ribs, and Tony says, 'Shut up, man.'

'What do you mean?' Linden says, leaning forward, elbows on his knees, looking down at Sameer.

But Sameer's nursing his ribs and groaning.

'Why d'you go and do that?' he protests to Victor. 'I didn't say nothing.'

'That means you did say something, you idiot,' Victor says coldly.

Linden glances at his brother. He forgets that even though neither of them really went to school much, Victor isn't stupid. In fact, for someone who's smoked a lot of weed tonight, Victor is acting pretty smart. And then he thinks, how much does Victor smoke? He never seems to be out of it or less than completely in control. For someone who's so deep into dealing, it's amazing, now Linden comes to think of it, that Victor's managed to stay out of jail. Either he's lucky, or he's sober enough to duck and dive when the law gets close.

He glances at his brother again. Victor's eyes are sharp and bright. No swollen druggy pupils there, no sleepy struggling to get to grips with what is going on. Victor's on the ball, no question. Linden feels a sudden surge of admiration for his brother. Victor mixes with idiots but he's not an idiot himself. He's smart. That's how he runs his little empire.

Linden looks down at Sameer, who's curled like a baby on the floor. He's snoring. Linden kicks him in the ribs, where Victor kicked him. 'Hey Sameer, what did you mean, like last time?' he asks, leaning over him.

Sameer peers dopily up at him.

'Leave it.' Victor gives Linden a sharp look, the kind that says he's not kidding.

Linden holds his brother's gaze, unwilling to retreat.

'Why should I leave it?' Linden asks his brother. 'I want to know what he means.'

'Nothing,' Victor says firmly. 'He means nothing. Look at him, he's wrecked, he doesn't know what he's saying. Hey,' he grins at Linden, 'you want to go dancing? I know some girls.'

Linden shrugs. 'My belly's hurting again,' he says.

'You hungry?' Victor asks him. 'I'll call for some pizza.'

Linden watches his brother while he calls for pizza. It's the first time since the banquet at McDonald's that Victor's gone out of his way to put food in his little brother's belly. Like he's got a guilty conscience.

Next morning, Linden's lost in misery. His head is bowed, eyes on his feet and on the ground immediately beneath them. Not really caring any more what's up ahead. Whatever it is, it can't be good. If he fell down a manhole in the next few steps, he wouldn't shout out or try to save himself. He would fall, silently and still, and disappear. When fate's this cut and dried, there's no point trying to mess with it. If he was paying attention, he would see that he has found his way into the warm of the arcade, and that he is surrounded by the Saturday afternoon swell of pre-Christmas shoppers. His ears must hear the piped-in Christmas tunes but his brain has decided not to process them in case their cheeriness torments him even more.

'Hey, Linden!'

Linden's not listening. There's nothing worth hearing. Nothing that can do him any good. Not listening means he can pretend that he's not here at all. He can move in his silent bubble and the world he's in is a seamless series of moving images. None of it has anything to do with him.

'Hey, Linden!'

The voice is closer, louder. It almost gets through to him. Still, somewhere deep in his head, he rejects the idea that anyone would want to speak to him, the biggest loser on the planet.

From the corner of his eye, he sees a girl and he raises his head to get a better look. Dark curls, jeans, a sweat-shirt, a scarf around her neck – she's striding across the mall with a sense of purpose. It's her – or is he hallucinating?

'Lin!' A hand grabs his arm and Linden swings around, fists rising, ready to hit out.

In front of him there's a guy about his own age with an expression of alarm on his face.

Linden lets his fists fall back to his side and the guy who grabbed his arm relaxes and grins.

'Marky!' The two young men hug, instinctively, then draw back quickly.

Marky had got out of Feltham a year before and Linden had missed him. The fact that Linden had heard no more about him made Linden think Marky must be doing okay. Thoughts of the girl leave his mind. He's pleased to see a friendly face for once.

'What's this?' Linden plucks at Marky's apron.

'I'm working,' Marky says. 'I'll show you.'

Marky's working in a shoe repair shop that opens on to

the arcade. He slips back in behind the counter, surrounded by key templates and rubber soles and packets of shoelaces. Behind him is the machinery for key cutting and for sewing and gluing shoes.

Linden laughs and Marky's face drops.

'What's funny,' he protests. 'Where are you working, then, in the City? Working in some hedge fund then, or what?'

Linden stops laughing. He shakes his head.

'No hedge fund, no way,' he says. 'I'm not laughing at you, Marky, it's just – shoe repair. It's not what . . .'

Marky leans over the counter. He says close to Linden's ear, 'You thought I'd be running around in a big fat car, with big fat music blasting out the window and a big fat pile of banknotes in the glove compartment?'

Linden grins and shrugs. 'Yeah,' he laughs. 'Yeah, that's what I thought, maybe.'

Marky grins too and then a middle-aged woman approaches, flourishing a pair of well-worn shoes. Marky's focus shifts to her as he asks how he can help, and Linden watches as his friend takes the shoes, fixes them, and hands them back to her, before taking her money, ringing up the sale on the cash register. The woman thanks Marky and he wishes her a good day.

'Do they know?' Linden asks when she's gone.

'What?'

'The people who hired you, this company. Do they know you were . . .?'

'Yeah,' Marky says. 'It's like a programme they have, for people who've just got out.'

'Yeah? That's cool.'

Marky shrugs. 'I'm not complaining,' he says. 'How about you? What're you doing?'

'I . . . well, I just got out, and I . . .' There's nothing that Linden can say that doesn't sound desperate. *I'm sleeping on my brother's sofa . . . I'm hungry all the time . . . I can't get a job . . . I've got no money . . . He wants me to go robbing again . . .* He shakes his head and turns away. He doesn't want to talk about his life and how it's sucking him down. If that means turning and walking away without so much as saying goodbye, that's what he's going to have to do. He's gone a few steps when Marky's voice breaks into his head.

'Lin,' it's saying. 'Hey, Lin, do you want me to put in a word for you?'

Linden turns around. He takes a deep breath 'Yeah,' he says. 'Yeah, I'd appreciate that.'

CHARLIE

9

In the forty-eight hours since Leah Martens looked at Charlie through her window and he gave her the finger, Charlie feels as though he can't keep up with his own emotions. He's never felt so angry at anyone. He's good at following, he knows he is. The girl shouldn't have spotted him, but she did, and on top of that she'd looked out through that window at him on purpose to make him feel stupid. He'd been looking forward so much to telling his dad about following the girl and finding out where she lived. He'd done exactly what his dad asked and done it brilliantly. He'd imagined his dad saying: *'That's amazing, son, I knew you had it in you,'* and she'd spoiled it for him.

At first he was furious and then the heat of fury cooled to an icy hatred. He would get back at her, the stupid bitch. In this new, cold way of thinking, it occurred to him that he didn't actually have to tell his dad that Leah Martens had spotted him. That was irrelevant. His dad wanted to know where she lived, and Charlie could tell him that. His dad would be impressed by that. Charlie could give his dad a street name, a house number. He could link to it on Google maps. He could click on the little yellow man and drag him on to the right street, and have his dad stand outside the girl's house, looking up at the window Leah Martens had looked out from.

But when he actually thought about his dad standing on the street looking into Leah Martens' window, another awkward question circled in his head.

What was his dad going to do with the address?

'*I've got some scores to settle*,' his dad had said to him in the coffee shop.

Well, his dad's scores were his now too, so Charlie wanted to wipe that smug look off the girl's face. He hoped his dad was going to let him be part of what he had planned. Whatever that was.

'I know where she lives!' Charlie can't contain himself. He'd planned how he was going to say it, building up to it, but in the end it bursts out of him.

His dad's sitting across from him in the same coffee shop where they met the first time. It had taken his dad quite a long time to text his phone number to Charlie. For a little while, Charlie had thought his dad wasn't going to get in contact at all. But he was sure his dad was just busy with all the things you have to do when you get out of prison. Eventually the text arrived from his father and Charlie rang the number immediately, his voice shaking with anticipation when he heard his dad's voice. His dad wasn't sure that he had time to meet up, so Charlie said he could always come round to his dad's house if he told him his address. Then his dad went silent for a bit and said that he'd find the time and actually Turner's café was the best place to meet. He didn't want Charlie getting mixed up with the reporters who sometimes hung around his flat, he said. The coffee shop was good and anonymous. They would be safe there. Charlie agreed that would be good, and he didn't say, *Safe from what?* although he thought it.

But now they are sitting across from each other, and Charlie can't wait to tell his dad what he knows about Leah Martens.

'Where who lives?' his dad says.

Charlie looks at him incredulously. He thinks his dad must be joking but he doesn't know him well enough to know when something's a joke and when it's not.

His dad is still looking at him blankly. Either he's a good actor or he's forgotten what he asked Charlie to do for him, and surely that's impossible, because it's all part of The Plan.

'Leah Martens, the girl who yelled at you outside the court,' Charlie says. 'You wanted me to find her for you.'

His dad's nodding slowly. 'Yes, I did,' he says. 'I've got scores to settle, that's what I said, right?'

'Right,' Charlie says uncertainly. 'She put you in jail.'

His dad nods again. 'I've been trying to think of a way to make her pay,' he says, 'the whole lot of them.'

'The whole lot of who?' Charlie asks.

His dad shakes his head. He's turned in on himself again, as though his head is filled with thoughts that are closed to Charlie.

'It's the girl you hate, isn't it?' Charlie says.

At last his dad raises his eyes and looks Charlie in the face. He sighs. 'I do hate her,' he says clearly. 'Let's think of a way to hurt her like she hurt me.'

Charlie stares at him. He'd assumed his dad had a plan. Surely that's what parents are for. They always have a plan.

That's why they get to be older and wiser. He thought that as soon as he gave his dad the address of the girl, they'd get going on revenge.

'If your mother had let me see you that day, I wouldn't have spent the past twelve years in jail,' Cheever says broodily. Charlie feels uncomfortable, like the first time they met, because it sounds like his dad is blaming his mum for getting killed. But Charlie doesn't open his mouth, because he doesn't know what to say. His dad is gazing at him with a strange expression on his face. Then his dad says, 'You're a lot like your mother, did you know that?'

'I know,' Charlie says. 'That's what my auntie says.'

'She was always thinking about things, your mother,' Charlie's dad says and Charlie doesn't know if he means that it's a good thing or a bad thing, to think about things.

'She was very stubborn,' his dad says. 'I know I wasn't as straight with her as I should have been but you were my son. I should have had the right to see you, right? I mean look at us now, perfectly civilized, sitting here having a coffee together. Father and son, as it should be. But she couldn't see it like that. You were hers and she wouldn't let me see you, wouldn't let me touch you. She wanted you all to herself.'

Charlie likes hearing that both his parents wanted him so much.

'That's what I like about our meetings,' his dad says. 'I got what I wanted in the end.'

Charlie feels like his dad just punched him. He doesn't know what to say. His dad seems to be saying he wants to have coffee with Charlie in order to get one over Charlie's dead mother. He doesn't seem sorry she's dead at all. Charlie stares down at the table top.

'I can't tell you how proud I am that you found the Martens girl,' his dad says, like he's hurrying to cover up what he just said. 'Because let me tell you, that's really fast. I've never known anyone be found so fast.'

Charlie sighs. He tries to put out of his mind the thing his dad said about getting what he wanted in the end. Maybe his dad wasn't thinking what was coming out of his mouth. Charlie does that sometimes, says things that sound all wrong, and then he hates himself because people get the wrong idea. He thinks that's what happened to his dad. He can't have meant those things about his mum. He's just angry that he's been in prison for something he didn't do.

Now that he knows he's impressed him, Charlie tells his dad all about looking for Leah Martens online and not finding a street address, and mapping the schools and clicking through the gallery of images from each of the schools. His dad listens intently.

'I can show you Charter Avenue online,' Charlie says eagerly. 'If you've got a computer at home I can show you her house. You can see it.'

His dad says, 'That's amazing. Charlie, I'm so proud.'

Charlie gulps. He's seized by the need to stay close to his dad. Perhaps he could go home with him. Perhaps he could even live with him. He could change his name from Brigson to Cheever, although he's a bit worried by the way Charlie Cheever sounds; he thinks he might get teased. He doesn't want his dad to walk away. He doesn't want his dad to go in one direction and him to go in another, back to his auntie.

'Seriously,' Charlie says. 'I can show you if you've got a computer at home.'

'I may take you up on that,' his dad says. 'But today I've got to go and see a man about a—' He sees Charlie's face fall and says. 'Hey, I'll see you soon. We'll look at it together next time, no need to be down.'

He reaches out his hand and ruffles Charlie's hair, and Charlie – who hasn't had his hair ruffled by his dad for twelve years – feels ready to explode with joy.

'What can I do next?' Charlie says.

His dad smiles. 'For me?' he asks, 'I don't deserve you.'

'For you,' Charlie confirms.

'Well . . .' His dad thinks. 'I don't want to ask too much of you. You've got school work to do, and you've got to help your auntie. I hope you're helpful around the house?'

'Of course,' Charlie lies. But then he doesn't like it when his dad reaches out and ruffles his hair again and says, 'I knew it, I knew you'd be a good lad. What do you do, eh, do you do the vacuuming?'

Charlie doesn't want to talk about what he does – or rather doesn't do – for his auntie. He doesn't like it when his dad's treating him like a kid, like he's making fun of him. He and his dad have got serious business in hand.

'I can think of a plan,' Charlie says helpfully, 'for getting back at the girl.'

His dad gives him a bit of a funny look, and for the first time Charlie thinks that actually his dad's blue eyes aren't like his at all. But then his dad nods in agreement.

'Yes, let's make her suffer,' he says. 'That's my boy.'

LINDEN

10

Linden's got lucky and he knows it. Marky's come through on his promise and now Linden's got his apron and he's behind the counter of the little kiosk learning how to repair shoes. He's even being taught how to cut keys, which makes him feel strange when he remembers all the car keys he's nicked from people's houses. It's only a try-out, Marky made that clear. The manager will see what he thinks, and if he says okay then Linden might get a permanent job. But even though he's not officially got the job, he'll still get paid.

'How's it feeling, Lin?' Marky asks him and Linden shrugs, like it's all right, like he's not fussed. The truth is, he's got a job and it feels brilliant. He's putting in the hours, and he'll be paid, and that feels like a real high. Better than the highs that Victor sells. But that's not the kind of thing that Linden's used to saying. Words like '*brilliant*' don't trip off the tongue easily. Brilliant sounds naïve, like you think there's no catch and there's always a catch. In this case, Linden hasn't found it yet, but he's wary, waiting for it to show itself. Something like, '*You can work here, but we cut your pay in half because you were in Feltham.*' Or, '*You can work here, but the boss will treat you like shit because you were in Feltham.*'

Linden hasn't told Victor what he's doing. He knows Victor will piss himself laughing. *Shoe repair?* he'll taunt. Linden is afraid Victor will take offence at his little brother choosing this over Victor's illegal job opportunities. Victor will think his little brother's spitting in his face.

Anyway, so far his boss seems nice, and Marky says he's okay and that they pay you like they say, so Linden's struggling to see where the catch is going to come from. But there's always a catch, there's no point in getting excited.

First thing in the morning, he thought he wasn't going to like standing right in the arcade like that. Victor's trained him to keep his head down, go unnoticed, melt into the crowd. Now here he is, wearing an apron and standing behind his counter in his brightly lit booth, for anyone to see. At first he stood there with his head bowed and his shoulders hunched over, so no one would recognise him, but Marky snapped him out of it. 'No one's looking at you,' he said, 'it's not a line-up!' And after a little while Linden realised that it was true. The people going past, they see you but they don't really look at you. You're just the shoe repair man. After a little while he even began to enjoy it. Just because people don't look at you doesn't mean you can't look at them. So in between learning from Marky he watches what's going on in the arcade, who's coming and going. He sees the elderly women walking slowly on their own, pulling their shopping trolleys, the young mums with their pushchairs or chasing after runaway toddlers; the couples bickering or kissing, and the kids just excited to be out on their own, nipping in and out of shops and never buying anything. There are Christmas decorations in the arcade: gigantic golden baubles hanging from the ceiling, and massive plastic white snowflakes and fairy lights. Add in the fact that there's a steady stream of pretty girls walking through the mall and compared to Feltham it feels like magic.

An elderly man approaches the kiosk and for a moment Linden panics. It's five in the afternoon and Marky's nipped out for a minute, to get a coffee to keep him awake til they close up shop at six o'clock, and Linden's not sure he can remember everything on his own.

The man delves into the plastic carrier bag he has looped over his arm and he pulls out a shoe, thrusting it at Linden.

Linden doesn't have any alternative. He reaches out and takes the shoe, turning it around in his hand. It's an ancient object, the leather so thin and tatty that it's nearly worn through in half a dozen places, and the sole is flapping off. Linden doesn't have a clue where to start or if it's even fixable.

The man wheezes something at him, but Linden can't hear. He spots a hearing aid in the man's papery ear and so he says, loudly, 'Sorry, can you say that again?'

And the man wheezes again.

Linden doesn't want to get it wrong.

'It needs resoling, is that right?' he says loudly at the elderly man, flapping the sole back and forward with his finger to illustrate what he's saying.

The man nods enthusiastically and says something that sounds like, 'How much?'

'You leave it with me,' Linden says, 'and come back in twenty minutes, yeah? We'll do it for a couple of pounds.' The man looks doubtful so Linden indicates twenty minutes on the clock face behind him. He's pretty sure Marky will be back in five minutes, so he can have it fixed for the OAP by then. Linden's pulled the price out of the air, but he thinks he can persuade Marky to give the old chap a discount on account of his age.

Again the elderly man nods in agreement. He gives Linden a quick smile and a thumbs-up, and Linden gives him a thumbs-up and a grin in reply. The old man turns and shuffles off, nearly colliding with a child who's escaped his mother's clutches and is running wild.

Linden watches the old man go. He doesn't know why, but the grin is still on his face. He feels proud to have dealt with a customer on his own, like he's found his flow. He thinks he's going to like fixing people's shoes for them. There's something noble about it. He's glad he's not working in one of the shiny-fronted shops selling sports shoes or mobile phones. He likes his booth. He likes standing here. This is it, this shuffling, skipping, sighing, frowning crowd of shoppers. This is his flow.

And that's when he sees her.

This time he's sure. It's the Martens girl from the trial, the one Victor stared at on the news.

She's wearing jeans and a long sweater, her hair loose and long, just like on TV. He's glad to see that she's recovered. Not that she's walking around with a big smile on her face – who does that? She looks serious, preoccupied by what's going on inside her head. But she seems in control at least. It's weird, even though he doesn't know her, seeing her screaming outside the courtroom had worried him. The way he felt, it had nothing to do with whatever connection she had with his brother. No, seeing her out of control and upset had made him worried for *her*. Now she's carrying some kind of kit bag, and she's walking purposefully, like she's got somewhere to be.

Linden closes his eyes and opens them again. Is it really her? What are the chances that this girl that he's been thinking about appears, out of the blue, in front of his eyes? He must be imagining it. But then he thinks, is it such a coincidence? The arcade isn't far from the park where she was attacked when she was small, which means she probably lives close by. It looks like she's familiar with the arcade, like she comes here all the time. The only reason he hasn't seen her before is that this is his first day. End of story.

She glances over towards him, as though maybe she's felt his eyes on her, and in that moment he sees the scar on the far side of her face, and then he's sure.

Leah Martens is walking fast, moving away from him. Soon she'll have disappeared. He wants to see where she's going, but Marky's still gone, and he doesn't want to leave the stall unmanned, doesn't want to get fired before he's begun.

Linden steps outside the stall, knowing he shouldn't. It looks untidy to be going in and out, like he can't stay still. Still, he takes several steps away from his post, and when he sees Marky walking back towards him with a coffee, he runs over to him and says, 'There's a shoe you've got to fix for an old man, it's on the counter, And he can't pay more than two quid. Don't worry, I'll be back.' And before Marky can argue he scarpers after the girl, unbuttoning his overall as he goes. If he's going to talk to her, he doesn't want to look like a shoe repair man. Life as a shoe repair man in this arcade may have been his flow ten minutes ago but he's not prepared to commit to it yet. Not in front of a girl like her. He's not sure exactly why he cares what she thinks, he just knows that he does.

When he gets within easy sight of the girl, Linden slows down. There's no way he can go up to her and ask her the question that keeps swirling in his head. He can't very well say, 'Hey, why does my brother look funny every time he sees you?' So instead he hangs back and watches where she goes. She walks out of the arcade, like she's used it as a short cut, not to buy anything. He follows her out into the cold air. It's late afternoon in December, and the sky's already dark. She's turning right then left and it's taking so long that Linden starts to worry more and more about Marky being annoyed at him for running off like this and he's on the edge of turning back, because she's just a girl and Marky's a job, but still he follows her. Now she's gone down an alley, heading towards what looks like a warehouse. She goes up to a doorway and pushes the door open, and he stands still and watches her vanish. After a moment, when there's no sight of her, he goes up and reads the little plaque by the door she's vanished through.

It's called the Empire Gym.

Linden stands there with his hand pressed against the door. What he wants to do is follow her inside. What he knows he must do is go back and apologise to Marky and explain about the old man and his shoe. Slowly, he lets his hand drop away from the door and he turns and heads back the way he's come.

Later, he'll find her. Next time. Now at least he has an idea of where to look.

CHARLIE

11

Charlie is racking his brains. He's been thinking a lot about his conversation with his dad and he thinks he understands why his dad said he didn't have a plan for settling scores with Leah Martens. Charlie understands now that it was another test for him. Like following the Martens girl and finding out where she lived. The new test is to come up with a plan for settling scores. He feels better when he understands what his dad is trying to do. He's trying to challenge Charlie. It's like the teachers at school always going on about thinking for yourself, and problem solving, not relying on other people. His dad doesn't want Charlie to rely on him to decide what to do, he wants to challenge Charlie to show him that he can come up with a plan himself. Charlie thinks that when he's done that, and come up with something that will impress his dad, then his dad will suggest he goes and lives with him. Charlie thinks his dad must want that as much as Charlie does. Charlie just needs to prove himself.

Understanding what's going on in his dad's head is one thing. Thinking of a plan is something else.

Charlie's not afraid of thinking big. But when he starts to think about actual revenge, and about things like knives and blood, he feels very queasy. He looks up online how to make a Molotov cocktail, because he's heard of people throwing things like that through letterboxes, and it seems better than sticking a knife into someone. But when he actually thinks about doing it, about setting something on fire and throwing it into someone's house, even the girl's house, and waiting for flames and smoke and wondering who's inside the house and when they'll notice, and if he might kill someone by mistake, then he feels ill, like he might throw up his lunch.

He sits in front of his computer and stares at the screen. He logs into Facebook using an account he made up once when he was playing a joke on his friend. No one knows the Facebook account is his and it doesn't have any identifying information on it. He finds his way back to her page and clicks to message her. He doesn't even stop to think, he starts typing, jabbing at his keyboard with two fingers, slowly, looking for the letters as he goes.

im the man hu folowd u and u shud be scayrd

He sits back, staring at the words on the screen. He feels excited. It's a lot easier to threaten the girl like this than face to face. This way, he doesn't have to do anything drastic like setting fire to her house and she doesn't have to mace him or knife him or trap him in a pit. It helps that he described himself as a man. It makes him feel bigger, more threatening, like he can be someone else on the screen, someone she should take notice of.

He clicks to send his message, and then he waits.

He glances at the clock. It's ten at night. He thinks of the girl sitting in her room, dark except for the glow of the screen. She'll be so scared when she sees his message. He thinks of her flinching away from her screen, starting to shake. He bites his lip in anticipation.

He waits, but nothing happens. Where is she? Asleep already? At ten o'clock?

He paces around the room. He wants her to see his message. He wants to know she's scared.

He goes downstairs to the kitchen to get a bowl of chocolate cereal. His auntie is sitting in there reading the newspaper. She's got the radio on too, not really listening, just for the company. Sometimes he wonders why she hasn't got a new boyfriend and thinks it's probably because she never makes an effort to meet anyone, or to dress prettily. She's always working and then when she comes home she's tired and just makes dinner and watches the TV or reads the newspaper. The last boyfriend was around for nearly a year, but Charlie never liked him, and he was pleased when they broke up. His auntie looks up, surprised to see him. He usually closets himself for hours on end with his computer and his computer games. He rarely even bothers to say good night. He wonders sometimes if it would be different if she were his mum. He thinks it would, that he'd care more, that she'd care more; but she's not and they both know it. When he was small, he'd said it to her a lot: 'You're not my mum,' and so she'd backed off, and that's how he liked it, her keeping her distance. Now he's bigger, once in a while they have a laugh together, and then Charlie sees how fun it could be if they were like that all the time, but then something always happens, like Charlie does something wrong, and the laughing stops.

'What are you up to, up there?' she asks him.

'Homework and stuff,' he says, lying as a matter of course. 'Biology.'

'Good,' his auntie says, recognising the lie for what it is. 'Let me know when you've discovered a cure for cancer.'

'What?' Charlie looks at her, irritated. He's not really paying attention, he's thinking about Leah Martens, sitting terrified in front of her computer screen. He feels about six feet tall, with broad shoulders and a short muscled neck, so big that his head looks little sitting on top of it. It's annoying to have an aunty bugging you about homework when you're so powerful.

'I'm joking,' she says. 'I mean all this homework should lead to something big.'

'Yeah,' Charlie says. 'Yeah, I think it will.'

When he gets back upstairs, he blinks at the screen. There are three new words there. Three little words, one big leap forward for Charlie's plan.

Who are you?

He grins. He types:

im yr wurst nitemayr

Then he deletes that and types:

u no who i am

He thinks that looks scarier. She won't know, she won't even guess, but she'll be trying to guess. She'll think of all the people it might be, all the enemies she has. It'll drive her crazy. He clicks to post his comment.

He doesn't have to wait long. She's replying.

I don't know who you are. Why are you trying to scare me?

Charlie thinks and thinks. What's the best answer? He wants to tell her exactly who he is. He wants her to know that his dad is going to settle his scores. But he also knows, instinctively, that it's scarier the less he says. He mutters possible responses to himself, and likes the sound of one in particular. 'Because I can,' he mutters to himself. 'Because I can.' He types it, so it's on the screen.

becos i can

He clicks to post his comment. Then, forcing himself, he turns the computer off and goes to bed. But he can't sleep. He's too full of excitement at what he's done. Too busy thinking about how proud his dad is going to be. He lies there with his eyes wide open, gazing into the darkness.

A night of silence will scare her even more.

LINDEN

12

Linden watches through the glass panel in the door. They're all shapes and sizes, the people in the gym, but most of them are men and when he scans the room for the Martens girl he finds her quickly. She's standing gathering her hair in a ponytail, securing it in a band. So now when she turns around, he can see her whole face for the first time, with the scar exposed. It's really not so bad.

It's more than not bad. Her face isn't perfect, but he can see who she is. And the fact that she's not trying to hide the scar makes her more interesting to him. He's been confused, since he got out of Feltham, about what girls look like. All he's seen of women since he was fourteen are his English teacher, women on TV and the models posing on the posters stuck on Feltham's cell walls, but none of the girls he sees walking around in town look like them at all. He'd have expected a girl to cover a scar like that with makeup, or wear her hair over it, hiding her face. But Leah Martens seems comfortable with it, proud of it almost, or perhaps defiant. Linden thinks of the young men in Feltham who bore their scars like battle wounds. He thinks of Victor with a knife scar under his eye. When he was younger his brother's scar had worried him. He didn't like to think of his big brother being threatened. He depended on Victor to protect him, so the thought of someone hurting him made him anxious. But when he asked Victor how he'd got the scar, he said he'd got into a fight outside a pub. He never knows whether Victor's telling him the whole truth.

A young man in black T-shirt and baggy trousers and bare feet looks like he's the instructor. He's chatting to Leah Martens, smiling, putting his hand on her shoulder in a friendly way, not like he's trying anything on. She's nodding, like he's giving her advice. Then the instructor calls the class together. Linden watches as they warm up. They're stretching, touching their toes and doing stomach crunches. To Linden, used to being surrounded by men in the gym, it's strange to see a girl in there alongside the men, doing the same as them. Soon he sees that she's not the only girl in the class, but she's the fittest and the most determined. The instructor tells them he's going to count them up to seventy push-ups and by the time he's reached twenty there are people dropping out, but even when Linden can see her arms are trembling under her, Leah Martens carries on until the count of seventy. The group drifts off to the side of the room, where they get stuff out of their kit bags, taping on shin pads, and winding their hands in long wraps that look like a bandage, pulling on their gloves. They all seem to be familiar with each other, chatting a little bit while they get kitted up. Then the instructor calls the class together again and demonstrates a move. He punches, kicks, punches again.

'Leah,' he calls, and she moves away from the crowd of students, standing ready, putting up her guard. She's obviously used to being singled out, Linden thinks. A few moments later, he can see why. She's perfectly controlled. Under attack, she doesn't flinch, she moves her gloves, minutely, to deflect blows. Then, when it's her turn to demonstrate the attack, she jabs, kicks and jabs again, fists and feet flying fast and to the point.

Softly Linden whistles in admiration. She's like a machine. He chuckles. It looks like she's making a point with every move.

I . . . don't . . . need . . . protecting . . . I . . . can . . . take . . . care . . . of . . . myself.

She looks so relaxed. How can anyone move like that and look so relaxed?

The instructor breaks away, and he moves so fast that by the time Linden realises he's headed for the door – for him! – there's no time to try to make himself scarce, but he turns to get away anyway.

The instructor throws open the door, 'Hey! What do you want?'

Linden thinks about running, but he hasn't actually broken any laws. Not this time. He turns back to the instructor. 'Nothing,' he says. Then, 'Just watchin'.'

'Watching? Well this isn't a public event. You either come in and give it a try, or you leave. First session's free.'

The sensible thing would be to leave. There were lads in Feltham who were into martial arts, but Linden was afraid of what he might turn into if he was actually taught to fight. He'd seen how Dave – the same Dave who set upon the new boy and hurt his spine – used MMA as an excuse to kick the shit out of anyone smaller than himself. Over the instructor's shoulder he can see the class waiting. Some of them are chatting, punching the air, stretching. He can see Leah Martens waiting too. She's standing watching Linden, almost like she's waiting for him.

'I don't have any kit,' Linden says.

'We've got kit we can loan you,' the instructor says. 'Spares. So, like I said, come on in or go on your way.'

The instructor waits for a second, watching Linden's face, which Linden can feel burning. He wants to turn and walk away, but Leah is right in front of him . . .

'Okay,' says Linden, 'I'm in.'

The instructor nods in approval and extends his hand. Linden stares at the hand – he can't remember anyone extending a hand to him before, not like this, a stranger making friends – he glances at the guy's face, expecting some kind of trick, but sees only slight impatience. He extends his own hand, tentatively, allows it to be shaken. And still the guy doesn't do some show-off martial arts thing and flip him on to his back on the floor.

'I'm Chris,' says the instructor. 'Let's give this a go.'

Linden follows Chris into the gym. He feels like a prize catch – a prize idiot . . . *Look what I found outside the door. He's big, but can he fight?* Everybody's eyes are on him and he wishes the floor would open up and swallow him down and deliver him back out on to the street. He knows the street. He can survive there. This though? A class . . . with girls . . . and rules . . . Fighting, but not fighting. Fighting so you hit but you don't actually break anything – like a nose . . . or a spine . . . How do you do that?

'Leah,' Chris says, 'help get – sorry, what's your name?'

'Linden,' he says. In that split second he can't think of a reason not to use his real name.

'Okay, Leah, help get Linden kitted up, will you?'

Leah jerks her head at Linden to follow her to a kit bag that's overflowing with jumbled pads and tapes. She hunkers down, digs around, then turns to face him, brandishing some pads.

'Have you done this before?' she asks him, brisk and businesslike.

He shakes his head, like he's gone dumb. Then he says, 'I saw you through the window, you're really good.'

She nods in acknowledgement of what he's said but she doesn't smile. He wonders what it would take to make her smile.

'These are for your shins,' she tells him, and watches while he struggles to put them on, telling him yes or no when he gets the taping right or wrong, but not helping, not touching him, which is probably a good thing because he can already feel himself red and hot with embarrassment.

Eventually, he's kitted up: shin guards, foot padding, hand wraps, gloves. He stands there watching. The class has moved on and the exercises have got harder, the combination of movements more complex – the experienced students stand out from the crowd, and the younger, newer ones are gasping and staggering, exhausted already.

'I can't do this shit,' he mutters.

'Yeah you can,' Leah Martens says, tight lipped. 'It's hard at first, you just need to put in the time.'

'Sorry,' he says, 'you should have a partner who can do all this kicking and stuff. You deserve someone good like you.'

She shrugs, which he takes for: *Yes but I'll put up with you.*

He raises his gloves to his face and grits his teeth. He's not scared of being hit, he's scared of being this close to a girl. Three years inside. Three years when he should have been learning how to chase girls, how to talk to them, flirt with them. Instead he's been sitting in his cell on his own or surrounded by other boys. Leah hesitates. He can see her thinking she's got to go easy on him.

'It's okay' he says. 'I can take it. I've been hit before.'

So Leah hits him, and he moves quickly to block her, her glove pounding into his. Jab, kick, jab and kick . . .

She doesn't pause, just runs through the sequence again. Jab, kick, jab and kick . . . Jab, kick, jab and kick . . . He watches her from behind his gloves. He moves quickly, anticipating easily. She's strong, but she's only using a fraction of her strength to hit him, he can feel that her power is there, behind the jabs and the kicks. She's not knocking him out, or knocking him over or anything, but he thinks she probably could if she put her mind to it and that freaks him out. He's never heard of anything like this before, girls who can fight like this, not scratching and biting, but learning techniques so they fight efficiently. What she can't see is, it's taking all his self-control not to hit back. It's lucky she's a girl. If it was a bloke, hitting him like that, he might have hit him so hard he'd have a broken nose by now.

They pause to switch roles. Leah raises her gloves to guard her face. Linden swallows. He's never hit a girl. Hanging around with Victor means he's met some girls who wouldn't hesitate to hit him. Still, he doesn't like the idea . . .

Jab, kick, jab and kick . . . Jab, kick, jab and kick . . . His first attempts are ungainly and keeping his balance is harder than he thought. His kicks and jabs are feints, fists and feet hardly touching her, hardly going anywhere near her, he's holding back so hard. He's been working out in a gym for three years. He's afraid if he hits her, it'll be like squashing a fly.

'Hey,' she says, signalling him to stop. She drops her guard and slips off her gloves so that she can gather up the strands of hair that have escaped from her ponytail.

'I'm supposed to be your opponent,' she says to him. 'You can hit me, I'm not a doll.'

Linden shakes his head.

'I don't want to hurt you,' he mutters. 'I'll hurt you if I hit you.'

She stares at him. 'You don't have to break any bones,' she says. 'There's, like, a happy medium, you know?'

He looks blankly at her.

'Like, a middle way, between breaking my neck and not actually making contact.'

He nods and mutters an apology.

She pulls her gloves back on.

He takes a deep breath, glances around, hoping no one watched that exchange. Then he goes through the routine again, still keeping control, but making contact now. Hitting hard enough for her to feel, but not hard enough to hurt. It's a good feeling, knowing he can keep control, knowing he's not going to go crazy hitting and kicking, knowing they're not going to have to drag him out of there screaming like a banshee with his fists flying.

Once, right at the beginning at Feltham, when he was small and scared, a kid called Ryan had taunted him about Victor, saying he was so thin he must have AIDS, and

Linden had lost it, hitting him so hard he'd broken Ryan's nose.

'Switch partners!' Chris yells, and they step apart, breathing hard from the exertion.

'Good job, Linden,' she says to him, and rewards him with a smile that transforms her face. 'I'm Leah by the way.' She holds out her hand.

He grins, takes her hand, biting back the words, *I know*. He's pleased by her smile, by the touch of her hand, by the praise. But a moment later she's already released his hand and she's walking away from him, looking for another partner.

When class is over, Linden hesitates. He could walk away. He wants to walk away. The thought of going up to her and talking to her is terrifying. Leah's unwinding the wrap from her hands. She seems isolated from the others but as he watches he notices that as they gather their stuff and go, each one of the class members waves to her, or touches her on her arm and she acknowledges each of them with a little wave, or a smile. Suddenly there's a burst of laughter from a small group, a shared joke, and Leah's face breaks into a broad grin. He likes watching her face. He likes the fact you can tell right away what's going on in her head. Outside the courthouse there was no secret, you could tell she was angry. Sparring in the gym, he could tell she was totally focused. Now, seeing her with her friends, she's having fun, but he thinks she's not really part of the group either; she likes being alone. He feels like he can read her emotions, even though they just met.

He likes watching her face and he likes watching her

body, which even in loose black trousers and T shirt looks way sexier than the Feltham posters. He likes the way she stands tall and straight, not coy or self-effacing. She's beautiful but he's trying not to stare, because he knows if he does she'll think he's a freak. Linden takes a deep breath and walks over to her. But then he stands there, shuffling, embarrassed. This is like asking for a job, he's setting himself up for rejection, bracing himself for the blow. He suspects Leah could deliver a knockout punch. Suddenly he has a flashback to the newsagent's shop, and the owner yelling at him, . . . '*Linden James. You've been in prison, haven't you? . . . You think I'll let you near my money?*'

Leah glances at him. 'Hi again.'

'Hi,' Linden replies, and swallows hard.

'So, are you going to take up kickboxing?' she asks. 'You're a natural.'

He shrugs, pleased. 'I might,' he says. Then he doesn't know what else to say. She looks at him again, as if to say, *Why are you hanging around?* He doesn't want to creep her out. But he can't turn around and walk away.

'Can I walk you home?' he says.

'You think I need protecting?'

'No, of course not,' he laughs, awkwardly. No one would think that. Then he shrugs miserably and says, 'It's me who needs protecting.'

Why didn't they have classes in flirting in Feltham? A basic life-skill, and he doesn't know where to start. It would've been full every lesson. Module One: pick-up lines . . .

She glances at him, straight in the eye. Then she smiles. *He got it right! He can't believe it*! He smiles, hopefully, but she turns her head away.

'Then you have to ask if I'll walk you home, not the other way round,' she says.

He winces, glancing around to see that no one's witnessing his humiliation.

'All right,' he shrugs. 'Scary Lady, will you walk me home?'

She grins. She likes that nickname. Scary Lady.

Then, just as suddenly, her face falls.

'I can't,' she says. No explanation.

'Okay,' he shrugs. He knows a brush-off. It's like the shop after all. His past somehow hanging around him like a bad smell. He's not going to embarrass himself. He turns to walk away.

'I'll see you next week, yeah?' she calls after him, but he doesn't look back.

Outside, in the street, he doesn't know what to do with himself. It's seven o'clock in the evening, and it's dark on this street with few streetlights, and it's freezing cold. He's not going to do any more following. If she doesn't want anything to do with him she doesn't want anything to do with him, and that's an end to it. When he was asking if he could walk her home, he felt like he should come clean, should say to her, '*Look, I followed you here, but I don't mean you any harm.*' That would have gone down well. So he's not waiting for her. He's standing there not knowing what to do next. When some of the others from the class come out, he stays where he is, doesn't know what else to do, nods at them, says bye as they pass by. Funny, like he's part of the class, when he just got hauled in by mistake. Anyway, he's still hanging around, so perhaps he is waiting for Leah after all, even if he's telling himself that he's not.

There she is, coming out the door with her kitbag over her shoulder. Her hair is loose over her shoulders, and she's pulled on a jacket over her jeans and sweatshirt. She's looking for someone. Suddenly he wonders if she has a boyfriend. Is that why she turned him down? That's probably it. Why did he assume someone like her didn't have a boyfriend? She'd have a million. The moment he feels jealousy hit, he knows this isn't just some crazy fascination with a girl that Victor is obsessed with. It's not just about finding out what the connection with Victor is any more. The moment jealousy hits, Linden knows he's got a whole new problem. Life is complicated enough without falling for a girl. Especially a girl who's linked in some way to Victor.

Two blokes walk up behind her, and Linden's thinking one of them must be the boyfriend, although she's got rough taste if so. He watches. They stop and talk to her, but the body language is all wrong. She doesn't know them and they're crowding her. She steps back, glancing impatiently along the road, looking for someone. One of them puts a hand on her arm, pulling her towards him, and quick as a flash she swipes him away, but they're loud and they've been drinking and they're not giving up. Without thinking, Linden crosses the road to help her. As he approaches he realises he's seen the two men before. They've been to the flat, doing odd jobs for Victor. Victor doesn't have employees, he has his high command, Tony and Sameer. Then there's a revolving band of companions who have either pissed him off or are in the process of pissing him off, kids or druggies that he slips a tenner to do him a favour. Linden's not sure if he's seen these guys since he's been out but he knows he's seen them before.

Linden says, 'Got a problem, Leah?' She glances at him, surprised to find him still there.

'No, no problem,' she says, standing her ground. 'As long as these jokers move along.'

Linden moves to stand at Leah's side.

The two blokes look up at Linden. He's not sure if they recognise him or not, but they glance at each other and then shrug and stagger off.

'I didn't need protecting,' Leah mutters.

'I know,' Linden says, 'but there was two of them and one of you. I came to even up the game.'

She looks at him again with that speculative look, as though she's weighing him up.

'Thanks,' she says.

'You're welcome. Maybe see you next time.'

She nods, says, 'Yeah.'

A car pulls up to the kerb a few metres from them and recognition sparks in Leah's eyes. She waves at Linden and walks over to the car. There's a man in the driving seat and from the way they greet each other – few words, easy familiarity – he assumes it's her dad. That cheers him up. That's why he couldn't walk her home then. A dad's way better than a boyfriend from his point of view.

The car pulls out from the kerb and drives slowly past him, under the streetlights, and he sees the man more clearly, first full face, and then in profile, then the back of his head.

Linden stares after the car.

He knows that face. But where from? He can't place it but it stirs his memory. He closes his eyes tight, trying to keep the face in his head. If he knows him, then the likelihood is Victor does too. Victor, who is fascinated by the girl. Victor, who probably sent his mates to bother her. Why would he do that? Because Victor knows her father . . . Linden's trying to piece together the links in the chain but he still can't place that face, so he's not getting the answers he's looking for. But anything that links the girl and Victor together scares him. He remembers her walking through the arcade, quick and confident. She doesn't know she's being watched.

When Linden opens his eyes and lifts his face, he thinks he's going mad. Having some kind of vision. If Victor could be called a vision.

Because there he is, his big brother, standing across the street, looking right at him. For an instant it comes into Linden's head that he could pretend he hasn't seen Victor, he could turn the other way and walk away. But Victor's all he's got. He can't walk away. Not yet. Probably not ever. So instead he crosses the street and walks up to him.

'I was wondering where you were,' says Victor mildly, 'and here you are. What a coincidence.'

Linden doesn't say anything, and he doesn't ask anything either. *What are you doing here? What's the girl to you?*

Because if he asks, Victor will lie to him.

There. The knowledge that Victor will lie to him has been there, clouding his mind, perhaps forever. But he's never said it to himself as clear as that. And once he's let the thought be thought, he knows it will not leave him: Victor will lie to him.

Walking beside him, Victor is silent. For an instant Linden has the panicked sense that Victor is listening in on what he, Linden, is thinking. He shakes his head, he's going mad.

'All right, Lin?' Victor enquires. 'You're very quiet.'

'Yeah,' Linden replies, 'I'm good. Got any plans for tonight?'

'Only the usual,' Victor barks with laughter.

So Victor can't hear what he's thinking – but he's suspicious, he knows something's up. Linden shivers to think what happens if his brother decides that his little brother's a traitor.

How can there be treachery in falling for Leah Martens?

Because that's what's happening. He's never felt this way before, wouldn't even have believed it could hit so fast. But the euphoria of finding Leah is shot through with fear. If Victor finds out what's going on . . . Linden vows to keep his thoughts on the subject of Leah Martens to himself.

Linden's noticed that Victor's evenings have a pattern to them. There's TV and beer and cigarettes, and just when you think things are winding down, Victor says he's off out. So Linden's surprised when he hears what sounds like a snore and looks up from the TV to see his brother lying on the sofa on the other side of the room asleep, his mouth agape. Linden gazes at him for a moment, then quietly gets to his feet and walks over to look down on his sleeping brother. Victor looks much younger like this and Linden thinks that once he would have felt a burst of affection for his big brother asleep and vulnerable, but that time is past.

Victor's phone has slipped from his hand onto the floor and silently, Linden squats down and picks up the phone. He hesitates. If Victor wakes up and finds him scrolling through the messages then Victor will skin him alive. He holds his breath and stands up, moving towards the door, avoiding the floorboards that squeak. He moves into the bathroom, closing the door behind him and turning the lock slowly so it doesn't make any kind of clicking or clunking noise.

Sitting on the edge of the bath, Linden stares at the phone. It's a smartphone and it's asking him for a password. He closes his eyes, thinks. What would Victor use as a password? He remembers what Victor sometimes calls himself for a joke, so tries typing in *King Victor*, and the phone lets him in. He scrolls through the messages, looking at texts from earlier that evening, around the time he'd gone to the gym.

There's an incoming message:

she's gone into the Empire Gym by the arcade

And then a reply from Victor:

stay with her. wait for her to come out. I want to know where she goes afterwards, follow her home, give her a fright from me

Linden stares at the screen. He hasn't been imagining it, then, Victor's fixation on Leah. His brother is having her followed. His brother is suggesting scare tactics. But why? What's in it for him? If there's a good thing to be said for Victor, he's not malicious just for fun. He usually has a reason.

From the other room there's the sound of a creaking

floorboard and then Victor's voice. 'Lin, hey, Lin, are you here? Have you seen my phone?'

Linden shoves the phone deep into his pocket. He'll have to 'find' it somewhere in the flat later on. Then he realises the next thing Victor's going to do is call his phone, and it's going to ring from inside his pocket. He snatches it out of his pocket. He has no idea how to turn Victor's phone off.

'Hey, it's in here!'

'What?'

'It's in here! Hang on, I'll be out in a minute'

Linden flushes the loo, although he hasn't used it. He washes his hands, although he doesn't need to. He walks out of the bathroom door, flourishing the phone. 'It was on the edge of the bath,' he tells his older brother.

Victor takes it from him. He gives his little brother a long look. 'Funny,' he says, 'I don't remember leaving it in there.'

Linden shrugs. 'Obviously,' he says, 'or you wouldn't have lost it.'

CHARLIE

13

Charlie frowns down at the newspaper that he picked up from the newsagents for his auntie like she asked. There's a picture of his dad on the front page alongside a picture of the waitress in the park. Charlie wants to read the article, see what the world is saying about his dad, but he's got to go, his dad will be waiting for him.

His auntie comes into the room still in her coat, carrying a bag of groceries – she's been at work for a couple of hours but it's Saturday morning and her office closes by lunchtime. She says she's got his favourite sausages for lunch. Charlie grunts, uninterested. He takes a deep breath. He wouldn't usually ask. Wouldn't usually risk his auntie knowing he can't read – or can't read quickly. Can't read well.

'What's this about?' He pushes the newspaper casually across the table, towards her, and she glances down at it, then looks more closely as she takes her coat off and pulls out one of the chairs so she can sit down.

'So,' she says, like she predicted this all along, 'his alibi's collapsing after all. Didn't I say he'd paid the waitress to say that?'

Charlie swallows.

'Is that what she says? That Dad paid her to say he was in the café?'

'*Dad*?' She repeats the word, surprised. 'You mean Cheever?'

'Yeah, Cheever,' Charlie mutters.

His auntie gives him a look, then she says, 'Why don't you read it for yourself?'

Charlie snatches the paper back, irritated, and leans over it, staring hard at the words, deciphering them slowly. But he hasn't got time for this. He boils with frustration. Reading hasn't bothered him much before, he's never needed it except at school where all his teachers know he's hopeless, but suddenly, in the past few weeks, he's needed to read all the time. All the finding out about Leah Martens. It's been exhausting and he knows that it shouldn't have been as hard as this. He knows something's wrong. He needs help. He just doesn't know how to ask for it.

'Her ex-boyfriend's got it in for her, hasn't he?' he asks, looking up at his auntie. 'He's just trying to cause trouble, saying she made it up for money. Why would anyone believe him?'

'Because no one really believes Cheever,' his auntie says bluntly. 'Everyone says the same as me, they don't trust him.'

'You're just prejudiced,' Charlie snaps.

'Prejudiced, am I?' his auntie says in a voice so soft it scares him. 'Well, if I am I've got reason. And so have you.' She comes up close to him and shakes her finger in his face. 'I don't care what you think of me but you're to have nothing to do with him, do you understand?'

Charlie won't look at her.

'Do you understand?' She's shouting at him now and he fears he might cry. He's got no time for this. Not for any of this. He has to get out of here.

'Yeah,' he mutters, 'I understand.'

She holds his gaze for a moment, then shakes her head and turns away.

'I don't know when you're telling me the truth and when you're lying to me,' she says sadly.

Charlie doesn't know what to say. Even he knows that saying he'd never lie to her is one lie too far.

'I'm off out,' he says and walks out of the kitchen into the hallway to put on his coat.

'Where are you going?' she asks, and there's no mistaking the suspicion in her voice. 'What about the sausages?'

'Just out,' he says, pulling his hoody on. 'I'll get something to eat.'

'Where's *out*?' She's not usually this insistent.

'I'm going to see a friend,' he says belligerently, 'if that's all right by you?'

'Charlie,' she pleads, 'promise me you're not going to see that evil man. Promise me this interest in his alibi is because of your mum, because there's just no way he's innocent, don't even think it.'

Charlie hesitates, but there's only one way out of this conversation.

'I promise you I'm not going to see an evil man,' he says coldly. 'I'm going to see a friend.'

He should be eager to see his dad. His dad's going to be so

pleased. Charlie's got his laptop in his bag, so he can show his dad what he wrote to the Martens girl, and how she wrote back. He'll show his dad he's worthy to work with him. That whatever his dad is going to do to get revenge, Charlie will be able to help. He doesn't know what his dad's plan is but he did say he had some scores to settle, so he must have something up his sleeve.

But if Charlie's honest with himself, what the newspaper said about his dad's alibi is preying on his mind. He knows Beth Cheever's ex-boyfriend is inventing things because he's angry with her for splitting up with him. But Charlie wishes he hadn't seen it, because it means this time there's a shadow over his meeting with his dad. It means that trusting him is a little bit difficult.

They're meeting at the coffee shop again, but Charlie is sure this is only because until his dad knows Charlie is serious about helping him he's worried about showing him where he lives. Maybe today once he's told his dad about the Facebook posts, they'll go to his house instead. It's like he's been through his initiation, and now he's going to become a man. He thinks again about the posts and he almost laughs out loud because they are the best thing he's ever done.

At the coffee shop, Charlie sits down without buying anything because he hasn't brought enough cash. His dad always buys him a milkshake or a hot chocolate, so he'll wait until he gets there, but he knows he won't be long, because his dad wants to see him just as much as he wants to see his dad. So Charlie picks a table and waits. The waitress behind the counter keeps glancing at him like, *Why are you taking up a table and not buying anything?* Charlie avoids her eyes. He plays with a cardboard mat, tearing it into pieces and building things out of it, little roads and bridges and a car. He thinks about getting his laptop out, but he's worried about using up the battery. He wants to save that for his dad. After a while, he checks his phone and sees that he's been waiting for an hour.

He texts his dad. *wayr r u?*

But when he looks up, there's his dad, pushing the glass door open and going to the counter and picking up a coffee, chatting to the waitress and then, only then, after doing all that, he turns towards Charlie. He brushes Charlie's cardboard bits and pieces out of the way and puts his coffee down on the table.

'Hi, Dad.' Charlie beams up at him. He wishes his dad had asked him what he wanted to drink. He's really thirsty now.

'Hi, son.' Cheever smiles. 'Sorry I'm late. I was afraid I might have missed you. But you waited.' It's not a question, just a statement of fact.

'That's all right,' Charlie says. He waits to hear what detained his dad, but his dad doesn't say anything else. Charlie watches as his dad takes a long sip of his coffee and sighs, glancing at his watch.

'The plan's going well,' Charlie says.

His dad looks at him blankly.

'The plan,' Charlie says again. 'To settle scores with Leah Martens.'

Charlie's dad gives him a long look. 'Really?' he says after a moment. 'Tell me about it.'

Charlie gets out his laptop and puts it on the table, carefully moving his dad's coffee so it doesn't spill. If he ruins this laptop, he's not getting another one, his auntie made that abundantly clear. He connects to the internet using the wi-fi password that's on a sign on the wall, and then he shows his dad his conversation with Leah Martens.

His dad leans in and reads intently, scrolling up and down, then scrolling up and down again. Charlie watches his blue eyes, behind his spectacles. He thinks again how his dad's eyes are just like his. But this just makes him think about what his auntie said about not being able to tell when he's lying and when he's telling the truth. And, for the first time, Charlie wonders whether his dad's like that too. Maybe the ability to lie is what got passed from his dad to him. He doesn't like thinking about that. He shakes his head, and Cheever glances up at him.

'What?' his dad says.

'Nothing,' Charlie says.

He can't see the screen from where he's sitting, so he watches his dad's face and recites the exchange in his head. He can remember it word for word.

im the man hu folowd u and u shud be scayrd

who are you?

u no who i am

I don't know who you are. Why are you trying to scare me?

becos I can

Who are you? What do you want?

you lyd

I never lied, you're the one who's lying

u r making it up. hes not the wun hu stabd u. u gest wont to hert him vishus bich

I'm not lying, cheever attacked me, I should know

u dont remember u cant say that

His dad glances up at Charlie, smiling, and Charlie waits on tenterhooks, glowing, for the words of praise he knows are about to come his way.

'You'll never get anywhere with spelling like that, Charlie,' he says. 'Are you dyslexic or something?'

Charlie's face falls.

His dad goes back to reading, then looks up again, sitting back on his chair.

'You really got her, son,' he says. 'You really scared her. That's exactly what I wanted.'

Charlie nods, but he's wary now, he doesn't know what's going to follow from his dad's mouth. All he can hear in his head is, '*You'll never get anywhere with spelling like that . . .*'

'Well, I'd better be off, I've got a meeting.'

Charlie is open-mouthed. He didn't think his dad would leave so quickly. 'But you just got here,' he says. 'I showed you all – all that. What about the plan?'

'Sorry, son,' his dad says, 'I've been running around like crazy. Got to get back on my feet, you know. Got to start earning a living. Then I can buy you something, a present to say thank you.'

Charlie nods again. A present sounds good.

'I'll come with you,' he says. 'We can talk on the way.'

His dad runs his hand through his hair. He's already half out of his seat, looking at his phone. 'What do we need to talk about?' he says.

Charlie starts to get out his seat. 'What comes next,' he says. 'Our plan.'

His dad looks at him and nods slowly. 'Tell you what,' he says, 'that was really rude of me, I didn't even get you a drink. What do you want? Hot chocolate?' He turns away, towards the counter. 'I'll get you a hot chocolate, with cream and everything, yeah?'

Charlie sits back down, confused. He watches his dad, joking with the woman behind the counter. She likes him, you can tell, smiling at him, laughing at something he says. When he puts the cash in her hand, he takes an extra moment, his fingers brushing hers. Charlie still feels like his dad's a stranger.

A minute later, his dad's put a cup of hot chocolate in front of him, with cream on top and a little biscuit on a saucer. Charlie stares at it. It's in a proper china cup, not a cardboard takeaway cup. Charlie knows what that means. His dad's not stupid. He knew what he was doing. He doesn't want Charlie to go with him. He's got the message.

So Charlie's not going to embarrass himself any more than he already has.

'Well, see you, son,' Cheever says, turning away. 'Enjoy the hot chocolate.'

'Yeah,' Charlie says dully. 'See you.'

His dad makes for the door, and Charlie reaches out and picks up the cup of hot chocolate and brings it to his mouth. It tastes like dishwater.

He watches as his dad hesitates outside the door then turns right.

Charlie stares at the laptop screen, still open on the table in front of him. The words glare out at him.

u r making it up. hes not the wun hu stabd u. u gest wont to hert him vishus bich

im not lying cheever attacked us

u dont remember u cant say that

He was so proud, and now he's so ashamed.

The words are weak, they're nothing. They can't hurt Leah Martens. He can't even spell. His dad could tell he's got it, the dyslexia thing Mrs Tepnall said. That was a letter he made sure his auntie never saw. And a phone call his teacher had with his fake auntie, the one with the breathy Irish accent. Extra spelling lessons is the last thing he needs, that's what his auntie told Mrs Tepnall.

How could he ever have thought his dad would be impressed by some words on a screen? Charlie can see what he's done for what it is now, just a kid playing at revenge. No wonder his dad wants nothing to do with him. That's why he left so suddenly, he doesn't think Charlie's up to the job. But Charlie's angry too, because he did try. And why does his dad think he's so much better than Charlie, anyway? He hasn't come up with any good plans to get the Martens girl back for lying. He hasn't even gone to the police and said who he saw in the park that day. Now Charlie even wonders if he did see someone. And if he lied about that, then maybe he did get the waitress to lie about the alibi too . . . Who knows what else is a lie? Charlie thinks again about his dad's lying blue eyes.

He glances out the window. Just because his dad wants him to sit in here drinking hot chocolate doesn't mean he's got to do it. Just because his dad doesn't want him to go with him doesn't mean he can't follow him . . . He can walk out of here any time. Charlie pushes back his chair and stands up. He makes his way to the door of the coffee shop.

LINDEN

14

Linden can't help himself. He's back at the Empire Gym, outside that door with the plaque on the wall. He feels like he's just ended up here, like he followed his legs and this is where they took him, but he knows there's more to it than that. He's taking a risk, meddling in Victor's affairs, whatever those affairs are. The first time he'd followed Leah, he'd just wanted to find out why Victor was fixated on her. Now he knows that Victor's having his thugs follow Leah, Linden wants those answers more than ever. But if he's being honest with himself, he's here because he wants to see Leah and he wants to make sure that she's safe.

He's arrived at the door but he doesn't push it open and go inside. He's got no money for kickboxing classes, no money for kit. He's not in a position to take up a hobby. So he just wants to see Leah and say . . . he'll say '*hi*.' But what then? She'll say. '*hi . . . so you're coming to class?*' And he'll say . . . he'll say . . . '*No . . . no, I just came to say – hi*.' And then what? She'll shrug. Perhaps she'll roll her eyes, because what kind of loser just hangs around outside a kickboxing class just to say hi to a girl? And she'll walk through the door and run up the stairs to the gym, and he'll be left out on the street like an idiot. Like a stalker idiot. A loser stalker idiot.

He turns, ready to walk away, head lowered, watching his feet on the pavement. He doesn't know what he was thinking coming here.

'Hey, Linden . . .' It's a man's voice. Linden looks up, and finds himself face to face with the kickboxing instructor, Chris. Linden grunts a hello, but he doesn't want to talk to anyone.

'You're going the wrong way if you're coming to class,' Chris says.

'I'm not going to class,' Linden says. In Feltham, if someone was talking to him and he didn't want to have a conversation, he'd just have pushed past him, kept on going. But Chris was okay. He hadn't had Linden arrested when he found him watching the class through the window in the door. He'd shaken Linden's hand.

'But you're right here and we start in five minutes,' Chris says, baffled. 'If you're here, why wouldn't you come in?'

Linden doesn't want to talk about it. He shakes his head, grunting again, hoping Chris will leave it and go on his way. But instead Chris won't leave it alone.

'You've got natural talent,' he says, 'a quick eye. If you put the time in, you could be good at this.'

'I've got no money for classes.'

Linden doesn't consciously choose to say it. It bursts out of him. An easy, ugly, way to end the conversation.

'Okay.' Chris looks at him speculatively. Then he says, 'Why aren't you wearing a coat in this weather?'

Linden shrugs. He's been cold ever since he got out of

Feltham because it's winter and he hasn't got a coat. The shoe repair shop hasn't paid him yet and he doesn't want to ask Victor for money. He could borrow but he really doesn't want to wear Victor's clothes. They smell of Victor. Still, he's not going to admit he hasn't got a coat. He doesn't want to sound like a beggar.

'Hi, Linden . . .' It's her voice, from behind him. He turns his head, and she's there, standing at his shoulder, hugging her padded jacket around her. He doesn't know how long she's been there, how much she's heard. Linden's eyes shift to the street behind her – are Victor's thugs following her this evening? But the street, as far as he can see, is clear.

'I'm freezing out here,' she says. 'I'll see you both inside.' She starts to walk towards the door, then turns, walking a few steps backwards. 'It's Christmas. Be nice, Chris.'

Chris sighs. 'Like the girl says, it's Christmas. I'll give you a month of free classes. After that, you have to find a way to pay.'

Linden shakes his head.

'I don't need charity,' he mutters.

Chris shrugs, and Linden can see he's offended.

'Suit yourself,' Chris says. He turns away from Linden and heads into the gym.

Linden stands on the pavement. It's humiliating, what Chris said, offering him lessons for free. But Linden can still see Leah walking backwards towards the gym. '*It's Christmas. Be nice, Chris.*' Why is she being nice to him? He groans. He really wants to follow her inside. He closes his eyes tight, trying to think. This is a big mistake. Why is he doing this? Is he doing it because he wants to find out what's going on with Victor, or is he just doing this because he fancies her? He's not sure himself where one begins and the other ends.

When he opens his eyes again, he starts to walk towards the gym. He pulls open the door and makes his way up the stairs.

CHARLIE

15

Charlie wasn't very good at this the first time round, but this time he has to get it right. The stakes are too high. This time it's not some crazy girl he's following, it's his dad.

He's not following his dad because he doesn't trust him, he tells himself. He's just finding out more about him. So he can help him.

Outside the coffee shop, he spots his dad a couple of shop fronts ahead of him. Charlie pulls his hoody up over his head. It's not a great disguise, after all the girl spotted him, but it makes him feel hidden.

His dad doesn't hurry. Which is a surprise to Charlie because he'd seemed in a rush to leave the coffee shop. He said he had to go to an appointment, and Charlie wanted to see who he was meeting, but his dad is strolling along like he has no one to think about but himself. The first time he stops and looks in a shop window, Charlie can hardly believe it.

You've got a meeting to get to! He wants to shout at his dad. *Hurry up!*

The shop is a men's clothes shop, the window full of headless mannequins wearing expensive-looking jeans and jumpers, with woollen scarves thrown carelessly around their truncated necks. Following his dad past the shop, Charlie glances at the prices and gulps. His dad must have some cash to even look in a shop like that.

At another clothes shop his dad doesn't simply stop and look, he goes inside.

You told me you had someone to meet!

He's gone for ages, like he's trying something on, and he comes out carrying a paper bag with the name of the shop on it.

Ted Baker.

Charlie tries to be pleased for his dad, like he's pleased for his auntie when she buys herself a new skirt or a blouse and she stands in front of the mirror admiring herself. But at the same time, he's thinking how his dad had said that when he had some money he'd buy Charlie a present.

Charlie doesn't know what to expect but he can't stop following now. He's got to find out.

His dad comes to a halt, joining the messy queue at a bus stop, and Charlie has to walk right past him. His heart's racing, but his dad is looking at the bus times, and there's a crowd of people waiting, so Charlie gets by without being noticed. He joins the people waiting at the next bus stop along. When a bus comes and his dad lines up to get on, Charlie waits until the last minute, then dashes on himself. He clambers on board just as the bus doors close behind him. His Oyster card is in the pocket of his hoody and he presses it against the machine, hoping he's got enough cash on it. He scans the faces around him, knowing full well he might see his dad's face looking at him, frowning. He's prepared for that. If it happens he's going to laugh and say, *Would you believe it? It's a small world.*

Charlie looks around again at the passengers as he makes his way down through the bus. Has he got it wrong? Is his dad still at the bus stop? But he saw him get on, he must be upstairs he tells himself, and he takes a free seat in the corner right at the back of the downstairs of the bus. From here he can see who comes down the stairs, and with any luck, if the bus doesn't get too crowded, he can push his way off after his dad.

The bus goes north. It's a part of town Charlie doesn't recognise at all. At first, every time the bus stops, Charlie waits, staring at the stairs from under his hoody, ready to leap into action the moment he spots his dad. But after a while he begins to feel like his dad's never going to appear. His excitement, the adrenaline rush of the chase, has flat-lined. He's lulled by the juddering motion of the bus, and the jumbled conversations that surround him, and the warmth of bodies . . . It's only when he jolts awake that he realises he's been asleep! For a moment or half an hour – he has no way of knowing. His heart is racing. He's messed up. Again! How could he be so stupid!

It's at that moment, when he's busy beating himself up, that his dad appears, out of nowhere, out of the heavens, coming down the bus stairs, the *Ted Baker* bag in his hand. Charlie stares. What next? His plan, to leap invisibly from his seat and get off the bus without his dad noticing, seems ridiculous now. The bus is braking, coming to a stop by a small row of shops, just next to a Ladbrokes and an HSBC. The doors open and passengers pour off on to the pavement. His dad is moving towards the door too . . . Charlie stands up, head lowered, elbowing his way past passengers standing in the aisle. He's causing them to swear at him.

'What's wrong with "Excuse me?"' One woman snaps, as he pushes past her.

'Excuse me,' he whispers, so his dad doesn't hear his voice and discover him.

He gets to the doors as they're swinging shut and he grabs them, holding them open long enough to jump out.

On the pavement, it takes him a moment to spot his dad, who's walking, faster now, down the high street. Charlie can see it's going to be harder to follow him here because all the other people from the bus seem to have disappeared and the street is almost empty. It's practically just his dad and him, so he hangs back. But he's not going to give up. Not after coming all this way.

His dad clearly knows where he's going. He has a sense of purpose now not looking at the street name when he turns right, or when he turns left a few metres later, past a brightly-coloured school and a block of flats and on to a road of terraced houses. Charlie thinks they must be getting close to where his dad lives because his dad seems to know exactly where he's going. He looks at home here. Charlie's sure he's about to find out what his dad's house is like, the street name and number. He doesn't know how he's going to use that knowledge. Would he be brave enough to go and knock on the door? The closer he gets the more futile this all seems. Even if his dad goes into one of these houses, all Charlie will have is an address. He won't know anything more about his dad than he started out with.

Suddenly Charlie realises his dad has turned onto a short path, through a front garden and up to a front door.

So this is it, 44 Marley Lane.

Charlie knows he's closer than he should be, he let himself catch up on his dad while he was daydreaming.

His dad's delving in his pockets for keys when the door opens.

There's a boy standing there. He's older than Charlie, maybe seventeen or eighteen. Charlie can see the similarity straight away. He looks like his dad. He looks like Charlie.

Charlie's dad holds out the *Ted Baker* bag and the boy takes it, grinning. He says something, and although Charlie can't hear what it is, he imagines that the boy is saying, 'Thanks, Dad!'

Behind them, a woman appears. She's plump and pretty in a faded way. Under the hall light, Charlie can see the grey roots to her blonde hair. Charlie blinks.

'I thought you were going to miss your supper,' she says.

His dad steps inside, and the hallway is narrow, so for an instant Charlie sees the three of them huddled together. The perfect family.

The boy moves to close the front door. He glances outside and sees Charlie standing there on the pavement, watching.

Their eyes meet.

Who are you? The question seems to reverberate back and forth across the street.

Charlie turns sharply away. He walks, mechanically. One foot in front of the other, in front of the other, in front of the other.

If only he could be sure that his legs weren't going to give out from underneath him.

LINDEN

16

It's the second time Linden's been to class at the Empire Gym since Chris let him attend for free. Last time, when he and Leah sparred together, they'd ended up in tears of laughter. He couldn't even remember now what it was that was so funny but he remembered that he liked her more the more he saw of her. And the more he saw of her the harder he found it to believe that she had anything to do with Victor.

Linden exchanges greetings with the others in the class. He's beginning to recognise the regulars. There are a couple of university students who carefully take off their spectacles before they start to fight, and a man who arrives in a business suit, then changes so you can see his belly spilling over the top of his shorts, and Warren, the class clown who's just broken his leg but does sixty push-ups in his plaster. There are things about the gym that remind him of Feltham: the odour of socks and the grunting effort of the warm up, the stretching and the pushups.

By the time they get started, Leah still hasn't arrived and Linden's watching the door, waiting for her to arrive. They finish the warm up and Leah's still not there. Linden puts on his shin pads like he's been doing it all his life and tapes up his hands. He's still using kit from the bag of spares but no one seems to care. He's worrying for no reason, he tells himself. Leah's got a right to be late. She's even got a right to miss class. She doesn't have to show up just because he's there. Still, he feels uneasy. He remembers Victor's thugs waiting to harass her outside class that first day he spoke to her . . .

They've just started sparring when Leah walks in. Relief floods through Linden . . . until he sees her face, set and white, as though she's had a shock. He catches her eye and smiles at her, but she blanks him.

'Okay, Leah?' Chris asks her, noticing her face.

Still she doesn't respond. Linden can see that Chris wants to go and check on her but he's got a class to teach.

She drops her bag on the floor, and Linden expects her to put on her kit and join the rest of the class, but instead her knees buckle underneath her and she sinks on to the ground where she kneels in among everyone's bags and shoes and mess and sits there staring blindly ahead of her.

Linden walks over to where she's kneeling and he squats down in front of her.

'Hey, Scary Lady,' he says quietly, 'what's the matter?'

Her eyes move to his face but she doesn't say anything.

'What happened?' he asks, more uneasy by the moment. No one looks like that unless something bad has happened. He saw this reaction once in a boy at Feltham after he got news his gran had died.

Leah shakes her head, and he sees that she is close to tears and that she's trying to hold them back.

'D'you want to get out of here?' he says, and in answer to that, at last, she nods.

Linden pulls off his gloves and helps her to her feet, picks up her bag, and turns to raise a hand in farewell to Chris, who nods at him, clearly concerned.

Out in the reception area, Linden sits Leah down on a comfy chair and goes to get her a glass of water.

'What happened?' he asks again, when he's sitting next to her.

'Nothing,' she mutters.

'Come on,' Linden says, 'something must have happened to make you look like this.'

She shakes her head, tight-lipped, tight-jawed.

He takes her hand from where it's resting on her leg, and holds it in the air in front of her. Both of them can see it shaking violently.

'What happened?' he asks again.

She shakes her head.

'Nothing,' she burst out, 'you'll think I'm stupid. It was nothing, I just got freaked out.'

'Tell me,' he says. 'For every stupid thing you tell me you've done, I'll tell you about a stupid thing I did, and then we'll be even.'

She smiles slightly at that, but she's shaking her head again.

'I was on my way here,' she says, 'I was almost at the gym, when these men came up to me . . .'

'What men?' With a sinking heart, Linden thinks he already knows the answer.

'The ones who were outside the first day you came to class, the ones who blocked my path.'

Linden feels an icy chill in his heart. He remembers the text message on Victor's phone:

give her a fright

'They were drunk,' she says, 'or they were pretending to be drunk, like last time. They surrounded me, like last time, and they were saying things – I'm not going to repeat that . . .'

'Were they threatening you?'

'Not with the things they were saying . . . the things they said . . . they were offensive . . . sexual . . . And I was trying to ignore them, and I tried pushing through them so I could get to the gym. But then one of them took out a knife . . .'

She catches her breath, and Linden sees her hand go inadvertently to her face, to her scar.

'He put it to my throat,' she whispers, 'and then he held it to my face, above my eye, and he was laughing about how he was going to cut me . . .'

Linden's got his head in his hands. A knife . . . he fails to see how she was being stupid . . . For Christ's sake, Victor, a knife . . .

'. . . and then he pushed the knife into my skin,' Leah cries out at the memory, and the rest of it she says in gulps, her face contorted with humiliation, 'but it didn't cut me . . . it was plastic . . . a toy knife . . . I . . . I . . . they laughed. They showed me the knife, they held it in front of my face and they laughed at me for being scared.'

Linden shakes his head. Victor the jester, the malicious player of games . . . Linden remembered so many cruel tricks played as jokes, friends humiliated, embarrassed, not talking to him any more. Linden knew how they felt. He tried to explain that he had been on the receiving end often enough. He'd heard Victor's laughter shaming him . . .

'I told you I was stupid,' she says, with a watery smile.

'You weren't stupid,' Linden says, ripping the shin pads from his legs and getting to his feet. 'I'm going to find them.'

'Leave it,' she says, 'they were just messing around. They didn't know . . . it was me . . .'

'They weren't just messing around,' Linden says. 'Someone put them up to it.'

He hurries out of the gym reception and down the staircase to the street below, pulling the tape from his hands as he goes. Outside, in the dark, there are no signs of life, no voices, no shadows moving through the pools of light cast by the streetlamps. He has no idea where Victor's thugs have gone but he jogs in the direction of the arcade . . . There, outside the glass doors, passing around a bottle, he finds them, shoulders hunched in their coats. One of them is still waving around the plastic knife . . . a toy dagger . . . and another one of them is wearing a plastic helmet, and they're laughing and fooling around, prodding each other with the dagger and pretending to be wounded, clutching their chests drunkenly.

Linden walks up to the man who is flourishing the dagger. With the advantage of surprise, he snatches the fake knife out of his hand and he prods him hard in the chest. Then he lunges towards him and shoves him up against the reinforced glass of a shop window, hearing a grunt as the air leaves his lungs.

'Who told you this was funny?' Linden snarls. He remembers this face from Victor's flat five years ago. He remembers this jerk opening the fridge and rummaging inside, stealing the meagre rations Linden had put aside for his dinner. He can smell the alcohol reeking from the man. His friends don't go for Linden, they don't try to pull him off. Instead, they laugh at their companion's predicament.

'Who told you to pull the stunt with the knife?' Linden shouts in his face. 'Was it Victor?'

The man takes a deep breath and then he spits full in Linden's face, pushing him away at the same time, shoving Linden to his knees, then kicking him in the stomach so that Linden cries out and collapses on to the ground. Somewhere close by Linden hears a girl cry out and he thinks of Leah – has she followed him? Has she been watching from the shadows? How much did she hear?

Linden lies writhing on the ground. He can hear them running away, still laughing and shouting, and then, in an instant Leah is leaning over him, helping him to sit upright, pleading with him to say that he's all right, scolding him for confronting her tormentors.

When the worst of the pain has passed and Linden's sitting on the pavement, curled over, his elbows resting on his knees, head hanging, Leah's voice reaches him as if from a great distance.

'Who's Victor?' she asks.

He closes his eyes. This wasn't supposed to happen.

'There's no Victor,' he says. 'You heard me wrong. I don't know anyone called Victor.'

CHARLIE

17

For Charlie, seeing his dad with another son – a son he buys presents for – is like someone dying. He can't keep up with his emotions, they come and go so fast. Disbelief, grief, anger . . . He's stuck on anger. He can't get around it. It's like a fiery red ball that spins inside him, ricocheting off his ribs and burning in his belly.

His dad lied to him. His dad didn't tell him that he was the second, the *lesser* son. Charlie had thought he was all his dad had and now he knows he's just a novelty, a toy, something to play with. When a small voice whispers in his head that he should have known, that his auntie had always told him about the other family that had driven his mother to despair, Charlie silences it. That was years ago, before his father spent twelve years in jail. If he'd thought at all about the other family, he'd assumed they'd disintegrated into dust long ago.

He's furious with his dad but it's the strangest anger he's ever experienced. Every time he thinks of his dad, he finds his eyes filling with tears he doesn't want and he sobs into his duvet, night or day, to muffle the noise.

He yells at his auntie but only because she's not his mum, who is twelve years dead, and because she's not his dad, who's lost to him for a second time because he belongs to someone else and because he lied to Charlie. Who else has his father lied to? Furiously concentrating, Charlie pores over the newspaper articles about the waitress, Beth Cheever, who may have lied when she gave his dad an alibi. She worked at the café in the park, that much she can prove, but the tale of Cheever being there on that day at that time and his credit card falling out of his wallet, well, her ex-boyfriend says differently. He says that she boasted that she'd been paid by Cheever to say that. If his dad has lied about this . . . He hates himself for his weakness, hates himself for not seeing through his father's lies.

Slowly, his fury crystallises into cold determination. If his father thought he was toying with Charlie, then Charlie will show him that he's not a toy. If his father was laughing all along at his childish plans for revenge, he'll show him that he's not a child.

The fireball of anger turns to poison in his stomach until one day, almost a week after he followed his dad home, he can't bear it any longer. His auntie is watching TV, so he sneaks down to the kitchen and searches for any alcohol that he can find. It's not the first time. When he plays truant from school, he likes to take a bottle with him for show even if he mostly swishes it around his mouth and tries to find a way to spit it out without anyone seeing. He doesn't know what lighter fuel tastes like, but he thinks spirits taste like he imagines lighter fuel tastes, like petrol or paint stripper.

But right now the poison-fury in his stomach is destroying him, and only alcohol can save him. His aunty's partial to a gin and tonic when she comes home from work on a Friday, so he knows where to find a bottle of gin, half empty. For his purposes, half full. He doesn't want to drink it in the house, doesn't want her to find him swigging from a bottle. So he slips it into the backpack he uses for school and leaves the house by the back door and goes to the recreation ground, sitting there in the lonely dark, with only his bottle for company. He's cold, shivering with it and with the adrenaline that's screaming around his bloodstream. He leans his elbows on his knees, and hangs his head, raising it only to drink. He doesn't want to look into the dark, or know what lurks in it. Wants only to breathe cold air and gulp down the foul alcohol that warms him inside. It doesn't take long for it to take effect. His shivering calms and soon he can't feel the cold. But his sour fury doesn't recede. Instead, the alcohol curdles it.

He stands and begins to pace around, drink and adrenaline fuelling him. There's been a light snowfall, and he kicks the snow.

He's going to show his dad.

There's nothing stopping him.

Then his dad will see which son is worth his time. Then his dad will be sorry. His dad will come to him on bended knee, begging for his time.

He's been a coward until now. But not any more. It's all that girl's fault. She told a lie and took his dad away. She made Charlie look stupid by not being scared of his messages. She's the one who needs to pay. And he'll show his dad that he's the one to make her.

Charlie bends and scrabbles in the dirt, picks up a stone and hurls it at a tree. He could hurl a rock through her window . . . He could scrawl graffiti on her house – *VISHUS BICH* – but he hasn't got any spray paint . . . He looks at the bottle on the floor – how flammable is gin? He stands for a moment, immobile, head bowed, eyes screwed shut, trying to get his brain to stop spinning.

Charlie raises his head. The world's still spinning, but the decision's made.

His fingers close over the lighter in his pocket.

Now all he has to do is to find the way to her house in the dark.

LINDEN

18

'Can I walk home with you?'

Linden braces himself for rejection. He's been watching her partnered with other people all evening, but they haven't come face to face once. Leah's already removed her gloves, and the taping around her hands and arms, and now she's removing the padding on her legs. He gets the impression that she's embarrassed because of what happened the last time they met.

'I'm sorry I was such an idiot about that toy knife,' she says. It's not really the answer he was looking for.

'Or you can walk home with me,' he says. 'It doesn't matter where we go . . . I . . . just want to walk with you.'

'It doesn't matter where we go?' She echoes it as a question, and he says, 'It doesn't matter to me.'

She looks at him for a long moment and then she turns her face slowly. Her hair is still gathered in a ponytail, so when she turns her face the scar is right in front of his eyes.

'Do you see this?' she asks.

'I see it,' Linden replies, not sure where she's going with this line of talk. 'I'm not blind. So what?'

'What do you think about it?'

Linden knows he should be careful what he says about that scar. He's not going to tell her what he really thinks, especially after that stunt with the fake knife. So he plays safe.

'I don't think anything about it,' he says.

'Don't you think about how I got to look like this?'

Linden hesitates. 'Yeah, I do think about that. I think that's why the toy knife scared you. You thought you were being attacked again.'

She holds his gaze, thinking hard.

'I think about my scar all the time,' she says. 'Not because of how I look. I don't care about that. I just want to know what happened. I want the truth. Does that make sense?'

'Yeah,' Linden says softly. 'I've got some stuff like that.'

'Have you got things that you're ashamed of?' she asks.

'You don't want to know,' he says, forcing a laugh. She's still not letting up on the whole looking him in the eye thing and he's beginning to get nervous. It feels like she can see right through him and into his head. Like she can see all his imperfections laid out: him handing over a bag of drugs, and breaking into a house, and driving off a car that's not his, and worse things too, waving the knife that Victor gave him, threatening people . . . He doesn't want Leah to see it. He doesn't want to look at it himself.

'All right,' she says, 'you can walk with me, if you like.'

'Your dad's not here to pick you up?'

'Not today, he's got a shift.'

'Yeah?' Linden says. 'What does he do?'

'He's a police officer.'

Linden feels like she's just slapped him.

'So better be on your best behaviour,' she says dryly, and when Linden doesn't respond, she says, 'That's what everyone always says to me when they find out what he does, "Oh, I'd better be on my best behaviour". I hate it. It's such a stupid thing to say.'

'Yeah,' agrees Linden. But what he's thinking is, *I'd better be on my best behaviour. Or get out of here now. One or the other.*

Linden pushes open the glass door, and they step out on to the street outside. The cold air hits them, and Leah shivers. She holds her hand out, catching something glistening in the air.

'It's starting to snow.'

He looks up into the black sky and sees a scattering of snowflakes falling lazily.

'Are you warm enough?' he asks her. 'We can always catch a bus if you want.'

Linden's got his hands jammed into his jeans pockets, trying not to shiver. He wishes he had a coat. He's layered every piece of clothing he's got one on top of another, but that's still not a lot of layers, and the cold is finding its way in easily enough.

Leah shakes her head, wrapping a scarf around her neck and pulling gloves on.

'I'm okay,' she says. 'I like fresh air.'

'This isn't fresh air,' he grumbles. 'This is freeze-your-frigging-balls-off air.'

'Lucky I don't have any, then,' she deadpans. 'Anyway, let's walk through the arcade. It's warm in there.'

So they walk along to the arcade and push the glass doors open, walking into its shining interior. Even though it's late, the lights are burning brightly. The arcade is still open because of the cinema on the top floor, but the shops are shuttered and locked up for the night. The shoe repair kiosk is up ahead and Linden is suddenly ashamed of it. He doesn't want her to know that's where he works. He starts to panic. What's he going to say when she asks him about himself? There's nothing about his life that he wants to share. Parents: dead and gone. Siblings: Victor, career criminal. Job: trainee shoe repairman. Past experience: entirely criminal. Previous address: Feltham Young Offenders Institute.

There's nothing . . . No, not true – there is something he's proud of: GCSE English Language and GCSE Maths, both taken and passed inside Feltham. But you can't have a relationship where the only topic of conversation is your two GCSEs. You can't even have a conversation where the only topic is your two GCSEs.

'How did you get the scar, then?' he asks. He can hear how blunt it sounds the moment it's out of his mouth.

There's silence and he risks a glance sideways to see what her face is saying. She's frowning, as though a whole argument is going on in her head.

'When I was four,' she says, eventually, 'I was in a park with my mum and there was a man – we saw him stab a woman, and then he went after us . . . It's just been in the news again because he got let out. You've probably heard about it. Everyone else has.'

'I don't pay much attention to the news,' he says, after a moment. 'What happened when he went after you?'

'My mum picked me up and we ran . . .'

Her voice trails off, and when he looks again, he can see the argument is still going on in her head. Suddenly she stops in front of him, so he comes to a stop too.

'Will you do something for me?' she asks.

'Depends,' he's getting nervous. Usually when people ask him to do something for them it's not good. Usually it's something that could get him put back inside Feltham. On the other hand, he knows that he'll do anything she asks of him. 'What do you want me to do?'

She hesitates.

'I know this is going to sound weird, because we haven't known each other long, but I've got no one else to ask . . . I want to go to the park where it happened. I need to remember what I saw.'

He stares at her. This is not what he expected.

'Now?' he asks. 'You want to go now?'

'Yes,' and her voice is urgent. 'I want to go now.'

'It's dark,' he says, trying to understand. 'Did it happen at night?'

She shakes her head. Her face is desperate. She's not asking for his help, she's begging.

'It's not about seeing it,' she pleads. 'It's about being there. I want to stand where I stood. It doesn't matter if my eyes are closed and I can't see anything. I want my feet on the ground. Then something . . . something will come back to me. I know it will.'

'You must have been there a million times,' he complains. 'If you haven't remembered before, you're not going to remember anything now.'

She gives him a long look.

'I haven't been back,' she says. 'This is the first time.'

Frigging brilliant, he thinks. *A trip down murder lane in the middle of the night and she picks me as her bodyguard.* Victor would be pissing himself laughing.

'You really don't remember what happened?' He feels like his brain is working at half . . . a quarter . . . of the speed it should be.

She shakes her head, angry with herself.

'I thought I remembered,' she says. 'I thought a man called Deryk Cheever did this to me. I've thought it for as long as I remember. When the court freed him last week, I screamed at him – screamed and screamed, outside the court . . .' She breaks off, shaking her head again. 'My dad nearly killed me for doing that. I'm so ashamed.'

Linden remembers the news, about how she'd never identified Cheever when she was four years old, although twelve years later she was screaming at him outside the court that she remembered him. So either she was lying, or she was messed up in her head about what she could remember. And from what he's observing right now in front of him, she's messed up. Linden knows that feeling. He knows it well. Like the night he was arrested before he got sent to Feltham. His memory of that night is so screwed up, he can't rely on it. He still can't work out how it happened.

'Well,' he shifts uncomfortably, looking at his feet, then up at her. 'Does it matter if you don't remember? Why not just forget it?'

She shakes her head. 'I got this scar but my mum got killed,' she says bitterly. 'It's not exactly something you just forget.'

Linden doesn't know what to say, so he doesn't say anything.

'Well, are you coming with me or not?' she demands.

'You really need to go now? Like at this minute? In the snow?'

But she's already started walking, striding fast. Striding away from him.

'All right,' He runs to catch up. 'All right, I'll come.'

They don't talk much on the way there. He's too caught up thinking *What on earth's happening here?* and maybe it's the same thing for her. At one point he asks her why she didn't ask one of her friends from the gym to go with her.

'They're great but the reason they're great is that I don't talk to them about any of this stuff. Maybe some of them know about me, Chris definitely knows about me. But they don't ask me questions, they treat me like anyone else, and it would ruin everything. My dad doesn't like to talk about it either. So instead I store it all up inside me until I can't bear it, and then I lose it. Then I scream it like an idiot and they put it on the TV. I'm just warning you, you know, in case I start screaming.'

He doesn't laugh. He can hear in her voice, she doesn't really think it's funny. She hates herself for what she did at the court.

'You're good because you don't know me,' she says. 'Or – actually, I feel like you do know me. Maybe you know me better than they do.'

'Oh,' he says, lost for words.

'Besides, you're big. No one will mess with you.'

'Are you saying you only want me for my body?' he teases her.

'That's exactly what I'm saying.' She smiles.

He doesn't entirely dislike that thought.

He acts like he's following her lead, but the closer they get he realises he knows the park they're going to.

Then they can see the park ahead of them, lining the far side of the road. This is where street lighting ends and the dark mass of silent trees and vast expanse of empty lawn begins.

Even Linden, who is accustomed to creeping around in the dark, is not happy. If there's anyone in the park at this time of night, it's people like him, low-lifes trading drugs or sex. The park has a reputation.

He wonders whether Victor's thugs are tucked up warm at home with mugs of cocoa tonight, or whether they're out here somewhere in the cold and dark, watching and waiting.

'You really have to do this now?' he asks. There is a biting wind and the snow is falling in flurries.

'I have to,' she says, turning towards him, 'or I'll lose my nerve. It's now or never.'

Reluctantly, he trails behind her.

'Come on, keep up!' she says over her shoulder, setting off across the empty road.

The snow is falling more heavily and wildly now, billowing this way and that, and the clouds have covered the moon. The path takes them across an expanse of grass which is turning white under the snow. A playground, to their right, looks sinister in the dark, the climbing frame a scaffolding, the swings hanging, shuddering in the sharp breeze as if ghost children are sitting on them.

Leah opens the gate, walking inside the fenced-off area. She walks slowly, making her way around the slide, the roundabout, the sandpit . . . She comes back and stands next to Linden, who thinks he has never been so cold in all his life. The wind is cutting through him. It's all he can do not to turn around and head home.

'I was here,' she says, 'with my mum. We were playing in here and Erica, the woman who he stabbed, was here with her little boy, Charlie, too.'

'That's what you remember?' asks Linden. 'Or it's what your dad told you?'

'Neither,' she says. 'I don't remember the playground and my dad doesn't talk about it. Like I said, we don't talk about any of this. It's like a taboo. The playground bit I read about in a newspaper report about Cheever's appeal. I don't really remember any of it . . . it's hard to explain. I find it hard now to know what I actually remember, and what people have told me, and what comes to me in dreams.'

'In dreams?' Linden says. 'That's made up, that's not like a memory.'

'I know what you mean,' she says. 'It's not like remembering something when you're wide awake. But sometimes there are dreams that are triggered by something that really happens, as though your brain is going over it time and again when you're asleep. For me, it's always the same dream. The same things happen. And I've researched it online, I've gone back over the news accounts of the murders at the time, and what I dream is pretty much what happened . . . So – I don't really know how to explain this – I feel like I remember, even when I'm awake. But am I just remembering my dream? Or do I really remember? Or do I dream the things I dream because I've been told that's what happened?'

He can just make out her expression and he can see that

she is tortured, but he can't think of a single thing to say that could comfort her. She carries on speaking.

'The playground's not in my dream, I only know that from newspapers. But I can see the path, and the trees, and the woman, Erica Brigson. But of course there are things I don't know in my dream. I didn't know Erica Brigson's name until I researched it online. Can you imagine that? My dad won't even tell his daughter the story of her own life? She has to go around digging it up from websites?'

He bites it back: *Lots of families have secrets; you're not the only one.*

'Dad won't tell me anything, he just talks endlessly about security, security, security all the time.'

You're standing in the middle of a deserted park, in the middle of the night, with a total stranger, Linden thinks. *I can think of a few parents who'd have a problem with that.*

'He'd kill me if they could see me now,' she says, as if she can read his thoughts. 'He talks as though there's still someone out to get me.'

Abruptly, she turns back to the path and continues on towards the copse of trees that looms ahead of them.

'My dad was born up north,' she says, 'on the coast, by Morecambe Bay. You look at it and it looks beautiful – sand for as far as your eyes can see, and the coastline dotted with pretty villages. But it's a deathtrap. You could walk across it for miles but you'll fall into quicksand and it'll suck you in, suffocate you. There's one guide who knows the way across, and it changes all the time, and he marks the path with twigs stuck in the sand . . . And then when the tide comes in, it comes so fast that it can drown you. Dad and I used to go up there when I was little. We'd stand by the bay at low tide and he'd point out over the sands and say, "That's quicksand, Leah. It'll kill you the moment you put a foot wrong. It's like life. It's treacherous ground. You can't trust anything or anyone. You can't even trust the ground under your feet."'

Linden hasn't had parents to speak of for years but even he knows this is a strange thing for a father to say to a little girl. He thinks her dad sounds like a prize jerk but he doesn't want to say it to her.

'Your dad sounds very . . .' he doesn't know what to say that sounds good, so he plucks a random word out of nowhere, '. . . inspirational.' He's embarrassed when she starts to laugh.

'Really? Inspirational?' Then she puts on a deep voice, obviously mocking her father, '"It's like life. It's treacherous ground." Seriously, you think that's inspirational? Because I can tell you, it's the opposite. That's what my dad is. He's the opposite of a role model. Whatever he does, I do the opposite. Whatever he says? The opposite. Keep your head down? I scream in the street. Don't go online? I'm on everything. Don't trust anyone? I've just brought a guy I hardly know to the park in the middle of the night.'

They're both silent for a minute. Then Linden says, 'That sounds inspirational to me,' and she glances at him, not sure if it's a joke. Then she starts to laugh and Linden smiles, because he likes that he made her laugh. It makes him feel good.

When Leah stops laughing she looks around her at the playground and she speaks in a sober voice.

'So, the papers said my mum and me were here in the

playground and so were Erica and Charlie. Charlie's dad, Deryk Cheever, followed Erica here and started to shout at her because she wouldn't give him access to his son . . .'

'Because she's discovered he's already married with a kid . . .' Linden completes her sentence without thinking.

Leah stares at him. 'How did you know that?'

'I'm remembering now,' he says, kicking himself. 'I think I did see something in the papers.'

She stares at him for a moment longer and then starts to speak again.

'Apparently, Cheever started pushing Erica around, trying to grab Charlie. So the other mothers gathered round to pull him off, send him packing. But Charlie was all upset because of the screaming and Erica didn't know what to do because his favourite stuffed toy, the one that always calmed him down, was in the car on the other side of these woods. It's not far, but Charlie wouldn't even let her push him in the pushchair, he was screaming so hard and fighting her when she tried to strap him in. So the other mothers told Erica to run and fetch it and they would watch Charlie for a minute. So she went back to the car and it was when she was running back to the playground that . . . that he attacked her.'

They reach the edge of the woods. Leah falls silent as they enter the trees. Above their heads, the branches sway violently in the wind, which howls through the trees. It is much darker here than out in the open and the trees shield them from the fierce wind. Her pace slows and she lifts her head, looking all around, turning around to look behind her, almost as though she expects something to happen. As though she thinks something – a memory – will literally fly out of the trees like a bird and land on her shoulder.

Linden watches her. He's beyond cold now. If anything or anyone attacked them, he'd be no help at all. It feels like if he had to move, he'd snap in two. He can see she's desperate. He wants to help her, he just can't help thinking this is a stupid enterprise.

Then Leah stops dead, staring down at her feet. Slowly, she starts to turn in a circle.

Linden holds his breath. He can't see clearly, but he thinks she's closed her eyes. He waits a moment.

'Is this it then?' he says, his voice sounding over the hiss of the wind in the branches. 'Was it here?'

'I don't know,' she wails. 'I don't know. I can't remember anything. Nothing looks like it does in my dream. ' She comes over to him and stands in front of him, looking up at him. She speaks calmly but he can see there's something else going on underneath the surface. 'What I know from the newspapers is that Erica got the stuffed toy from her car, then she was hurrying back along this path. That's when we saw her, coming the other way. Charlie's stuffed toy fell out her bag but she didn't notice. I saw it and I ran after her with it. This is the only part I remember clearly . . . I mean I know it from my dream, I've dreamed about it over and over. Erica turned towards me when she heard me shouting and that's when he came out of the trees and started . . . stabbing her. But after that . . .'

She stops speaking and Linden can see she's getting upset but he doesn't know what to say. He doesn't want to touch her or do anything that might scare her, so he just stands there and listens.

'Mum comes running up and grabs me and runs that

way,' Leah points, 'towards the road. He's chasing us. He's so close behind us that I can hear his footsteps and he's catching up because mum is slower because she's carrying me . . . We get to the side of the road but the traffic is so heavy – there's no break in it . . . and I'm looking over her shoulder and he's right there, in reach of us . . .'

Leah's staring at Linden, but she's not seeing him any more. She's looking through him, like she's watching something in her head.

'After that . . . it's like flashes of memory, nothing complete . . .he jabs the knife at me . . . I try to swipe him away . . . knock his arm, the arm with the knife, and . . . and he staggers, lurching forward . . . and the knife catches him . . . right under his eye,' She looks at Linden, frowning. 'That's the first time I've remembered that part. Is my memory coming back?'

'I don't know,' Linden says. 'What can you remember?'

'I tried to push him away and made him cut himself with the knife. I even see it start to bleed. I see it. And then he yells and lunges at me with the knife. It cuts me. I scream, and mum runs out into the road . . .'

Linden's staring at her.

She shakes her head.'That's all . . . but I remembered something new,' she says blankly, as though the importance of this has stunned her. 'I remembered the knife cutting his face . . . why can't I see his whole face?'

'So you can't see his face?' Linden doesn't know whether he wants her to see a face, or not to see a face, but he has to ask.

She shakes her head, her face distressed. 'Not the whole

of it,' she says, 'never all of it. If I dream about him and I wake up, little pieces of a face stay with me . . . nothing to get hold of, or put together to make a whole face.'

What can he say? Nothing. Not yet. Even his frozen brain can think this far. Wait. Think about it. Process it. Keep it under control. Maybe he's jumping to conclusions. He stands there, and he can feel the expression on his face, baffled and anxious.

Leah takes one of his icy hands in her gloved hands, and lifts it to her lips and blows warm breath on to it. Then does the same with the second. He could stand there all night, like this, the rest of him frozen numb, with her lips against his fingers.

'Come on, snowman,' she says, slipping her hand through his arm. 'Let's go.'

He walks her home then, her hand tucked inside the crook of his arm the whole way. She doesn't say much, which is just as well, because his head is reeling from what just happened; from her lips on his fingers. From her warm breath on his frozen flesh.

And reeling from what she has remembered.

When they get to her door, Leah stands in front of him and reaches up. Her lips are on his cheek. So soft and warm.

'Thank you,' she says. 'I knew I could trust you.'

He nods, unable to say anything, and waits until she's turned and let herself into the house. Then he turns and walks away. His head is filled with her eyes, looking up at him. With her lips.

'I knew I could trust you.'

CHARLIE

19

Later, Charlie wishes he'd got lost. Or that he'd tripped and broken his leg. Or his neck. Or that an alien spaceship had arrived and whisked him off to space to conduct experiments on him. Anything, really, to make sure that what happened next didn't actually happen.

Afterwards, he couldn't explain how he got there, he couldn't remember the route or the names of the roads, but he made it anyway, battling through bitter winds, as though there was a sonar calling to him.

He stands in front of her house on Charter Avenue, like the time he followed her. She'd looked out of that ground-floor window at him, bold as brass. Looked him in the eye.

Now, standing there, the house looks like a fortress. The Martens girl seems unreachable.

He swallows. Even in his drunken state, he knows that this is serious and that he's never done anything like this before. But the adrenaline is still circulating in his veins and, mixed with the alcohol, it's like a slow-burning fuse that has to burst into flame.

He remembers he came here to burn her house down, but now he's here his courage begins to fail.

He's going to throw a rock through the window instead.

That's what he's going to do. Throw a rock through the window.

He bends over and starts to scrabble around, like he did in the park. But of course – as a more sober person could have told him – this isn't the park and, apart from a few shards of gravel, there are no rocks around. He stands up again and staggers slightly, and as he does so, the lighter falls out of his pocket. He bends over, almost toppling, to retrieve it.

The sense that he can do nothing to hurt her makes the fury begin to rise in him again.He can feel the lighter in his hand. Its hard, cool lines remind him again of the most simple solution. He strips off his hoody and then his T shirt, standing bare-chested for a moment in the street, but the alcohol protects him from feeling ridiculous, or even cold. He pulls on his hoody again, then goes up to her front door and drops the T shirt in the doorway, takes the bottle of gin from his back-pack, and splashes some on the T shirt. For a moment he stands there, swaying, bent over the T shirt. He's forgotten what comes next . . . Then he remembers. He's going to set fire to the T shirt and shove it through the letterbox . . . He's breathing hard. He doesn't want to do this, but this is the only way. He's got to show his dad what he can do. He's got to show *her* that she can't get away with what she's done.

He gets the lighter out of his pocket again and picks up the T shirt in his other hand. Shaking he holds the lighter to the fabric . . . the flame starts to lick at the fabric . . . the fabric begins to blacken and smoke, and he starts to try to shove the T shirt through the letterbox. He's rammed a handful of fabric into the slot when he realises the flames are taking hold much quicker than he expected – he hadn't thought that the flames would move up, towards his hands. He swears as the flames scorch his skin, then cries out in pain and let's go of the T shirt. It hangs there, on the door, suspended from the letterbox, in flames.

Charlie steps back from the door. He nurses his left hand, which is raw with pain.

He can't take his eyes off the letterbox, which is engulfed in flames, whipped higher by the frozen wind.

What has he done?

He feels ridiculous. He feels like someone who's drunkenly shoved a burning T shirt through a letterbox.

But he might be a mass murderer.

The thought hits him like a hammer through his drunken skull.

Are the flames eating through the wooden door? Maybe the other side of the door is alight already, with flames racing up the stairs, galloping up along a nylon carpet, nibbling at the wooden banisters, making them glow orange and then burst into flame too . . .

'Fire!' He yells, at the top of his lungs. 'Fire!'

LINDEN

20

By the time Linden gets back to the flat from going to the park with Leah, he's shivering from the cold. But he hardly notices, because when he thinks about Leah, he feels as though he's burning up.

His head is thinking: *Don't trust me, Leah, stay away from me.* But when he thinks about her lips on his fingers, or her hand tucked inside his arm, or her mouth on his skin, then he doesn't want her to go away. That's the last thing he wants.

And then he thinks about Victor, and the scar under Victor's eye, and he's overwhelmed by waves of self-disgust. He has to forget Leah. He has to stay out of her way. Because if the pieces of the puzzle are fitting together like Linden thinks they are, then he's the last person on earth that Leah should be kissing.

If he's right, then he knows why Victor is so interested in Leah. If she's with Linden, he'll lead her straight into danger.

His phone beeps to tell him he's got a text message. It's from Leah.

R u going 2 the empire 2morrow?

He stares at the text. He really wants to see her. He wants to feel her lips again and the touch of her hand.

can't . . . got things to do

He keys in the killer words. He presses Send.

He watches his screen while the little arrows take his rejection to Leah. He curls up like a baby. He's tired but he's too hungry, too cold, too miserable, to sleep.

Sometime later, Linden's mobile rings and he snatches it from his pocket, thinking it's Leah.

'Lin!' It's Victor, speaking urgently. 'I need you now.'

'I'm asleep,' says Linden.

'You get out here now, this isn't bloody bedtime. This is an emergency.'

An emergency.

Linden buries his head in his hands. After tonight, it seems more important than ever to say no to Victor. But it's one thing to know that in theory, it's another thing to do it in practice. It's just not that easy.

Victor reels off an address, then hangs up. Linden sits there trying to think. He doesn't know why he ever resisted his fate. Why did he think he could go with the flow in the shopping arcade? Why did he think that he could have a proper job? Or Leah – why would he let himself believe that he could be with her? This – a call from Victor – was always bound to happen. How could he think he would get away as easily as that? He paces up and down in the flat – should he go, or should he stay? But without Victor, he's got nothing. Nowhere to stay, no family . . . There isn't any choice in this, there's only his miserable fate.

Linden gets in Victor's car. Or at least, a car that Victor's been using for the past few days. No one asks where it came from. Linden doesn't exactly have a licence but he's a good driver. He's got a lot of experience. He drives to the address Victor gave him. It's a tree-lined suburban street of Victorian houses set back from the road. Linden drives slowly along the street until he sees a car parked, with two figures inside. He pulls up alongside and lowers his window. Victor also lowers his window and they talk, vehicle to vehicle.

'Lin.' Victor greets him. He seems nervous, on edge. He nods towards one of the houses, a semi-detached house with large bay windows. 'Sameer's gone in, but he's not coming out, and we can't make contact. Can you go in after him, see what's going on? I think he's got lost in there or something.'

Linden's heart sinks. You go into a house like that, you're out as fast as you can, you don't hang around admiring the décor, so something must have happened to Sameer. Linden hasn't done this work for three years and he doesn't know whether he's still got the knack. It used to be that the moment he went through the door or the window, he could tell where the owner kept his car keys. He'd be there in a flash, with his hand in the bowl, or taking the key off the hook. But he's not sure he can still do it.

'Come on, man, I'm worried,' Victor says. 'Sameer gets freaked out too easily. What if someone's pulled a gun on him or something?'

'A gun?' Linden's pretty freaked out himself. 'Why don't you go in, Vic? Why did you call me?'

'Lin . . .' Victor has opened the car door, and he's pulling his little brother out now. He grabs both of Linden's shoulders and makes him stand in front of him, looking him in the face. They're under the street light and Linden's thinking this is not discreet. He doesn't want to be seen with Victor, doesn't want to be seen anywhere near him.

Linden's so close to Victor's face he could rub noses with him. He's trying to look his brother in the eye but instead he finds his line of sight keeps slipping to the scar underneath his brother's eye. How did he get that scar?

Linden can't concentrate on anything. All he can see is the scar. Victor said he got it in a pub brawl, but now Linden thinks about it, he's never seen Victor fight outside a pub, he's never really seen him fight anywhere. Victor's too careful for that. He lets the others drink and brawl and kill each other on his behalf.

'Lin, I need you,' Victor is saying, shaking him. 'And if you ever want to freeload off me again, you help me out here.'

Linden shakes his head but he knows he's got no choice really. He pulls away from Victor and moves carefully around the perimeter fence of the front garden, ending up by the front door. He tries the door and finds it open. Sameer is certainly inside then. No one around here would leave their front door unlocked at night. He steps back for a moment and sees that the house is dark. So maybe Sameer has lost his way in the dark? Some of these houses are cavernous.

He takes hold of the door handle and pushes the door open, stepping softly inside. Hands outstretched, feeling for obstacles or for Sameer, Linden moves carefully into the hallway. He wishes he had a torch. His eyes are taking a while to get used to the dark. He can't see a thing.

'Sameer,' he hisses, but there's no reply, and no sound of movement.

Linden curses his predicament. He doesn't feel safe at all. There's something about this house, about its darkness and the way it's set so far back from the road, and Victor's nervousness outside, as if he knows that nothing good is going to happen in this house. Outside, the wind whistles around the walls.

There's a sudden creak from above and Linden freezes.

It could be anything. These houses talk to themselves. He just hopes it's that and not someone other than Sameer lurking in the darkness. He can scarcely move. There would have been a time when he would creep around a house like this silently, getting to know it by touch, moving fast, getting hold of what he needed. Now he doesn't want to spend a moment longer here than he has to.

He moves slowly along the corridor, gently pushes open a door. The curtains are open in here and the night sky glows into an empty room. No Sameer.

The house is empty, there's no furniture, no sign of habitation at all. Now he thinks about it, he realises something's been niggling at the back of his mind ever since he entered the house. There were no cars parked outside, except for his and Victor's. Usually it's cars that Victor is after, that's the easy pickings – send someone in to grab the keys and get out as quickly as they can. But why send Sameer inside to get keys to a car that isn't here? No keys, no car. That realisation makes Linden think he should never have broken in, or Sameer before him. All this risk for nothing? Or has Victor changed how he operates? Is

Sameer after something else? Is he here for another reason? Linden's anxiety deepens – what is Victor up to?

He hesitates . . . then he softly pushes open the next door. This room is darker, the window covered. Cautiously he creeps forward, arms outstretched.

His foot touches something soft.

He recoils, gasps.

He bends over to touch, feels fabric give underneath his fingers – something thick, like a jacket. If this is Sameer, he's not moving.

Linden curses under his breath. What is he doing here? Where is Victor? This is his doing. This is his mess, let him fix it. The howling wind is preying on his nerves.

Suddenly there's a noise behind him, but before he can turn and fight, someone's pushed him, and he's fallen on top of the soft mound on the floor. There's yelling and he hears the word 'Police!' but nothing is making sense.

Now someone's kneeling on his shoulder, and they've grabbed his wrists and they're pinioned behind his back. Linden's heart is pounding and all he can feel is fear. Not about what's happening here and now. But fear of Feltham. Of doors closing on him again. Of being trapped inside, losing the arcade, and his flow, and Leah . . .

'Get off me,' he shouts. 'Get off me!'

The voices around him dissolve into laughter.

'Take a picture, take a picture,' he hears a voice urge.

Then someone flicks a switch and light floods the room.

Slowly Linden cranes his head to get a look at his captors.

He swears.

Victor's doubled over. 'I'm pissing myself,' he gasps. 'Pissing myself.'

Sameer is standing there with his smartphone, grinning, and Tony's giggling like a maniac. 'He was so scared,' he's muttering to himself, delighted. 'So scared.'

Linden pushes himself to his feet. He kicks the mound he thought was Sameer and turns out to be a pile of cushions. He swears at Victor, grabbing his shoulders and pushing him back against the wall.

'Why did you do that?' he yells in his brother's face. 'What have I done to you?'

Victor's still grinning, although the back of his head is flat against the wall and he's shaking his head.

'Lin,' he gasps, 'Lin, you don't understand. This is a lesson, this is education.'

'What?' Linden can hardly speak. 'What the fuck do you mean?'

Suddenly Victor explodes out of Linden's grasp and turns on Linden, shoving him up against the wall, twisting his arm across his back, so that Linden shouts out in pain. His cheek is pressed hard against the wall.

'There's no need to get so aggressive,' Victor hisses in Linden's ear. 'I want to show you that this is your life. This is it. This is as bad as it gets, and as good as it gets, do you understand?'

Linden shakes his head, at least as much as he can, which isn't a lot. 'No man,' he croaks, 'this is your life, not mine.'

'You've got a girlfriend and a job in a shitty little shoe repair shop, that's your life is it? Well, you watch and see how long they last!'

'What are y—' But Victor hits him across the side of the head before Linden can finish speaking.

'Don't mess with me,' Victor hisses, 'and don't challenge me. I can twist you around my little finger.'

As he speaks, he twists Linden's arm higher and higher up his back and Linden shouts out again in pain.

'I could snap your arm like a twig,' Victor hisses in Linden's ear. 'Or I could snap your neck like a twig. Do you have any preferences?'

Then he releases Linden as quickly as he's seized him, turning away from him to chat to Sameer and Tony as though nothing has happened. As though they're not standing in an empty house in the middle of the night. A house they've broken into. As though Victor hasn't just threatened his little brother with his life.

Still unsteady on his feet, feeling as though his arm has been torn from its socket, Linden walks out of the house, closing the door behind him. His shoulders hunched against the biting wind, he walks back to the car he's not licensed to drive and sits for a moment in the driver's seat, still trying to work out what happened. He drives back to Victor's flat, a flat he has no claim to. A flat he shares with a brother he fears. He walks in the door and his belly growls with hunger. Over the noise, the whisper of Victor's voice comes to Linden: *'You've got a girlfriend and a job in a shitty little shoe repair shop . . .?'*

So Victor knows aout Leah. He has been watching, or his thugs have been reporting back.

Linden buries his pounding head in his hands.

'Well, you watch and see how long they last . . .'

CHARLIE

21

Charlie has always played truant on Sports Day. He didn't know he could have won the hundred metres and the four-hundred and the eight-hundred, maybe even a marathon. He didn't know he could run so fast. Didn't know he could keep running until the Martens house and his attempt at arson was far behind him. Didn't know fear could do that . . . He breathes sharp and hard, sometimes a sob interrupts his breath and his throat is tight, but still he keeps on running. His left hand, scorched at the wrist and across his knuckles, feels as though his skin's been surgically peeled from his flesh.

He's not thinking straight. He knows he's not. His thoughts come in ragged scraps. He's a killer . . . His auntie is going to cry . . . His legs are slowing . . . He's really thirsty . . . He's heading for his dad's house.

That's not something he decided – he's not in any state to make decisions. He's more in a state to gasp and gulp and moan in horror at what he's done than to think sensibly about his best strategy. Still, the pain in his hand sharpens his brain, trumping the alcohol. He dredges up the memory of the journey he made when he was following his dad to Marley Street, and he finds the stop for the night bus, and he waits and waits, and gets on to the bus, and fumbles his Oyster card out of his pocket, and sits at the back of the empty bus, so full when he was last on it that he could hardly elbow his way off. He sits there, shifting and moaning, unable to sit still because of the excruciating pain in his hand, and the bus drives him out into the unknown again, and in the dark and the snow and the wind it's even stranger than it was in the day. If it wasn't for the Ladbrokes next to the HSBC he wouldn't have recognised the stop. Falling off the bus, still snivelling, half drunk still, he could have made a dozen wrong turns. Instead, he finds himself on Marley Street outside the door that opened on his dad's other family and broke his heart and drove him to this.

Going to his dad's house is not a good idea. He knows that when he arrives there, but there he is, nevertheless. He's standing, panting, outside the door he saw opened by . . . his half-brother. He remembers the woman at the door too, the perfect family framed in the hallway before the door shut in his face.

He can't remember why he came. He wants to go home. He wants his auntie to make his hand better.

Charlie, collapsing on the icy pavement, is wracked by crippling sobs.

Drunken possibilities trickle through his weeping head. *This* is the house he should have burned down . . . This is the house he could still burn down . . . Charlie's still got his lighter in his pocket. He could wait for the flames and watch them burn . . .

Lying huddled on the pavement, crying, the sound of approaching sirens cutting through the night sky confuses him. Why are the sirens here? They're in the wrong place. Surely the sirens should be racing to put out the fire at the Martens' house . . .Then the horrible realisation: these aren't the sirens of fire engines, they're police sirens. Police Officers who've been called from their beds, pulled on their uniforms over their pyjamas and got into their patrol cars, all to come after him. How did they track him? Is it his mobile phone that's giving him away? He's heard that people can be tracked that way. Panicking, he pulls it from his pocket, fumbling to pull it apart, pull out the batteries and the SIM card, and drop the bits back in his pocket.

Charlie scrabbles to his feet, shrinking out of the street light and into a dark garden, where he presses himself into the snow-laden shrubbery just as two police cars pull up outside his dad's house.

He's right. They've come for him.

His heart plummets into his stomach as officers get out of the cars, slamming doors behind them. Charlie gets ready to run. But once out of their cars, they don't seem interested in the street at all, they don't look around to see if they can see Charlie. They go straight up the path to his dad's front door and ring the bell.

Up and down the street, people are coming to their windows, and some to their front doors, to peer out at what's causing the noise.

Charlie doesn't understand. And then he thinks, they've come here because they think that this is where they'll find him. They know, somehow – they seem to know everything about him – that he's been hanging out with his dad. Or rather, Charlie can now name it for what it is, he's been hanging around his dad, hoping his dad will look in his direction.

The front door opens and Charlie isn't surprised to see the same woman from before. What does surprise him is that the woman is in tears, wailing and beside herself. Her knees collapse underneath her and one of the officers catches her before she hits the floor. The police seem to try to calm her down, but before he can see anything more, they all go inside and the door slams shut, and Charlie's left outside waiting. He can hear her wails even with the door closed. He's both more scared and less scared than he was a few minutes before. He's pretty sure the woman's wailing has nothing to do with him but the police are still here at his dad's house, so if it's not about him, then what is it about?

He starts to shiver. He's cold but this shivering comes from deep, deep inside and it shakes him like a leaf. He can hardly feel his feet. He stamps. He blows into his scorched hands. Nothing helps. His jaw is rigid with cold. His whole body keeps getting shaken by shivering fits.

After a few minutes, one of the officers comes out of the house and he's speaking into his phone as though something important is happening. Charlie strains to hear but he can't catch a single word. And even as the officer's on the phone there's another siren shrieking louder and louder, and an ambulance pulls up and paramedics leap from it and head straight into the house, pushing past the police officer.

Charlie doesn't know how much time passes as he huddles in the shrubbery. He feels like an animal caught in headlights. He can't move. He's paralyzed, watching and waiting and shaking. His greatest fear is dogs. He's terrified of police dogs, can't think of anything worse than a ball of muscle and fur and teeth launching itself at him and sinking its incisors in his arm. He has a sense that something is waiting in the shrubbery close to him to pounce. Perhaps it is a dog. His ears, hypersensitive to threat, pick up breathing and the shifting sound of earth underfoot . . . He could not be more afraid than he is, more frozen to his patch of ground. Even the pain of his hand seems to retreat into a dull throb as his fear takes over.

The front door opens and people spill out into the street. They seem subdued. This is a pause in the action, a necessary delay. Then something else appears at the door and at first Charlie's brain can't comprehend what's happening. It is illuminated only by the hall light that spills out on to the street and by the flashing lights on the vehicles in the street. He can't make head or tail of the thing they're carrying. He blinks and his brain begins to piece together the information from his eyes. There's a stretcher and there's a shape on top of it. And the shape, which is roughly the shape of a body, is covered completely. Zipped up. Whatever's inside can't struggle, can't see, or hear, or breathe.

In the air around him, Charlie seems to hear a sigh of satisfaction, a deep breath expelled.

Charlie is finding it difficult to breathe. He's taking short, panicky breaths. Behind the stretcher, the boy who looks like him appears in the doorway, his face stunned. So if the woman and the boy are OK, Charlie knows of no one who could be that shape upon the stretcher.

Except for his dad.

'No,' Charlie starts to mutter to himself. 'No, no, no.'

He starts to chant it. He doesn't know if he loved his dad or hated him but either way this wasn't supposed to happen.

Across the street, the ambulance pulls away and Charlie falls silent. Still, the boy seems to stare in his direction. Has he seen Charlie there? Or heard his chants? And then the front door to the house closes on the grim-faced son.

Now Charlie can't keep still. He starts to pace around and then he starts to make noises. He can't help it. Shouting, howling noises, soft at first, then louder and louder.

A cold hand lands roughly on his mouth, clamping itself over his lips, his teeth.

Charlie's heart stops. He can't make a noise. He can't shout, he can't scream.

The police have found him. They were looking for him after all and now they've got him.

'Shut up!' Someone hisses in his ear.

As if Charlie has a choice.

The hand doesn't move from his mouth. He's shoved down, so he's kneeling in the earth.

'You need to shut the fuck up if you're going to get out of here,' the voice hisses in his ear. He can feel someone's mouth against his earlobe, the hot breath on his eardrum. 'Follow me. If you make another noise, I'll shut you up.'

The hand removes itself from his mouth and Charlie doesn't make a sound. The dark mass releases Charlie so that he can get unsteadily to his feet. Charlie doesn't dare so much as glance up at the face of his companion. When the person next to him starts to move, he follows carefully behind. His companion doesn't lead them back on to the road. Instead, for as long as they can, they hug the houses, moving from garden to garden, scrambling over low walls and hedges, Charlie gasping in pain as branches and thorns catch on his burned hand. Once, a light goes on in the house whose garden they are creeping through. Once, a window opens and a woman sticks her head outside. Both times, Charlie and his companion freeze.

At last they're confronted with a wall so high that they're not going to get over it and the man turns reluctantly back towards the road. He turns to Charlie, saying in a low voice, 'Act natural,' and strolls down the garden path on to the pavement as though he's leaving his house to go to work. Like he does this all the time.

Charlie walks a step behind, shivering in the bitter wind. He's never felt so unnatural, acting natural. At any moment he expects to be confronted with a police officer, or to hear a barked order to halt, or to feel canine teeth buried in his arm. He scurries alongside the man until they have turned the corner at the top of the road, and the sirens and the police cars and the ambulance are out of sight and earshot. Still his companion strides on, putting ever more distance between them and Marley Street. Charlie pants behind him. He can't even hear the man breathing. Charlie's afraid, after the catastrophes of the past few hours, that he's being befriended by Death himself.

At last, the figure ahead of him comes to a halt. He half turns, his face still in shadow, and says to Charlie, 'Okay, fuck off home now, all right? And not a word about tonight to anyone, you'll only incriminate yourself putting yourself at the scene of a crime.'

Charlie can't speak. He shakes his head. He can't go

back to his auntie. Not tonight. Not after what he's done, and what he's seen. Even Charlie, who lies to his auntie on a daily basis, hasn't got enough lies inside him for tonight.

He takes a deep breath. 'I've got nowhere to go. Can I come with you?'

There's an all-night café open in a row of closed-up shops and they go inside. Now Charlie can see the man's face, lit by the strip light on the ceiling. He's very pale, Charlie thinks. Like shocked pale, like something he's seen or done has sucked the blood out of his face, or like he never goes out in the sun. And he's thin as though he never eats. The paleness is made paler by the man's clothes, which are black, from head to foot. There's an even whiter scar underneath the man's eye.

Charlie sits at a table and waits while his companion buys drinks, coming over to the table with two paper cups. Hot chocolate for him, like his dad would have bought him. His dad . . . When he thinks about his dad, he can't breathe very well and he certainly can't drink hot chocolate. He sits there staring at the cup and occasionally glancing at the man who's sitting opposite him. He's shaking from everything that's happened. He holds his throbbing hand underneath the table, trying not to let it touch anything, to reduce the pain. He glances out the window and sees the street still dark outside. How can one night last so long?

'I'm Charlie,' Charlie says eventually, because he realises he hasn't said it yet. His jaw is so tight from trying not to show the pain that he feels, like he has to unlock it before he can speak at all.

'Victor,' the man says, nodding and sipping his black coffee.

'I think my dad got killed,' Charlie says, eventually.

Victor glances quickly around, but they're on their own. Even the man serving behind the counter has gone into the back of the shop.

'What are you talking about?'

'He lives there, at that house they brought the body-bag out of,' Charlie says.

Victor doesn't say anything but Charlie sees a strange expression cross his face.

'My dad was Deryk Cheever. He's been in the news a lot lately, he was quite famous,' Charlie volunteers to fill the silence. He glances around the shop. He wants to plunge his hand in a bowl of cold water. It feels like it's still burning.

Victor sips his coffee.

Charlie sips his hot chocolate. He can talk about his dad and right now he feels nothing. He does feel like crying but that's because of the pain in his hand. . He feels very, very tired and, the more he sips his hot chocolate, the more tired he feels. He's grateful to his new friend but he doesn't want to spend all night talking to him in this café. Perhaps if he sneaks back home his auntie will never know he was gone and he can curl up in his bed. He doesn't know what he's going to do about his hand. He doesn't know how to stop it hurting and he doesn't know what she's going to say when she sees it. Right now it looks red and sore, but he has a feeling that all the skin will come off it before it gets better. A thought strikes him, a memory of smoke rising from his belly, and he glances down, seeing the black patch on his hoody, where the flames licked. His aunty's not going to like that either. He tries to think about something else.

'Why were you waiting in the garden?' Charlie asks Victor.

Victor gives him a look like he doesn't like the question.

'A nosy little boy, are we?' he says.

'No,' Charlie says, 'it was just lucky you were there to help me get away. I expect you live there or something. Do you know my dad?'

Victor doesn't say anything. He just sits back in his chair and gives Charlie a really long look. The kind of look that makes Charlie feel as though a lonely, dark space has opened up inside him.

'I want to go home,' he says.

Victor nods, gets to his feet and gestures to the boy to follow him.

'Okay,' he says, 'I'll drive you home.'

Charlie nods, relieved. *I'll drive you home* sounds so normal after such a strange and terrifying night. Sometimes his auntie gives him a lift, or a friend's dad gives him a lift. This strange man isn't very friendly, but at least he looked after him and helped him escape, and now he's giving him a lift home.

Charlie follows his new friend to a car, parked outside the kebab shop on the street, and Victor tells him to get into the passenger seat. On the dashboard, a clock flashes 3:13. The man switches on the heater and Charlie falls into a half-sleep, giving vague directions when he's asked, until at last they're pulling up outside his house. Charlie's head is lolling against the window, his eyes half closed. He's dimly aware that they're parked and Victor's turned the engine off. From the corner of his eye, he can see his friend carefully removing an object from inside his jacket and wiping it with a cloth. Charlie shifts in his seat, waking up, wondering what's going on.

Victor hurriedly slips the thing, whatever it is, down the side of his seat.

'Okay, get out of here,' the man says, 'and remember – not a word about tonight. You'll only get yourself into trouble. You don't want anyone knowing you were there.'

Charlie nods. He's too tired to speak.

'And I don't know what you've done to that hoody,' Victor says, 'but you might want to get rid of it in case someone wonders what you've been up to.'

Charlie nods. He pulls the hoody over his head, wincing at the pain in his hand.

He climbs out of the car, bare-chested now, and runs, shivering and stumbling, to the wheelie bin in the yard. He opens the bin and shoves his hoody inside, then staggers to his front door. The keys are still in his jeans pocket in spite of all his scrambling and climbing over fences. He lets himself in and tiptoes as quietly as he can up the stairs. It's amazing, after his night on the frozen streets, to be back in his warm home. He feels as though he's been away for a decade. He falls on to his bed, lays his hot hand on the cool pillow, and his eyelids close.

He hears the smallest of sounds.

Something stirs deep inside his head. His eyelids flicker open. He hauls himself upright, leans over to the window, and plucks back the curtain.

Outside, the car he drove home in is still parked. The man who drove him home is on the pavement outside his house, turning away from the wheelie bin that belongs to

Charlie's house. The man slides back into the driving seat, the engine starts, and the car moves slowly away.

Charlie lies back down, blinking at the ceiling, trying to kickstart his brain, but his eyelids are too heavy. Within moments they have closed over his sleeping eyes.

LINDEN

22

'This is as bad as it gets and as good as it gets.' That's what Victor said after tricking Linden.

Linden thought Victor was crazy. He wanted life to get better. A great deal better.

But the next day, when he got up and went to the shoe repair shop, Marky didn't want to look him in the eye. The manager was there, too. And they stood there behind the counter facing him, blocking his way in.

'Sorry, Linden, this isn't going to work out,' the boss said. And for the first time Linden saw a harder look in his eye than he'd seen before. The soft, friendly, contours of his face had sunk, as if in disappointment.

At first, Linden was under the impression that he could fix this. There had clearly been a mistake.

'What do you mean?' he said, blinking in shock. 'What do you mean, it's not going to work out?'

'Linden,' the boss said, 'in order to make this work, we have to be a hundred per cent sure of who we're employing.'

'Yeah,' Linden protests, 'but you know – about Feltham. You know that! I didn't lie to you.'

'That's in your past,' the boss says. 'We need to be a hundred per cent sure of your character now. Do you understand that? It's not only the money, although we can't afford to have that disappear, it's our customers and their security. Do you understand?'

At first Linden doesn't understand what he's talking about, and then he does. *The customers and their security* . . . The key copying machine.

Linden nods. Mutely.

'If we get word that anything's out of order now, if you're up to stuff outside of work, well, we just can't go forward . . . Do you understand that?'

Linden glances at Marky, but Marky's head is bowed.

'Yeah,' he says. 'I understand.'

He doesn't want them to see him cry, so he turns away. He walks slowly, like there's no hurry for him to do anything. He swings his shoulders a little so he looks carefree. He knows who to blame. Victor told him as much. '. . . *a girlfriend and a job in a shitty little shoe repair shop . . .? Well, you watch and see how long they last . . .*' How could they have known about what happened last night unless someone told them? Had Victor spoken to Marky and told him about Linden driving the stolen car, or breaking into the house? Most likely Victor texted Marky a photograph from the fake robbery the night before. What would Victor have written to Marky? *See what Linden's up to all over again? Can't keep a good thief down.* Linden knows how Victor manipulates situations for his own ends. Marky's own job is on the line. If he had information like that, he'd have had to tell his boss. You couldn't blame him. If Marky recommended Linden, and Linden was going to go bad, that would come back on Marky. No, you couldn't blame Marky.

Linden knew who to blame.

Back at the flat, Linden grabs his stuff and puts it in his bag. There's little enough of it. He's got one last chance, and that's his uncle, the brother of his heart-sick dead mother. He doesn't know whether his uncle will let him stay. They've never been close. They haven't kept in touch. His uncle never visited him in Feltham. Still, Linden has to leave this flat. He has to get away from Victor.

He wants to ring Leah. He wants to ring her so badly.

He keeps thinking about what Victor said: '*a girlfriend and a shitty job . . .*' Victor's taken care of the job. What's he going to do about Leah?

He should ring her and warn her. He should tell her to get away, go and stay with someone. He should tell her she must stay away from him. That he's too dangerous and that's without whatever history Victor and Leah share, making things even more complicated.

Don't trust me, Leah. Don't trust me.

He walks out the door. No backward glance. Leaving Feltham felt more like leaving home than this feels. He's on the street outside when Leah rings.

He stands in the street staring at the phone until, at last, a half dozen rings in, when she's in danger of giving up on him, he answers. At once he knows, he shouldn't be doing this. He should have fallen silent, vanished from the face of the earth. No good's going to come from this.

'Linden?' Leah's voice is urgent.

'Yeah?' Linden aims to sound non-committal, but then he can't help saying, 'Are you all right?'

'I know I can trust you,' she says, like she said the night before. He wishes she wouldn't say it. It sounds like pressure. Like if she says it, he has to be worthy of her trust, and he's not sure he's worthy of anything.

'Yeah,' he says, 'you can trust me.'

'I need to see you,' she says. 'I've got to talk to someone.'

He wants to say, *Why don't you talk to a friend? You can't trust me. Not really. Not if I'm right.*

But instead he thinks about her lips on his fingers and he says, 'All right.'

'The park,' she says, 'now.'

When he finds her, sitting on a park bench, she's shaking uncontrollably although she's wearing about a dozen more layers of clothes than he is.

'Cheever's dead,' she tells him, the moment he gets there.

Linden puts his bag down on the bench. He sits down beside her.

'How?' he says.

'Somebody stabbed him in the yard at the back of his house. Apparently he went out there for a smoke and he was attacked. Someone must have been watching him.'

They both sit there shivering.

She shakes her head, as though she can't believe what else she's got to say.

'There's more . . . We think someone tried to burn our house down.'

'What?' Linden turns towards her, startled. 'Are you all right?'

She nods. 'I'm fine, the house didn't catch fire, but I heard someone shouting "fire" in the night, and I got up, and we found a burned T-shirt hanging out the letterbox, like someone had tried to set a fire. The only thing damaged was the paint on the door. But both things happening on the same night? It can't be a coincidence.'

Linden thinks hard. He never has believed in coincidences. Not really. There's always an explanation. Arson and murder on one night. And where was Victor? Victor who has a scar on his face. Victor who's given order to his thugs to follow Leah and harass her . . .

'When did it happen?' he asks.

'I woke up at midnight. The T-shirt was still smoldering, so it must have just happened.'

Linden frowns. A burning T-shirt didn't sound like Victor. A burning T-shirt sounded improvised, amateurish.

And what time was Victor playing stupid tricks on him in the empty house? It must have been about midnight . . . It looks like his brother has an alibi.

Linden feels relief rush over him, warming him up. He's been wrong about Victor. His brother couldn't have had anything to do with the arson, and since the arson and murder must be linked, he had nothing to do with the murder. Linden begins to feel light-headed. He's been so scared, thinking what Victor's capable of, too ready to think the worst of him . . .

He remembers Leah sitting next to him, shivering. Tentatively, he reaches out and touches her hand. He'd like to wrap her in his arms but he's not going to risk freaking her out.

She turns to look at him and he's expecting fear, maybe a little frailty. Instead, the fury he sees in her eyes startles him.

'He thinks he can scare me off,' she hisses.

'I don't get it,' Linden says. 'Who thinks he can scare you off?'

'Cheever said he saw someone else in the park when Erica was killed, he said he was going to tell the police.' Leah speaks fast – she's already worked it out in her head and she's frustrated that Linden hasn't. 'The newspapers say that when I was a kid, right after the attack, I identified someone else. That has to be it. That's the link. Cheever was killed to stop him identifying the real killer. Whoever stabbed Cheever wanted to kill me too, in case I could remember.'

Linden nods slowly. But what he's thinking is, it's two different things, sticking a burning T-shirt through a letterbox that might catch fire or might not, and watching someone's back yard, waiting patiently to stick a knife through them. The T-shirt business is amateur, the stabbing is professional.

'Maybe . . .' he says. 'What time was Cheever stabbed?'

'They're saying one-thirty in the morning,' Leah says. 'Apparently he always stays up late, always goes out into the garden for a smoke around then.'

'It might have been the same person who did both,' he says. But what he's thinking is, Victor wouldn't have had time to attempt the arson, but he'd have been through with the malicious prank he played on Linden by about twelve-thirty at night. Victor could have done the stabbing.

'Definitely,' Leah says, 'there's no doubt about it. It must have been one person who did both. That's the only way it all fits together. Someone went after Cheever, and that person tried to kill me too.'

Linden shakes his head. Already he can see that his relief about Victor was premature. The house fire doesn't sound like Victor, but the Cheever murder . . . ? he really doesn't want to think it, but it could have been his brother. The brother with the scar under his eye. The brother who said, '*a girlfriend and a job . . . ? You watch and see how long they last . . .*' The brother who looked after him when he was a kid and visited him every week in Feltham – the brother whose blood he shares. He should walk away. The safest thing for Leah would be for him, Linden, to stand up and walk away. He thinks of her lips on his cheek, her lips on his fingers.

'We stick together, yeah?' he says to her. 'We'll find out what's happening and keep you safe.'

She looks at him and nods, businesslike. It's a deal. They stick together.

She thinks she's safe with him.

She trusts him.

Linden can't find it in himself to tell her that she really shouldn't.

CHARLIE

23

It's all over the TV and the papers. How could it not be? Charlie can't escape. His auntie leaves the TV on at dinner, or he goes to the shop to buy sweets, and it's there in his face.

ARSON ATTACK ON STABBING VICTIM'S HOME

If he looks away, he gets a face-full of another front-page headline.

FREED CONVICT CHEEVER FOUND DEAD

He stands there staring at the newsstand, blinking. All the papers make the link. If Cheever went to prison for twelve years for a knife attack and the same night he's murdered his supposed victim's house gets torched, there has to be a link.

Charlie's head is reeling. He's beginning to wonder if he murdered Cheever in his sleep. Everywhere he moves, he moves in a dark cloud of guilt. He knows he tried to burn Leah Martens's house down. He knows he did this and he knows it was wrong, and somehow fate has taken his sin and doubled it, so that now whoever is guilty of arson – which is him – is implicated in a murder. He wanted someone dead and somehow someone ended up dead.

In the few moments that he's not panicking, he can see that none of the headlines make sense. He's heard people talking about it on the radio and everyone thinks that there must be a link but no one can work out what it is. Besides, thinks Charlie, if his dad wasn't guilty of the knife attack, which is what the judge said when he let him out of prison, then that girl and her mum weren't even his victims. Which means they're nothing to each other.

Charlie thinks he, Charlie, must be the link. He was in both places and he's Cheever's son – but he can't understand why his dad was killed. Every time he thinks about that, he feels an empty hole inside him, so he's trying not to think about it. But that's hard too, because how do you not think about a thing like that?

The morning after his dad was killed, his auntie woke him and told him what she'd heard on the news. She was on her way to work, in a hurry, relieved he didn't cry, didn't in fact show any emotion at all. She didn't know he was gritting his teeth, trying to hide his hand from her. His head pounding with a hangover from the night before.

That evening, when she gets back from work and it's on the news, she can't help letting her feelings show.

'I know he was your flesh and blood,' she says, 'but good riddance.'

'I'm his flesh and blood, so would you say good riddance about me?' Charlie bursts out.

'No, oh no, Charlie,' his auntie says. She goes over to him where he's sitting on the sofa and sits down next to him and tries to take his hands in hers, but he snatches them away. 'Biologically he was your dad. But he was a nasty piece of work, and you're nothing like him. You're like your lovely mum, and she was my sister, and she was lovely when we were kids, and lovely when she grew up. She'd never hurt a fly, and for all your faults, neither would you . . . Charlie?' She's seen his hand. He's been trying to keep it out of her sight but he's been careless and now she's seen. 'Charlie, what happened?'

She's putting out her hand to touch his.

'No,' he screams, 'don't touch it!'

'What happened?' she says again.

'It got burned,' he says, and begins to cry.

'I can see that,' she says, but she can't get any sense out of him, and in the end she gives up, and goes to the bathroom cupboard to find cream and a bandage to make him more comfortable.

Charlie's acting suspiciously and even he knows it. No matter how long has passed since it happened he can't behave like nothing happened. He sits in his room, because he's afraid of talking to his auntie in case she asks him more questions about how his hand got burned. When he comes down to eat, he can't put anything in his mouth. So he's hungry and shaky, and his hand hurts, but all he can eat is sweets because they don't make him feel like throwing up, so he runs back and forward to the newsagents buying sweets and glancing nervously each time at the newspapers in case there's some news that's new.

Charlie hears the hammering noise of a helicopter overhead and assumes it's looking for him. He knows they'll come for him. He expects, any moment, to hear a voice booming through a loud hailer, calling his name. He supposes it has something to do with the DNA on his T-shirt. He must have sweated into it a lot before he burnt it. But then wouldn't it have been nothing but ashes after the fire? Maybe his fingerprints were on the letter box? But how would they match them to him? He's never been fingerprinted in his life. Still, he knows the police have their methods, he knows they'll find him. You don't get to set fire to a house and not take the consequences.

So when the doorbell rings in the afternoon, and his auntie calls him downstairs with a worried voice, he knows they've come for him. For a minute, he thinks about climbing out the window, but it's a sheer drop of ten metres. Or pretending not to be there, hiding under his bed. But if they've got to him already, they'll find him again. They'll send a sniffer dog to get him and the dog will fasten its teeth into his arm and drag him out, or they'll set that helicopter to chasing him through the streets, his feet pounding on the ground, and the thwack-thwack-thwack of the helicopter rotors above his head.

'Coming,' he shouts back down. He takes a deep breath, but it doesn't slow his heart down at all. He goes down the stairs, wondering if this is the last time, thinking should he have packed for prison first, because he's got nothing, not even a change of underwear.There's a man in uniform and a woman in normal clothes, and they come into the sitting room and talk to him and his aunty there. They ask him where he was the night before and he lies by telling part of the truth. He says he took a bottle of gin to the park, because years of lying have taught him that it's always as well to stick to the truth as much as possible. And his auntie shakes her head and looks as though she's going to cry, but she doesn't know the half of it.

Then the woman asks him whether he went anywhere after that, and he's expecting that the street she's going to talk about is the street where Leah Martens lives, Charter Avenue. But it's not.

'After spending some time in the park, did you make your way to Marley Street?'

He hasn't thought about that question. Hasn't thought it through, because he didn't think anyone knew he was there.

He shakes his head.

How did they know?

His mind races. He thinks about all the text messages to his dad, and he thinks, how hard would they have had to look to find him? If they've got his phone, then they've got him.

'Charlie,' the woman police officer says, 'I've spoken to your auntie and she's told me that you know that your father has been found dead.'

He nods, trying not say too much. He can see she's trying to look sympathetic. She's got a face on for little children or stray dogs, but behind it, her words aren't soft at all. She wants him to get upset, because she wants something from him and she knows that if he loses control, she's got him.

'We know you've been in contact with your dad, Charlie.'

Still Charlie doesn't say anything. It wasn't even a question, they can't blame him for not answering when they can't be bothered to ask a question.

'Isn't that so, Charlie, that you've been contacting him?'

He nods.

Beside him, Charlie can feel his auntie stiffen and stare at him.

'Can you tell us about that contact, Charlie?'

'I texted him,' Charlie says, reckoning that's the least they know. The less everyone knows, the better.

'And he texted you back?'

'Sometimes.'

'What did you text him about?'

Charlie sighs. There's no way around it. If they know this much, they know everything.

'About when we were going to meet up,' he says.

'Where did you meet?'

Charlie gives the name of the café, Turner's, where they'd met every time. The woman officer writes everything he says down and Charlie remembers sitting in the Old Bailey and watching police officers read from their notes. What he's saying now, what the officer is writing down, is evidence. It could be read out in court, with him in the dock. He glances quickly at his auntie, who's murmuring, 'Charlie, oh Charlie,' over and again.

'And what did the two of you talk about when you met, Charlie?'

When Charlie thinks about sitting in the sunny coffee shop with his dad, it seems as though there was a dark cloud hanging around them, a gloomy fate. When he thinks about the things they talked about, about revenge and how to hurt Leah Martens, he feels so ashamed that he knows he will never be able to speak about it.

'Did you argue about anything?' the officer presses.

He shakes his head. He feels as though the cloud from the café has moved into his auntie's sitting room, and is enclosing them. He will never be able to explain it to anyone else. They didn't argue, but there was nothing good, either. He can't understand, now, why he even kept pursuing his dad. Because he knows now that's what it was. He pursued his dad. His dad never texted him, except that first time, with his number. Charlie always texted his dad. His dad just went along with it. Perhaps he was curious about this long-lost son. The boy that he was so keen to see that it cost him twelve years in prison. But Charlie can see he wouldn't have gone along with it for long. It was nothing to him. Nothing. Charlie was a disappointment, not worthy of the time wasted, inside prison or when he was out.

The policewoman's speaking again. 'The reason we ask,' she says, 'is that Mr Cheever's other son, who lived with him, says he saw someone who answers your description outside the house right after Mr Cheever's body was found.'

Charlie gazes at the policewoman. Behind her, through the window, he can see other police officers gathered around the wheelie bin outside. One of them reaches down inside the bin, then withdraws a gloved hand, holding something aloft. The others gather around to look. Charlie stares.

'Charlie,' his auntie says. She's crouching in front of him, with her hand on his arm. 'Charlie are you all right?'

'Charlie,' the policewoman says, 'can you tell us what happened to your hand? Have you hurt it? Have you got a cut?'

Charlie gazes into the face of his auntie. He can't speak. He blinks. Like Morse code, only he doesn't know Morse code. SOS. I'm drowning.

'He burned his hand in the kitchen, that's all,' his auntie bursts out, standing and facing the officers. 'He can't answer any more of your questions, he's too upset, now be off with you, we'll leave this for another day.'

While his aunt's seeing them out, Charlie races upstairs. He can't face his auntie's questions. She's going to kill him for going to see Cheever. He throws himself into his bed, and pulls the duvet over him, fully clothed. When he hears her knock softly and then open the door, Charlie closes his eyes tight.

He can hear her walking across the room, floorboards creaking, and then he can feel her standing over him. She's bending over him. He can feel her breath on his cheek. Softly, she kisses him and he tells himself not to flinch.

'Are you awake?' she asks softly. 'Charlie, you can't be asleep, it's only four in the afternoon.'

He doesn't respond. Head down, eyes closed, steady breathing.

What did they find in the bin?

He can feel her leaning in close. He wants to push her away so he's got space to breathe, space for his heart to pound, but he doesn't move a muscle.

'What kind of trouble have you got yourself into now?' she murmurs. 'What would your mother have said?'

His eyes prick at that. There it is again. He's always disappointing everyone, no matter what he does. He even disappoints his dead mother. Not many people can say that. Still he doesn't let on that he's heard.

'I think they think you killed him,' she says, after a moment, with fear in her voice. 'You know that, don't you, Charlie? If you can hear me . . .'

Still he ignores her.

After a few minutes, he can tell she's turning and walking away, out of the room. When he's heard her footsteps on the stairs, receding, Charlie opens his eyes and stares at the ceiling.

What did they find in the bin?

His life choices stare down at him, bleakly.

Either he stays in bed and pretends to be asleep for the rest of his life.

Or he gets sent to jail for the rest of his life.

Or . . . he runs away.

LINDEN

24

Outside the café window, the snow is falling heavily. Linden is wearing a scarf that Leah's brought from home for him. She doesn't say but he supposes it's one of her dad's because where else is she going to get men's clothes? She's brought him gloves too. He feels weird wearing clothes chosen and paid for by a police officer. But at last he feels warm, so he's not complaining. Now, inside the café, taking a seat opposite Leah in a little booth, he unwinds the scarf from his neck and takes off the gloves.

'D'you think she'll come?' Leah's gaze is fixed on the door of the café, watching everyone who steps inside.

'I don't know,' Linden says. He's never met a journalist in his life, doesn't have a clue how they operate. One thing is, he's afraid they won't recognise her if she doesn't look like the photos they found online.

'There she is!' Leah almost jumps from her seat, then changes her mind, stays where she is. This isn't a secret meeting – you can't have a secret meeting in a café – but the less fuss the better.

Linden twists around in his seat and sees a woman in a sheepskin jacket standing, frowning, scanning the room. He raises his hand, but not like a wave, just a small movement, as he imagines men might call for a waiter in a posh restaurant. A moment later she's at their table and Linden is sliding along the bench to make space for her, so she can sit opposite Leah. Linden looks at the profile of the woman's face. He can't work out how old she is. Her hair has grey roots, but mostly it's a dark black-brown with red streaks, and it hangs around her face, which is lined and made up. She's got foundation in the creases around her eyes and her mascara is flaking on to her cheeks and her lipstick's worn off to a dull purple-pink. She hardly gives Linden a glance. It's Leah that she's interested in.

'Hi.' The woman reaches out across the table, and Leah shakes her hand awkwardly. 'I'm Stella Crosby,' the woman says, 'thank you for getting in touch, I'm glad of a chance to meet you.'

Linden can see Leah doesn't know how to respond. Small talk is not her thing.

'I've seen you before,' Leah says. 'You're the one who came after me outside the court. You wanted to interview me.'

'And you told me to get lost. Yes, that was me. I was assigned to cover Cheever's appeal. I thought it was a one-off story. But what you shouted outside court that day, it made me think there's more to this case than meets the eye. That's why I've stuck with it.'

Leah looks at Stella Crosby's face for a long moment. Then she starts to speak. 'I read what you wrote about me. You said that after this happened,' Leah indicates her scar, 'you said the police tried to get me to identify who did it and I didn't choose Deryk Cheever.'

Stella Crosby nods.

'That's what I was told.'

'Who told you?'

'A source,' Stella Crosby says. 'I can't tell you his name.'

'Why not?'

'It's not what journalists do,' Stella Crosby replies. 'Our sources speak to us on condition we don't use their names. We have to respect that, or no one would give us any information. They have to know it's safe to speak to us.'

'Your source used *my* name,' Leah says. She's sounding agitated. Linden shoots her a warning look. He doesn't want everyone in the café looking at them. 'He didn't ask me whether I wanted him to use my name and you didn't ask me whether you could put my name in the paper. If you can use my name, you should at least tell me his.'

Stella Crosby looks amused.

'My name wasn't his to give and the information wasn't his to give either,' Leah continues angrily. 'It must have come from a police file and police files are confidential.'

'I understand how you feel,' Stella Crosby begins to say, slowly. 'But there's really nothing I can do, it's the way things work.'

'Well I don't like the way the way things work,' Leah snaps.

'Fair enough,' Stella Crosby says, 'I hear what you're saying. Look, I'll have a word with my source, see if he's willing to meet you. You never know. I've got your number, I'll pass it on to him.'

'How about you give us his number?' Linden says.

Stella Crosby turns abruptly towards him, as though it's the first time she's noticed him there.

'Who are you?' she says.

'Linden,' he says.

'Is that your surname, Linden?'

He shakes his head.

'Then do you have a surname, Linden?'

He shakes his head. He's been thinking how his surname always leads back to Victor, and he doesn't want anything leading back to Victor. Especially not with a journalist.

'He's my friend. That's why he's here,' Leah says.

'Okay,' she says. 'Well Linden, I think you know I can't give him your number. That's not how this works. The most I can do is talk to him and see if he wants to contact you.'

Linden and Leah exchange a look.

'Can you tell him it's really important?' Leah says. 'Can you tell him that if it wasn't Cheever who did this to me, then someone else did and I need to know who, because maybe that person will go after me again, or he'll go after someone else. If I identified someone else after it happened, your source would know, wouldn't he?'

Stella Crosby looks speculatively at Leah.

'Have you got anyone in mind?' she asks.

'Just tell him,' Leah says.

'Okay, okay.' Stella Crosby holds up a hand in surrender. 'I'll tell him.'

Leah stands up. 'Let's go,' she says to Linden.

'Hey!' Stella Crosby leaps to her feet and stands in front of Leah, blocking her way out of the café. 'Hey, not so fast. I didn't come here to take instructions from you!'

Leah hesitates briefly, then sits back down. She doesn't say anything. She glances at Linden, who shrugs.

'I want you to tell me everything you remember about that day,' Stella Crosby says.

Leah shakes her head. 'That's not why I'm here,' she says.

'It may not be why *you're* here,' Stella Crosby says. 'But it's why *I'm* here. I've offered to speak to my source to see whether he's prepared to contact you, but this is a two-way street.'

Leah scowls. 'I don't want to talk about it,' she says.

Stella Crosby leans across the table.

'You stood on a public street and accused Cheever of murder and days later he's dead,' she says. 'You're going to have to talk, whether you like it or not. If it's not me, it's going to be the police. Maybe some vigilante heard what you shouted and decided to take matters into their own hands with Cheever, because *you* said he should never have been let out.'

Linden sees the blood drain from Leah's face. Suddenly she looks ill, her scar white and stark, cutting through grey skin.

He wants to get rid of the woman, tell her to get lost, leave them alone. But he's beginning to realise she's right. Leah could be getting into something else, something bigger than she wanted to.

'You know what I think?' Stella Crosby says. 'I think the timing in all of this is important. First Cheever's freed because he's come up with an alibi, and my source tells me you didn't identify him at the time of the murder anyway, so everyone thinks he didn't do it. Then Cheever's alibi begins to wobble. The waitress's story begins to sound a bit weak, her ex-boyfriend says she's attention seeking. So someone who thought Cheever was guilty all along might be furious that he was freed at all. Say, for instance, someone like your dad, who thought Cheever killed his wife and scarred his daughter for life. He'll have seen Cheever released and he may not have liked it but Cheever did have an alibi. Now he's furious because it's all looking like lies . . .'

Leah's shaking her head, not wanting to hear this.

'You see, Leah, we all need to know the truth, or people like your dad are going to keep falling under suspicion . . . You're the one who saw the attacker, Leah, you're the only one who can get us closest to the truth so innocent people don't suffer. Don't you want the person who killed your mother to be punished? So, tell me, what do you remember?'

Leah stares at her. She swallows. Her eyes flick towards Linden. He knows what's going through her head. Should she tell Crosby how she's remembered that the attacker stumbled and that the knife cut him too? Linden feels panic rise in his chest. He tries to warn her with his eyes not to say anything and hates himself for it. Why is he protecting Victor?

'I don't remember much,' Leah says.

'Do you remember his face? Colour of hair? Eyes? I'm assuming you'd have said if he wasn't white?'

Leah stays silent, her face carved in stone, lips tight together.

The woman nods, satisfied, as though she'd expected this non-compliance.

'Have you ever tried hypnosis?' she asks.

Leah stays silent and still.

'It's all in there,' Stella Crosby says. 'Lodged away, hiding. But it's all there. All you've got to do is unlock it. Then you'd know. I bet you'd really like to know . . . It must tear you up, not remembering what happened.'

Leah doesn't move, but her eyes flick towards Linden, entreating him to help.

'She doesn't want to,' he says to Stella Crosby. 'Don't you get it?'

'I get that Leah's afraid of what she'll find hidden in her head,' Stella Crosby replies. 'But put it this way. We're running a story today that Cheever had an appointment to speak to the police about what he saw in the park on the thirtieth of May twelve years ago. That appointment would have taken place the next day. Apparently he had a description of someone, the person he said actually attacked you. And what do you know, before he can speak to the police, he's killed. Do you want that to happen to you, Leah?'

Leah stares at her. Stella Crosby is confirming her worst fears.

'Because you've got information too, whether you know it or not. Which means the same could happen to you. You must have thought about that. But if you dig those memories out of your head and put them in the newspapers you're protecting yourself, because what's the point in the killer coming after you if you've already put the information out there?'

She looks from Leah to Linden.

'If you're her friend, you should advise her to cooperate,' she says. 'You look like a nice kid and you're sweet on her, right?'

Linden forces a laugh.

'It's all right,' she says. 'That's how it's supposed to be at your age. And if you're in love with someone, you want to protect them, right?'

'Leah doesn't need protecting,' he says gruffly, trying to ignore the fact that Stella Crosby just said he was in love with Leah.

'Is that what you think? Seriously?' Stella Crosby shakes her head. 'Believe me, she needs protecting. So get her to give me a call and we can set up an appointment with a hypnotist. You can be in control, I'll come along and observe. No tricks.' With that Crosby stands up. 'Goodbye,' she says, extending her hand to each of them in turn. 'Call me again when you really want my help.'

When she's gone, Linden buries his head in his hands. Leah stretches her arms across the tabletop and lowers her head on to them, twisting her neck to look out of the window.

On the other side of the glass, Stella stands on the pavement and the snow falls heavily all around her. She steps out into the road and within moments she is swallowed up in the snow.

CHARLIE

25

In the middle of the night, Charlie's eyes snap open. He stares into the pitch dark and knows he has to go now, this minute, or the police will come back for him. He doesn't know what they found in the bin but he has a bad feeling. He remembers putting his burned hoody in there and he remembers the way Victor was standing there, by the wheelie bin, the way he walked back to his car, trying too hard to look nonchalant. He remembers the police gathered around the wheelie bin, pulling something out . . . If they pull out his hoody, they'll know it's his. If they find something else in there, they'll assume that's his too . . . His heart starts to race.

Maybe they're surrounding the house now . . . he kneels up in bed and looks out of the window, but he can't see anyone or anything moving. Everything is in place: the wheelie bin, the cars on the road, even next-door's cat on the wall. If he goes now, no one will see him, but if he waits 'til the morning . . . he can't wait. They know he was at Marley Street, they can put the rest together. He's almost sure that he isn't to blame for what happened to his dad, not unless he's lost his mind, but setting fire to that girl's house . . . No, he hasn't got a moment to lose. He jumps out of bed and starts to pull on layer after layer of clothes. It's going to be cold out there and he doesn't want to carry a change of clothes, so he wears them instead. He starts picking things up, then putting them down again, desperate to go and reluctant to leave all his stuff . . . His room is full of things he wants. Not anything special, just like all the rubbish that piles up. He knows he doesn't need any of it but it doesn't seem right to leave it all behind, either, because what if he can never come back? He grabs handfuls of rubbish – a plastic model of David Beckham, a ping pong ball, a chocolate bar he doesn't even really like, a nail clipper and an empty cigarette carton – and stuffs them in his pockets. Then he hurries from the room and down the stairs, quietly unchaining the front door and letting himself out on to the street.

When he shuts the door behind him, he has a feeling like he wants to run back inside. It's not that he hates his home. He hopes his auntie understands this because he doesn't want to hurt her feelings. He knows that if he doesn't go, then the police will come back and even if they don't arrest him for murdering his dad they'll arrest him for trying to murder Leah Martens. His hand will be evidence enough, and probably his auntie will go to prison too for saying that he burnt it in the kitchen. He would have tried to write his auntie a note explaining that he's not running away from her but he's so bad at writing that his note would look stupid. He knows he's been an idiot. He knows he deserves to suffer for trusting his dad and for putting the burning T-shirt through Leah Martens's letterbox.

As he reaches the corner, a dark figure detaches itself from the shadows and Charlie stops in his tracks.

‘Hello, Charlie,’ says a voice he knows. ‘What are you doing out here at this time of night?’

A lighter glows in the dark and Victor hands Charlie a lit cigarette, which he puts straight between his lips, inhaling quickly. It’s not only tobacco, there’s weed in there too, and he feels the smoke begin to wash the tension from his muscles.

‘Me?’ Charlie says. ‘What about you, what are you doing here at this time of night?’

‘I’m checking on you, Charlie boy,’ Victor says, ‘making sure you’re all right.’

‘How did you even know I was coming out the house?’ Charlie asks, baffled.

‘Call it a good guess,’ Victor says. ‘I wouldn’t want to stay in a house with police sniffing round, digging in my bins and everything.’

Charlie stares at Victor.

‘What did they find?’ he asks.

Victor shrugs and says, ‘How should I know?’

‘I saw you put something in there,’ Charlie says.

‘No you didn’t,’ Victor says. ‘Because I didn’t put anything in there. Maybe you’re getting me mixed up with you. Maybe you put something in there.’

Charlie thinks that this is exactly what he’s afraid of. If they find the hoody, the police will assume that whatever else is in there is his too. But whatever else could be in there? Charlie remembers how nice Victor has been to him. Victor wouldn’t do anything to hurt him, he’s pretty sure of that. So probably Victor’s telling the truth. Probably Victor didn’t put anything in the wheelie bin. He knows he saw Victor on the pavement, walking away from the wheelie bin. But it could be true that Victor didn't drop anything in the bin. He didn't see Victor actually put anything in the bin. He'd been so tired. He didn't know why he'd imagined that Victor had put something in the wheelie bin.

'Anyway,' says Victor, smiling, 'if I put something I shouldn't've in your bin, I'd hardly come back now, would I?'

No, Charlie thinks, *you wouldn't*. And he's relieved, because although he wouldn't say he likes Victor, he does admire him, and he does remember that Victor helped him before. If Victor's rescued him once before, maybe he can do it again.

'I'm on the run,' Charlie tells him. 'The police came to ask me about that night. They think I killed my dad, so they asked me where I was, if I was there.'

Victor thinks about that.

'What did you tell them?' he asks.

'Nothing,' Charlie says. 'I said I didn't go there, but someone saw me.'

Victor breathes slowly, thinking.

'Did they ask about me?'

'No.' Charlie shakes his head. 'Why would they? They know who I am but they don't know who you are.'

Victor nods, satisfied.

'Can you help me?' Charlie asks. 'I don't want anyone to find me.'

Victor nods.

'Yeah,' he says. 'I'll make sure no one can find you. Come on.'

Charlie follows him a few paces down the road to a car.

Victor opens the passenger door for him, holding it open.

'Hop in,' he says.

Charlie clambers in.

Victor shuts the passenger door, walks around to take the driver's seat, and a few moments later, the car pulls away.

LINDEN

26

Stella Crosby messages Linden's phone. When it beeps to announce the message, Linden is at his uncle's house. He hasn't been back to Victor's flat. Not since he packed his bag and left, and Leah called him to meet her in the park. It seems like forever since he left Victor's flat but it's only forty-eight hours. His uncle has given him a bed, but he's not happy about it. It's '*a bed for a couple of nights*,' that's all, a bed belonging to a seven-year-old who's been moved in with his nine-year-old brother while Linden stays. The seven-year-old's complaining loudly, the nine-year-old's complaining, and his uncle thinks that because of Feltham Linden's not the kind of boy who should be around his kids anyway. He thinks he'll be a bad influence. Linden knows that because he heard his uncle saying so to his wife in the kitchen.

'*We have to show a little charity*,' she'd said, '*the boy had a bad start in life.*'

'*Three days, maximum*,' his uncle replied. '*And make sure he cleans up after himself, washes the dishes and tidies up; he has to pull his weight.*'

After he overheard that, Linden washed up every last teaspoon after every meal. He'd never done so much washing-up in his life. He knows he's not welcome here, but there's food aplenty. He's never seen a fridge like it, bursting at the seams with leftovers that are entire meals. He doesn't want to be thrown out on his ear, because his choices are Victor or the street. So he's in the kitchen, up to his elbows in soapy water, when his phone buzzes and he dries his hands and pulls his phone out of his jeans pocket and he sees Stella Crosby's name. Linden reads the message.

Tell your friend my source will talk to her.

He stands there in the kitchen, leaning against the counter and staring at the screen on his phone. He thinks about Stella Crosby, about her tired, hungry eyes and her fidgety hands. She reminds him of Victor. A woman on a diet of adrenaline.

A woman with a plan. He doesn't trust her an inch.

Two hours later, Linden and Leah are standing on a path by the Thames. The wind chill makes it bitterly cold and they're stamping their feet to keep warm. Leah has stolen one of her father's coats for Linden, a padded jacket that he takes gratefully even though when he puts it on Leah laughs because it makes him look so much heavier than he is.

'Doesn't your dad notice that someone's nicking all his stuff?' Linden asks when he's zipped it up. It feels strange to be wearing stolen goods belonging to a police officer.

At first Leah doesn't reply, and then she says, 'I don't know. I never know what he sees and what he doesn't. He doesn't talk much, he's so wrapped up in his work. He's hardly ever at home.'

Linden thinks about her dad. He remembers again how

he thought he'd recognised him inside the car when he picked Leah up from the gym. It's driving Linden mad that he can't remember where he's seen that face before. The memory keeps flitting into the light, then retreating again.

'Doesn't he worry about you?' Linden asks. 'I mean, especially after the attack, didn't he get scared because you could have died like your mum?'

Leah doesn't answer at once and Linden can see her struggling to explain.

'I don't know what he was like before it happened,' she says. 'But as long as I can remember, he's been scared. Everything's about security, about caution, about not getting sucked under, keeping your head down, locking doors, keeping things under control. He won't let me on Facebook or Twitter or anything. I mean I'm on them anyway . . . I do everything he tells me not to do . . . I refuse to cower behind my door. He's never there. He crawls out of the woodwork to lecture me about security and then he runs away again and leaves me to it.'

'It's like you brought yourself up,' Linden says.

Leah nods slowly. 'Pretty much,' she says.

'It's why you act older than you are,' he says. 'Not like a kid or a little girl. You . . . you're really confident.'

She's looking up at him.

'What about you?' she says. 'I don't really know anything about you.'

'And that worries you, does it?' he teases her. 'When you're dragging me off to parks and to hang around by rivers in the dark?'

She laughs softly in the dark, tucking her hand through

his arm, like she did in the park, and then she says, 'I told you, I trust you.'

They fall silent. Linden's thinking how much he likes the feel of her hand tucked in his arm. He's also thinking, *I didn't answer her question, I joked my way out of it. She's got to notice that.*

'Tell me about your parents,' she says.

So she did notice.

'Nothing to tell,' he says. 'They're gone. I don't know anything about my dad and my mum died when I was little. Heart disease. Before . . .' Before Feltham, but he's not going to tell her about that. Not as long as she's got her hand tucked in his arm.

She glances at him in surprise.

'So who brought *you* up?'

Linden shrugs. 'My brother, I guess. He's a lot older than me.'

'What does he do?'

'You mean for a living?' Linden says, playing for time, and when she says yes, he hesitates for a moment and then blurts out, 'He's in management in the pharmaceuticals industry. He's always busy with . . . like . . . managing . . . pharmaceuticals . . .'

'So we're the same, you and me,' she says, after a moment. 'We've both had to grow up quickly. Bring ourselves up.'

Linden grunts. *I had a bit of help from Her Majesty's Young Offenders Institute at Feltham,* he thinks. But he doesn't say it out loud. And he knows that not saying this fact, now when she's asking him outright about his past, is the same as a lie.

* * *

Footsteps approach them on the riverbank and they both turn quickly towards the sound. They can't see his face in the dark but they can see from his build that it's a man. No Stella Crosby. Linden breathes a sigh of relief. Maybe he was wrong. Maybe she doesn't have a plan. Maybe it's just the fact he can't seem to trust anyone any more . . . except Leah.

The man slows as he reaches them.

'Leah Martens?' he asks. He's got a scratchy voice, as though he's smoked about a million cigarettes too many. 'You can call me Smith.'

Linden wishes he could see Smith's face more clearly, but they're working in moonlight here, and all he can see is a broad, large-featured face.

'Does he have to be here?' Smith asks, nodding towards Linden.

'If I'm here, he is,' Leah answers firmly. 'Is Smith your real name?'

Smith laughs grimly. 'You've grown up,' he says. 'Last time I saw you, you were a tiny little thing.'

'You worked on the case?' Leah asks.

Smith doesn't reply. Instead, he starts walking and Leah and Linden are forced to walk alongside him.

'I have access to information about the case,' he says carefully. 'I hear you want to trade information.'

'I don't want to *trade*,' Leah says sharply, stopping in the middle of the path. 'No one said anything about trading. I just want you to tell me what you know.'

'Okay,' he says, 'if that's how you want to play it.' He turns around, walking back the way he's come.

Leah stares and then runs after him.

'What are you doing?' she shouts.

He stops again and speaks to her quickly, dismissively.

'I'm a busy man,' he says, 'I've got things to do. I want to find out what happened twelve years ago. I want to get to the bottom of this. I can tell you what I know but I need to hear what you know too. This is about cooperation, working together . . . I thought you'd be wanting to do that so you know who killed your mother.'

'You mean you're *still* working on the case?' Leah asks.

Linden shakes his head. Something's wrong.

'Since Cheever got out, it's been reopened,' Smith says. 'If it wasn't him in the park then it was someone else. We can't let a double murder drop.'

'Let's get out of here, Leah,' Linden says to her. 'He's messing with you.'

'If you don't speak about what you remember, you'll be obstructing a police investigation,' Smith says. 'I wouldn't want that on my conscience but that's a choice you've got to make.'

Leah stops walking and Smith comes to a halt in front of her.

'Come on,' he says, friendlier than before. 'Tell me your half of the story and I'll tell you my half, you can put them together then. No harm can come of it.'

Leah takes a deep breath and when she starts to speak she sound calm, as though she's saying something that she's thought through.

'My story won't help you,' Leah says slowly, 'it's patched together from what I've read, and what people have told me, and from my dreams. I was four years old. I think I can remember little bits of what happened – I have images in my head, like snapshots – but I don't trust my memories any more. I was sure Cheever was guilty and now we know he's innocent. Why would you want to know what's in my head? It's just a mess.'

'I can tell you why you thought it was Cheever,' Smith says.

Leah runs her tongue over her lip nervously. Linden knows she wants to hear this but he wishes she would walk away.

'Tell me,' she says.

Smith laughs softly, shaking his head.

'Ladies first,' he says.

'Really?' Leah says, 'You want to hear about my dreams, I'll tell you, but it's just a dream . . .' And then she tells Smith what she told Linden in the park, about walking with her mother through the trees, and the other woman coming towards them, and the stuffed toy falling on to the path, and Leah picking it up and running, taking it to the woman, then seeing the man coming out of the trees with a knife. She describes the stabbing as it happens in her dream, and Erica Brigson bleeding to death, and the man chasing them into the road . . .

'Do you see his face in your dream?' Smith asks.

'I must have seen his face,' Leah says. 'It was right in front of me.'

'Was it Cheever?'

'Leah,' Linden tries to intervene. 'Leah, you don't have to talk to him . . .'

But she's not listening any more, she's thinking aloud.

'I . . . I can't see the face in my head any more. It's like it's disintegrated. I think perhaps his face disintegrated in my head right after the attack. Perhaps it scared me too much to be able to see it, even in my head. When I shouted outside the court that it was Cheever, I thought it must have been him because everyone told me it was.' Her voice is clear. It rings out over the river and into the trees, and Linden glances around nervously. *Who's listening, in among the trees?*

'Not because you remember his face?' Smith presses again, although she's told him already.

'No.' She's frustrated at having to explain herself, ashamed of what she's done, the mistake she's made. 'Because I thought I must have identified him when I was four. I thought that was why they arrested him. Then I saw the newspaper article saying I didn't ever identify him and Stella Crosby said that came from you. That was when I realized that I don't know whether I have a real memory of his face, or whether I've made it up.'

There's a moment's silence, broken only by the sound of Leah's agitated breathing. Linden thinks if he listens carefully, he can hear the sound of them all shivering. Linden wants out of here. This was stupid. No good ever comes from meetings on a riverbank in the pitch dark and now Leah's gabbling away her secrets to a man whose only name is Smith.

She's been taken in. Tricked . . . Stella Crosby's got a plan, that's what he thinks.

Smith shifts, pushing his hands further into his pockets, hunching his shoulders high around his neck, trying to block the creeping cold.

'Your mother was killed outright when the car hit her,' Smith starts to speak in his gravelly voice, 'and whoever attacked you took advantage of the traffic accident to scarper. You were thrown clear. You were in shock, you couldn't speak a word, and the paramedics were afraid there were internal injuries as well. Your face was a bloody mess. They rushed you to hospital, and you spent hours in surgery being sewn up. No one spoke to you before that about what you'd seen. There didn't seem any point. You were such a tiny thing, and you didn't even seem to hear anything anyone said to you . . . Even when your dad came to find you in the hospital, you looked at him as though he was a ghost. The doctors said they couldn't see any brain damage on scans but no one knew how hard you'd hit your head, so no one could be sure.'

Even Linden is paying attention now. He'd thought the guy was a complete fraud, some bit actor playing a part. Now he thinks, *If this is an actor, he's a good one.* Leah's standing there gazing up at the man as he speaks. She doesn't move. She's like a statue. She's never heard this before.

'When you came out of surgery, we – the police – left you alone for forty-eight hours while you recovered. There didn't seem any point in rushing it. We thought the longer we left it, the stronger you were, the more we'd get out of you. Then, no one wanted to tell you about your mother, so that was another delay. When your dad did tell you, you were so upset that we had to leave it again. Meanwhile, word's getting back to us from all over the place that Deryk Cheever had a violent argument with his mistress, Erica, in the park a few minutes before the attack, so he becomes prime suspect. When you do come around, someone shows you a photo line-up. It wasn't me but I know who it was. You don't pick Cheever. Next day, someone shows you a different line-up. Different except for Cheever. He's still there. But still you don't pick him. Third day, they show you another line-up, all different, except for Cheever again. He's the only one in all three line-ups. The officer starts to taunt you: "*What, can't you see him?*" Maybe he points at Cheever: "*Does he look familiar?*" You get very upset, you cry. Finally, you point to Cheever.'

'So I did identify him!'

'By then you'd seen him three times. He was the only face in all three line-ups. If he didn't look familiar by then, nobody would. The officer led you right to him, the police needed their man. The positive ID should never have been allowed in court.'

For a moment Leah is silent. Then she says, 'Why did they allow it? Why didn't someone tell them to stop?'

'Everyone wanted it to be Cheever,' Linden says. 'He already said it, Cheever was prime suspect. The only suspect.'

Leah is shaking her head. 'But if it wasn't him, then who was it?'

She sounds so fierce that Smith, all six feet of him, takes a step back, away from her. 'Cheever said he saw someone else . . .' he says. 'If he hadn't been killed, he'd have been speaking to the police the next day.'

'I'll never know,' Leah mutters angrily. 'I'll never know.'

'But you do know,' Smith says, tapping his head. 'It's all in there. You're the one who knows. You're the one who saw him.'

'I was four,' Leah says. 'No one remembers faces from

when they were four, but I stared at him and I knew he wanted to kill me, so his face must be in my head somewhere. When I dream, I see him, but it's never whole, it's like – in splinters . . . I feel as though I'm on the brink of seeing his whole face. I think – maybe I'd remember him if I saw him again. I think my memory would put his face back together then.'

'Okay,' Smith says. 'That's something. You'd know him if you saw him. That's something.'

Linden shakes his head. That's not what Leah said.

'Are there new suspects?' Leah asks.

'I don't know anything about that,' Smith says. He speaks as though he's got what he came for. It's time to move on.

'But you said you were investigating . . . you said the murder investigation was reopened.'

'Maybe,' Smith says. 'But not by me. I'm retired. I'm working for Stella Crosby now. She's the one who's opened an investigation, for the newspaper.'

Leah's jaw drops. She stares at him.

He shrugs, glances over his shoulder towards the trees, and then says, 'I never said I was with the police, not any more. You should be more careful who you speak to, love.'

Linden lunges towards him but suddenly, out of the trees, a motorbike revs on to the path. It speeds towards them, deafening them, and swerves to a stop in front of them. The driver is clad in black, helmeted, his face hidden by his visor. Smith climbs quickly on to the back. He twists around, with a camera in his hand, and a flash goes off in their faces.

Linden swears. He grabs hold of Smith's arm but the

driver accelerates. Linden tries to hang on but the bike is already moving away and he finds himself dragged, the bike lurching forwards against his weight, Smith kicking him, until he lets go and falls, hard, into the snow, and the bike speeds away.

Leah runs to him. With her standing over him, he shakes his head slowly to and fro in the snow. 'Bad move,' he's saying. 'Bad decision. We should never have agreed to meet him.'

She crouches down and shakes him, speaking urgently. 'Come on, you've got to get up. You'll freeze to death.'

Slowly, he props himself on one elbow, then sits. Leah stretches out her hand and he takes it, pulling himself to his feet.

CHARLIE

27

When Victor parks the car outside an anonymous block of concrete flats five minutes' drive away, Charlie is disappointed.

'I thought we were going on the run,' he says.

'You're going on the run, I'm going home,' says Victor. 'You can hang out at my place if you want to, or you can get lost, it's nothing to me.'

That stings. Charlie wishes someone in his life would actually want to spend some time with him. But he's got nowhere else to go. He can't go home because the police will be waiting for him, and the night's so windy and dark and cold. When he said he was running away from home, he had no intention of sleeping in a park. Not in this weather. He's not sure where he thought he would go.

'I'll hang out with you,' he says to Victor, who makes no comment.

Inside, Charlie walks from room to room with eyes like saucers. His auntie's house is all purples and pinks, and flowers – anything to try and jazz up a gloomy home; this place is like the opposite of that, all blank walls and modern gadgets.

'Is this a bachelor pad?' he asks Victor, staring in awe at the vast TV screen and the gaming console.

'I'm a bachelor and this is my pad,' Victor replies drily. He looks amused. It occurs to Charlie's sleepy head that Victor is looking at him like a cat looks at a spider.

Charlie sits himself down on the sofa and gazes around him in awe. He doesn't see the mess, just the masculinity. It's like a weight's been taken off his shoulders. There's no auntie making his tea and asking him how school went, there's no tablecloth to wipe crumbs from, no coat rack to hang up your coat. When he'd walked through the door, he'd watched Victor chuck his coat on to a chair, where it landed in a heap, and Charlie had followed suit.Victor reaches for a pack of cigarettes on the table and offers it to Charlie.

'Smoke?' he asks, and Charlie licks his lips and takes two from the pack, sticking one between his lips and the other in his pocket for later.

Victor flops into an armchair opposite Charlie. He picks up the remote and switches on the TV.

'So,' he says, sounding bored, one eye on the TV screen. 'Your mother giving you grief about being out that night? About the police coming round?'

'I don't have a mother,' says Charlie, 'she was killed twelve years ago.'

'Oh, yeah, I remember now,' says Victor, who has not for a moment forgotten exactly who he's speaking to.

'The police think I murdered my dad. Someone stabbed him and they think it was me.'

'Why –' Victor says, tapping his cigarette on the edge of an ashtray on the table to the side of his armchair, '– would they think that?'

'They think I hated him.'

Victor runs his tongue over his lips. 'Did you?'

'No,' Charlie says miserably. 'I couldn't hate him, he was my dad. But I was angry with him. He was pretending to like me.'

'Ah,' Victor says. He blows a smoke ring towards the ceiling. 'That's bad. Unrequited love.'

'He was my dad,' Charlie protests. 'It wasn't unrequited anything.'

'I hope they don't come and interview *me*,' Victor says, and stops, apparently to think for a moment. 'Because *I* can put *you* at the scene, Charlie boy.'

Charlie glances at him fearfully. 'You won't though,' he says, suddenly unsure. After all, he doesn't know Victor at all, doesn't know if he can trust him. 'You won't, will you?'

'Probably not,' Victor says. 'If you tell me what you were doing there.'

'I was angry at him,' Charlie says. 'I was going to yell at him. I'd come from the girl's house, the one who shouted at him outside the court—'

'The house where someone set a fire?' Victor isn't even trying to disguise his interest any more. 'What were you doing there then?'

Charlie gazes back at him without saying anything, but he raises his bandaged hand to show Victor.'

Victor stares.

'You burned it?' Was it you that did that?' He sounds excited, almost happy about the arson, and Charlie can't resist taking the credit. He so rarely has anything to take credit for.

'Yeah,' he says, smiling for the first time. 'That was me. I nearly burned the house right down.'

'Way to go, Charlie,' Victor says, grinning, and Charlie grins back.

'The girl wasn't hurt, right? She walked out.'

Charlie nods. He's really happy that no one got hurt, but he's not sure whether a lack of victims counts as a good thing or a bad thing to Victor.

'Well, Charlie,' Victor says, 'I think you and I are going to get along fine. We're birds of a feather, you and I. I'm going to adopt you as my little brother. The position just became vacant.'

He smiles brightly at Charlie and Charlie smiles brightly back.

'Great,' he says, and Victor roars with laughter.

Charlie is confused. He doesn't know why Victor is laughing. He thinks that having an adopted big brother is rather like meeting your father for the first time in twelve years, very strange and unfamiliar.

'Well, if it's great, why don't we drink to it?' Victor says. He gets to his feet and heads to the kitchen, which Charlie has glimpsed through an open door.

Charlie's ravenously hungry and actually he's desperate for food. For an instant, an image of his aunty's spaghetti bolognese fills his head, and he feels a tug in his tummy. But if drink is what's on offer, then at least it will fill him up.

When Victor comes back into the room, he has a bottle of vodka in one hand and two glasses in the other.

'Your drink of choice?' he asks Charlie, flourishing the bottle.

Charlie nods because he wants to please. Alcohol is alcohol and even though the last time he drank didn't go too well, right now he thinks it might help him not to be scared. He watches as Victor pours until the glasses are full and he takes the glass offered to him.

'Do you have any other brothers?' Victor asks Charlie.

Charlie shakes his head and says, 'No, do you?'

'No, I don't, not any more,' says Victor. He raises his glass, clinks it with Charlie's, and says, 'To brotherhood!'

'To brotherhood!' Charlie echoes, and they drink.

LINDEN

28

Stella Crosby's story explodes on to the front page.

TWELVE YEARS TOO LATE
Attack Victim Admits She Did Not Tell Truth
Cannot Remember Face of Attacker

The moment Linden enters the coffee shop and catches sight of Leah, he can feel how angry she is, and how upset. He slides into the seat opposite her and she hardly acknowledges him. He watches her reading, eyes furious, flicking across the newsprint. She's got a cup of coffee in front of her. He'd kill for one of those but he's got no spare cash for anything. They'd paid him for his days at the shoe repair shop, put some cash in his account, but it was only a few days of work and the cash would run out any day. He walked for forty minutes from his uncle's place to get here because he couldn't afford the bus fare.

He's read the story already, from a paper abandoned at a bus stop on the way. It's got photos with it, of Leah's mum and of Erica Brigson. Linden thinks they look alike. Both young, slim, blonde. They're both smiling at the camera with babies on their laps. There's a photograph taken on the riverbank, the one Smith took from the motorbike as he left. In the picture, Linden can see himself, standing behind Leah. The photograph cuts him off at the neck. Linden's glad about that. He doesn't want Victor seeing him in the newspaper.

There are word-for-word quotes in the story, so Smith must have been wearing a wire, and Stella Crosby must have had a transcript in front of her when she wrote the story. But it's not a story Linden recognises. The way Stella Crosby's written it, it looks different.

To Linden, the big news from what Smith told them that night on the riverbank was that the police had tricked and bullied a frightened four-year-old Leah into picking Cheever from the line-up. After that, she'd grown up with everyone around her telling her Cheever was guilty. She respected the police, her own dad was a police officer, everyone expected the police to get it right, so why would she have questioned it?

But Stella Crosby tells it a different way. What she's written doesn't even look like news to Linden, it looks like Stella Crosby's opinion, as though she's just stirring things up.

Leah Martens has tried to make us all believe that Deryk Cheever, who was stabbed to death last week, was guilty of the murder of her mother and another woman. The reason we believed her? Twelve years ago, she came face to face with the killer, who also brutally knifed her. If anyone knew the face of the killer, she did.

The truth is, twelve years ago, and just days after the attack that left her scarred, the police showed Leah Martens line-ups, two times, and she did not identify Cheever. Only after police believed they had other evidence pointing to Cheever's guilt and suggested to the girl that he might have been in the park, did the child decide to go along with what was suggested. Now a teenager, Leah Martens tells this paper she cannot remember ever having a complete picture of her attacker's face in her head. Just days ago, she screamed accusations at Cheever when he was freed on appeal. Yet she admits to our reporter, 'his face disintegrated in my head right after the attack'. It's one thing for a four-year-old to go along with what she's told, quite another for a teenager to accuse someone she knows to be innocent. Her initial false identification meant Deryk Cheever was imprisoned for twelve years, but we cannot make a four-year-old accountable. But now, as a young adult, her accusations may have led indirectly to his murder . . .

Without lifting her head, Leah reaches towards her coffee cup and pushes it towards him.

'Have this,' she says. 'I don't want it.'

He doesn't argue. He slides the cup of coffee towards him, starts to drink, doesn't care that it's five minutes colder than it was when she bought it.

'Why didn't she write a story about what the police did back then?' Leah says. 'Because making a little kid identify the wrong man is wrong.'

'Because Stella Crosby is working with Smith,' Linden says. 'He probably still drinks with the same police officers, he's got no interest in getting them in trouble. He probably only gave her the the transcript of what you said. I bet she never even saw what he admitted to you.

Linden's eyes are flickering across the page again. He

notices that Stella Crosby has quoted another thing Leah said:

'I think maybe I'd remember him if I saw him again . . .'

Linden wonders if Leah even remembers saying that. He wonders if it's true – it was an awfully long time ago. And he wonders what the killer would think if he saw it on the page. Linden thinks a killer might worry about Leah. Linden thinks a killer is already worrying about Leah.

Someone knocks on the window and Leah looks up, startled.

On the other side of the glass there's a photographer standing in the snow. He's got his camera pressed up against the glass.

'Come on,' Linden grabs her hand, 'let's get out of here.'

Outside, they start to run through the snow and the photographer starts to run behind them. They're slipping and sliding, holding hands for balance. When Linden glances behind him, he sees the photographer has lost his footing and is sitting in the snow on his backside, and he swings Leah around to see. She laughs. When they reach the park, they stop, heaving great breaths. There's no one behind them, no one for miles around, just a great expanse of white.

'Let's forget about Stella Crosby and all her bullshit,' Linden says. 'No one reads her stupid newspaper anyway, everyone knows it's full of lies.'

Linden crouches down and gathers a great ball of snow, then stands, lobbing it at Leah, and she shrieks as the snowball hits her. She leaps away from him through the snow, leaving deep footprints behind her. But when she turns, he's right behind her, grinning with great handfuls of snow in his palm, that he hurls and that thud into her, as she stands laughing with her arms in the air in surrender.

'I'm not running any more,' she yells at him when he's run out of ammunition. 'I'm going to get you now.'

She gathers handfuls of snow and yells, 'You better run!'

But he stands there smiling at her, with his arms outstretched, waiting for her to reach him, and when she does, she smears the snow over his face and in his hair, and she pulls him towards her, and they kiss and laugh, and then they kiss some more.

It's getting dark when they head back home. Cold and damp, they walk with their arms around each other, hip to hip. He walks her to her door. Outside, they kiss again, pressed close together, oblivious. Leah pulls away, disentangling herself from Linden's arms.

'I wish this afternoon could last forever,' she said. She's looking serious now, coming back to earth so close to home. 'But it can't, can it? This isn't over, I know it's not. I should never have screamed at Cheever. I should never have spoken to Stella Crosby. I should have left well alone.'

Linden shrugs, reluctant to come down to earth so fast. 'It doesn't matter what's in the papers,' he says. 'People get bored, they move on to something new.'

'Cheever's dead,' she says grimly, shaking her head. 'And whoever did it might want to do the same to me.'

Linden pulls her to him. He doesn't want to say it but he's scared too. Any time he stops and thinks about what's going on, and *who* he suspects is involved, he's scared.

'Hey,' he says, 'I'm going to be here with you. I'll do everything I can to protect you.'

'I know.'

'Even though I know you don't need it.'

She smiles and turns away from him and puts her key in the door.

'Even though I know you'll end up protecting me.'

She laughs.

'Take care,' he says to her.

She rolls her eyes.

'I mean it,' he says. 'Take care. Lock all your dad's locks. Put the bolt across. Don't answer the phone or the door unless you know—'

'You're sounding like him,' she says, and that makes him shut up. He doesn't want to sound like her dad, the jerk.

She turns the key and disappears inside her flat. Outside, Linden waits until he hears the locks turned.

He can only have walked ten paces when the first blow hits him from behind. A moment later, someone kicks his feet from under him and he's on his knees.

'I know you now,' says a voice. 'I know you who you are, you lying piece of shit.'

CHARLIE

29

'You know whose fault all this is, don't you,' says Victor. Or rather, he slurs. Not that he's drunk, quite the opposite, he's entirely sober. But he wants to keep Charlie company, wants to seem as out of it as the boy.

'S'hers,' Charlie says, from his position curled like a puppy – a drunken puppy – on the sofa.

'S'hers,' Victor agrees.

Between them on the floor lie the day's newspapers. Victor is not generally interested in current affairs, but in this case, the front page was what even he would call news.

The girl, Leah Martens, wired and transcribed.

There's a photograph of the girl standing by a river in the dark. There's someone standing next to her. The photograph cuts that person off at the neck, but Victor knows his brother when he sees him, even headless.

Linden. Standing right behind his girlfriend.

Victor thinks that's very sweet.

He thinks it's very interesting.

He thinks by now Linden would have understood that his relationship with Leah Martens is dangerous.

'Twelve years your dad was inside,' Victor says, 'all because of her lies. It's a shame she didn't burn in the fire.'

He's afraid he might be sounding too sober, so he belches loudly.

Charlie snorts, and for a moment Victor thinks the boy's passed out. But then the boy says, 'Yeah . . . yeah . . .'

'Could have another go,' Victor suggests. He waits for the boy to say something, but he doesn't. 'Or have a go at her, give her a scar on the other side of her face. Try not to burn your hand this time.'

Victor barks with laughter, but the boy doesn't respond.

'You know what I think?' Victor says. 'I think *her* dad might be the one who killed your dad.'

Charlie frowns, blurry-eyed, across at him.

'Think about it,' Victor says, crouching down in front of Charlie, speaking just centimetres from his face, trying to make sure Charlie remembers this one thing through his drunken haze. 'Think about it, her dad has always hated Cheever for killing his wife and hurting his kid. He couldn't get at him when he was inside, but once he was out . . .'

'But my dad didn't kill his wife or hurt his kid!' Charlie slurs.

'But he'd believe his daughter, wouldn't he?' Victor says. 'And she always said it was your dad. I'm not saying it was definitely Leah Martens's dad who killed Cheever, I'm just saying it's possible . . .'

The boy lifts his face towards Victor with a look of intense concentration and Victor thinks he's about to agree. But instead he suddenly turns a horrible green colour, shudders once, then vomits all over the floor.

Victor swears violently, then watches helplessly as the boy vomits again.

'You're going to fucking clean it up yourself!' he yells.

But Charlie's not going to do anything. He's passed out on the sofa.

Victor stares at the pool of vomit spreading across the floor, soaking the newspapers, and pooling in the cracks between the floorboards. The smell of alcohol and stomach bile fills the room.

He swears again. He can't believe the kid got this drunk so quickly. He's sure when he was Charlie's age he had a stronger constitution.

Gingerly, trying to step only on the shores of the lake that is his floor, he gets and starts to go and search for whatever it is that people use to clear up vomit.

Ten minutes later, wads of toilet paper in hand and expression of disgust upon his face, he's clearing up.

This isn't what he was intending. The boy's no use to him like this, passed out and snoring.

This wasn't in his plan.

'I think maybe I'd remember him if I saw him again . . .'

He hears it in his head as he crouches, cleaning up the foul-smelling mess. *'I think maybe I'd remember him if I saw him again . . .'*

Time for a new plan.

LINDEN

30

Normally, Linden would be aware of where he is and he'd be on alert. He wouldn't hang around near the shadows. He doesn't think of himself as particularly vulnerable but he knows he's not immune. It was true in Feltham and it's true out here too.

But he's not paying attention. His head is too full of Leah.

So when the blows start to rain down on him he's completely unprepared.

'I know you who you are, you lying piece of shit.'

Taken by surprise, he doesn't have time to hit back.

'You think I don't remember you but you're wrong.' The man spits the words out, covering Linden's face in spittle. 'I know you and I know what you're doing to me.'

Now, face to face, Linden recognises his attacker. It's Leah's father. And now, he's quite certain that he's seen him before.

'I'm not doing anything to you, man,' Linden tries to struggle to his feet. Leah's dad comes at him again, grabbing his collar and pulling him close, so their faces are centimetres apart.

'You're trying to pay me back, right?' he says, panting.

'You think you're getting to me through my daughter? Well I'm wise to you now, and you're never going to see her again.'

'Hey,' Linden says, still backing off, 'that's up to her.'

'No,' the man snarls, 'it's up to you.' And he punches Linden hard in the face.

Linden cries out, his hands flying to his face where his fingers meet blood pouring from his nose.

'What are you doing?' Linden cries out. 'You're a police officer, not a fucking vigilante.'

'I'm whatever I want to be,' Leah's dad says. 'And you're a piece of shit.'

He kicks Linden's legs from under him, and when Linden collapses on to the pavement, he kicks him again and again, until Linden is screaming out and curling around, trying to grab the foot to stop it. The man stops kicking for a moment and squats down next to Linden, who is moaning.

'Stay away from her,' the man says, 'or I'll put you inside again. I've done it once, I'll do it again without a second thought, and then I'll do it again, until you're stuck in there for good and you never see the light of day.' He stands and walks away.

Linden lies there. He doesn't want to move ever again. It's going to hurt too much. He's going to stand up and he's going to fall down again, and that's going to happen about a half a dozen times, he can feel it. He can't go back to his uncle's, not like this. So he's going to drag himself back to Victor's miserable flat and he's not going to be able to move. He lies there for a while, flexing his limbs one by one, making sure everything's functioning. Which still doesn't mean he wants to get up. Actually, the freezing snow is acting like an anesthetic, numbing everything that hurts.

For a moment he loses consciousness. Then, when his brain sends out an alarm signal, his eyes flicker and he stares up into the night sky. The snow falls steadily. It feels like a blanket. Like someone is covering him. When he thinks about a blanket of snow, he knows that either he gets up, or he dies in the snow.

He flips over, so he's on his belly, and then he pushes up against the ground, so he's on all fours, and then he's kneeling, and finally he's standing. He staggers, slipping through the snow, back en route for Victor's flat. He hears Leah's dad's voice in his head.

'I'll put you inside again. I've done it once, I'll do it again without a second thought, and then I'll do it again . . .'

He blinks. The snow is hypnotising him. He can't let his mind wander. The streets are deserted. Everyone except him and Leah's psycho dad are sipping hot chocolate in front of a fire. His feet are numb. The snow has worked its way inside his shoes. The shoes will be finished – even Marky won't be able to fix them . . . He finds his mind wandering to the shoe repair shop . . .

He's got to stay on track, or they'll find his body frozen solid.

'I'll put you inside again. I've done it once . . .'

The words echo inside his frozen skull.

He sits down on a kerb so covered by snow he can't really see the kerb itself, just feel it underneath him. He's going to have a rest. His stomach is still hurting and his head is spinning from the kicking that it got. He closes his eyes for a moment.

In his mind's eye, he sees the face of Leah's father again, and with the image comes a flash of another image. So momentary that he can't hold on to it. It flits into his head, as if to say, *I'm here, keep on looking.* And slowly faces come into focus. Leah's father, standing with other police officers, watching him as he's dragged into the station . . .

He feels something, another human being close by; he is afraid that Leah's father has come back.

He forces his eyes open and finds, peering into his face, another face. Serious eyes examining him.

'Leah,' he tries to say, but his lips won't move. He takes hold of her hand in his and squeezes tight, absorbing its warmth, drinking it in.

'My dad came home, I could see he'd been in a fight.' She's talking quickly, angrily, but Linden understands foggily that her anger isn't directed at him. Which is a relief, because he's had enough of Martens' anger for one night. 'He told me he'd warned you off. I know what he means by that, so I came looking for you. I hate him! Why would he do this!'

Linden keeps tight hold of her hand. Tries to tell her through frozen lips, 'Leah, he's right to warn me off you. I'm not good enough. He . . . he was with the police who arrested me and sent me to Feltham. He knows I'm a piece of shit.'

Leah shakes her head, frowning. 'He told me . . .' she says. 'I don't want to hear about it now. You've got to get up or you'll die of cold,'

She has to push and shove to get him upright, and then he drags his feet and can't walk straight because his feet are so cold that he can't feel them. Leah remembers from some television programme or other that if a horse is sick, you've got to keep it on its feet and this is how she thinks of Linden for the next half an hour, as they make painfully slow progress. He, so much bigger and heavier than her, is the horse that must be cajoled and chivvied on, and never allowed to rest, or he will stop and die. She has to keep asking directions from him. *Left or right? Straight ahead here? You're sure this is the right way?*

'Where is this?' she asks, as Linden staggers to a stop outside a block of concrete flats.

'Victor's . . .' he mutters, unable to explain more. It's fate again. It won't let him escape. It makes him want to weep. Victor won't be surprised. He'll have known his little brother would be back.

He tells her which bell to push and, when no one answers, he bashes on the door until someone looks out the upstairs window.

It's Victor.

'It's me,' Linden starts to say, and then he sees it – Victor's face when he spots Leah. This shouldn't be happening. He's brought her to the wolf's lair, delivered her . . .

'Get out of here,' he says, turning to Leah.

Her face falls. She doesn't understand.

'Go!' he says. 'I don't need you any more. Haven't you seen what your fucking father did to me?' And he curses and swears about her father, until she covers her ears and starts to back away from him.

'What are you doing?' Leah says. 'Why are you being like this?'

'Get the fuck out of here,' Linden yells at her. He takes a threatening step towards her. For a moment she stares at him. And then she backs away.

Linden feels himself collapse against the wall. What has he done?

Victor is opening the door. He's stepping out into the snow, looking up and down the street. Linden looks at his brother's face, clearly illuminated in the streetlights.

'Where's the girl?' he says.

'Gone,' Linden says. 'I got rid of her. She's nothing to me.'

'What happened to you?'

'Her father beat me up.' Linden's teeth are chattering. He wishes Victor would let him inside. If this is where he's got to be, if this is his fate, then he wants to be inside it, not out here in this freezing wind.

'I've got a house guest,' says Victor, 'You'll have to sleep on Sameer's floor.'

Linden's relieved that he'll be on Sameer's floor, not on Victor's. He nods. As he turns to follow Victor inside, he sees movement from the corner of his eye and he looks back. Leah is at the corner of the street. She has stepped into the streetlight and he can see her face clearly. He can see her startled expression.

Linden knows that she's seen Victor.

'I think maybe I'd remember him if I saw him again. I think my memory would put his face back together then . . .'

He thinks she's remembered now.

Quickly, he turns away and follows Victor inside.

CHARLIE

31

Charlie wakes up. It's pitch dark and he doesn't know where he is. There's nothing, not so much as a shaft of light, to give him a clue. He stretches out his hand and it comes into contact with nothing. He scarcely knows which way is up and which way down, let alone where there is a window or a door, some form of exit. Panic and stomach acid rise in his throat. He closes his eyes again. There's no point, after all, in keeping them open if there's nothing to see. He has never felt so ill in his life, as though the contents of his brain have been removed with a spoon and the contents of his stomach have been injected with curdled milk and shaken up and down. Something or someone inside his head is pounding at his skull with a hammer, trying to break out. He wants to die. He never wants to drink again. Somewhere, on the other side of a door, he hears Victor's voice. He's on the phone to someone.

'Sameer? Yeah, what is it? Really, he's gone? Risen from his sick bed? I didn't think he had it in him. Run off to his girlfriend, no doubt. Everyone's on the run tonight . . . Sameer, take care of business, I'm going to do a little chasing myself.'

Suddenly, light invades the room. Charlie cries out as it

hits his eyes, blinding him and sending an arrow of pain through his skull.

'Up we get, Charlie boy.' Victor grabs his right hand and pulls, until Charlie, whimpering and moaning, is at the edge of the bed.

'Come on, Charlie,' Victor says. 'Weren't you the one who wanted to go on the run?'

He pulls Charlie off the edge of the bed and the boy collapses on to the floor, lying sprawled and gasping.

'For Christ's sake,' Victor says, 'if you puke again, I'm going to hold you face down and drown you in it!'

Somewhere deep in Charlie's head, he begins to understand that he has not been lucky. Not in the death of his mother, not in the nature of his father and not in this adopted big brother. His auntie has been his one true friend – and he has betrayed her. Tears run from his eyes, down the side of his face and on to the floor. His hand has started hurting again, worse now. His auntie changed his bandages but he hasn't changed them since he ran away . . .

'It's all the girl's fault. All her fault.'

He's aware that something is going on in the room. Cautiously, he opens his eyes. Victor is pulling a box from a broken wardrobe. He puts the box on the floor and removes the lid, reaching inside.

He pulls out a gun.

Charlie, immobile on the floor, is now paralysed with fear. Some part of his brain sobers up out of sheer necessity. He wants to cry out, to plead for his life. But to do that will attract attention to himself. If there is even the tiniest possibility that Victor might forget that he's lying drunkenly on the floor, then Charlie will seize that possibility. He holds his breath, trying not to twitch so much as a muscle.

'You see this?' Victor turns towards him, flourishing the small black gun. 'This means we have the power, you and me. Nobody messes with us now, right?'

Charlie stares.

'They'd better watch out for you, right?' Victor pokes Charlie in the ribs. 'Because you're the man with the man with the gun.'

LINDEN

32

Linden can see the patch of black on the door, where the burning T shirt has scorched the paint. He rings the bell, but he can't hear it ring, and no one comes, so he bashes on the door and yells her name.

The door opens, and suddenly Leah's there in front of him, looking at him silent and unsmiling.

'I'm sorry,' he says desperately. 'I'm sorry. I didn't mean what I said. I had to stop you seeing him. I wanted you to get away from there before he hurt you again—'

'I trusted you,' Leah replies, stony-faced.

'You should trust me,' Linden says. 'I'll never hurt you, Leah . . . I made a mistake. I should have told you. About me and about – him. I should have warned you, instead I took you there, where he could see you and he could get hold of you. I'm sorry.'

He starts to weep, then, head bowed, shoulders shaking, and Leah watches him, taking in everything about him. She lets him weep for what feels to him like a long time and he wonders if this is his punishment.

'Come in,' she says eventually, 'you'll freeze out there.'

Leah lets him into the ground-floor flat and leads him to a small sitting room, where she waves him to a chair and sits down herself. She's only a couple of metres away from him but it feels like a yawning ocean of space. Linden wants to reach out and touch her but he doesn't dare, so he sits there, hunched over in his seat, hands rubbing his knees.

He looks around nervously.

'Is he here?' he asks.

'You mean my dad? No, he's gone.'

He opens his mouth to speak, but she's talking already.

'Who was that man last night, the one who let you into the flat?'

He hesitates, but he can't lie to her. He can fail to tell her something but he can't lie.

'He's my brother.'

He watches her face fall. 'Your brother,' she echoes, as though she can't believe it. And again, 'Your brother?' Then she says, 'He has a scar under his eye, doesn't he? I could see it clearly . . .'

Linden could say no. She might even feel better if he said no.

'Yes,' he says. 'He has a scar under his eye.'

She takes the news as though she'd expected it. She must know, Linden thinks, she has to know, or at least suspect.

'How did he get it?'

Linden shakes his head miserably. 'I don't know. He's had it as long as I can remember.'

'You haven't asked him how he got it? Even after I told you about the man in the park getting cut on his knife?'

'I knew he'd lie. He always lies. He's not . . . safe.'

He raises his head, afraid to ask the question they're both avoiding.

'Do . . . do you remember him?'

'When I saw him . . .' Leah pauses, 'I felt as though I was falling backwards in time. It wasn't that I remembered his face . . . it was as though his face suddenly slotted in. As though there was a space waiting for it . . . If it wasn't for the scar, I'd have said I was just freaked out by everything else. I wouldn't have said I could identify him just from the way I felt. I couldn't have gone to the police or anything. But the scar and the strange way you'd acted. Even the way we first met, with you looking through the window at the gym. My dad told me what you used to do. He said your brother was worse. So was it your brother? Did your brother tell you to follow me?'

Linden is paralysed. Ever since he met her he's kept thinking, *Don't trust me, please, because I don't trust myself.* And now all he wants to say is, *Please, please trust me* . . .

At last, Linden opens his mouth to speak. He keeps his eyes on hers.

'No,' he says, his voice low and desperate, his head hanging, 'you've got to believe me. I'd seen him looking at you on TV, like he was fixated. Then I saw you in the arcade and I . . . I just wanted to find out why he was behaving like that. He didn't tell me what to do, I did it on my own. He doesn't give me orders any more. I make my own decisions . . .' He breaks off and looks up at her face. 'I'm not like him. You know that, right? I'm not like Victor. I'd never hurt you. I went to the gym to follow you, I wanted to find out who you were and why he was so – obsessed . . . But then I met you and we talked and . . . and then it wasn't about Victor any more.'

She's watching him, weighing him up.

'He scares me too,' he says simply.

Still Leah says nothing. He's never felt so scrutinised.

Linden opens his mouth. He wants to tell Leah everything now, about Feltham and everything. He wants to get rid of it, so she knows everything. He wants her to hear it from him, not from her dad. He's got a sudden feeling, like euphoria or elation or something, that if he can tell her everything about his life, if he can explain, then he'll feel light and free, as though it's been lifted from him. And what they have won't change, because then everything will be out in the open, like it should have been from the start. But she's talking already, about something completely different. It's as though between a millisecond ago and now she's made some big decision that she's not announcing. Linden can't keep up.

'What? Say that again,' he has to say.

'I *said*,' she's irritated by his lack of attention, 'if it *was* him . . . if it *was* your brother in the park that day, why would he have done it? Did he know Erica Brigson? Why did he do that to her?'

He shakes his head. 'I don't know,' he mumbles.

He doesn't really want to talk about Victor and whether he might have murdered two women and attempted the murder of a child twelve years ago, because he doesn't want to think any more about the answer to that, or how that makes him feel.

'Did you see Stella Crosby's article today?' she says, getting up.

He shakes his head. He can't keep up with her, with what's going on in her head. He thought they were talking about Victor and now they're talking about a newspaper.

'Perhaps it has something to do with that . . .' It's as though she's thinking aloud.

She gets up and disappears, reappears with a newspaper, handing it to him and talking at the same time so his head is filled with trying to understand what's happening.

'It's about Dad,' she says. 'Stella Crosby claims he was working undercover at the time of the attack.'

Frowning, Linden starts to read, but his head is too full to make much sense of the words.

'I thought your dad was just an ordinary policeman? But is that what he does?' he asks. 'He works undercover?'

'It makes sense,' she says, unsmiling. 'It's why he's so paranoid, it's why he seems to always be half a dozen people at one time and none of them live here. He's always something else, somewhere else. I suppose I knew but I didn't have a name for it.'

Linden lowers his head again over the newspaper.

> Documents leaked by police sources reveal that at the time of the murders in the park, Martens had been working undercover for five months on an assignment known as Operation Gold Medal . . .

'Operation Gold Medal,' Linden says, looking up at her. 'Why was it called that?'

She shakes her head. 'I don't know,' she says, 'I think the police choose random names, maybe it didn't mean anything.'

> According to our source, Operation Gold Medal was an undercover investigation into a drugs ring operating in South East London. Martens was posing as a drug dealer and had infiltrated the drugs-distribution organisation. Shortly before the murders in the park, that investigation collapsed. The drug ring went to ground, its leadership apparently descending into mutual recriminations. Martens left London and attempts by colleagues to find him were unsuccessful. When his wife was murdered and his daughter attacked, a family member told police that he was in the north of England. At that point, he returned to London, refusing all media interviews.

Linden closes his eyes and rubs his palm over his face. Drug dealer . . . Operation Gold Medal . . . Leah's dad . . . He can feel his brain piecing things together . . . He opens his eyes and looks at Leah, he doesn't think she's going to like what he's about to say, but everything is starting to fit with an idea that has been hanging around his head ever since he saw the photo in the newspaper the other day. Erica Brigson and Leah's mother, each with a child on their lap, two murdered women who looked so very much alike.

'Say, just say, for argument's sake, that my brother is the man who attacked you. And we don't know if he is,' he begins, hesitantly. 'Well, what if it wasn't Erica Brigson he was after . . . What if it was your mum? Maybe even you?'

Leah is frowning at him.

'Then why kill Erica at all?' she says. 'Why not just go after Mum and me?'

'Say it was a mistake,' he continues. 'Say this man, let's say my brother, he's waiting in the trees for a child and a mother, and then he sees a woman and a child running towards her, holding out a teddy. This other woman, she looks like your mum. What does he think? Maybe he thinks that the woman you're running towards is your mother?'

Leah's looking at Linden like he's crazy.

'But my mum was right there. Why would he get it wrong?'

Linden shrugs. 'Maybe he doesn't see your mum. He just sees the other woman from the back and you running towards her. Maybe it was a case of mistaken identity.'

Leah hasn't stopped looking at him like he's mad, but she's still listening.

'But, even if that's all true, we still have the same problem,' she argues. 'Why would your brother want to kill Mum and me? He's got no link with Erica but he's got nothing to do with us either.'

Linden is silent for a long minute.

'Maybe he does,' he says.

'What do you mean? I don't understand what you're getting at.' Leah's patience is running thin.

'I'm thinking . . .' Linden trails off. If Leah's already looking at him like that, what's she going to think of him after he's said what he's about to say?

'Well? Spit it out, Linden, whatever it is.'

He shakes his head. 'You're going to laugh at me,' he says. 'You've had longer to work this all out than me, and you're the smart one. It's you who should be doing the thinking, not me, I don't know what I'm doing.'

Leah comes over to him and crouches down in front of him.

'Linden,' she says, seriously. 'Say it. I'm not going to laugh at you.'

Linden gazes at her for a minute then he takes a deep breath and says.

'I'm just thinking . . . Operation Gold Medal. Who gets gold medals?'

'Athletes? Champions? Winners?' Leah stares at Linden and he thinks he can almost hear her brain whirring around as she tries to catch his train of thought . . . Maybe he is crazy . . . Then she whispers another word: 'Victors.'

Leah stares at him. 'What does Victor do for a living?'

'I told you – well I kind of told you,' Linden says. 'Pharmaceuticals – but not the good sort. Drugs, any drugs. And car theft for pocket money.'

She stares at him.

'It might be that it's a coincidence,' Linden warns. 'Maybe it's just random, like you said. Maybe the name's got nothing to do with Victor.'

'Maybe,' she says. 'But say Operation Gold Medal *was* Operation Victor. Dad could've been working undercover with Victor . . .'

For a moment they are both silent.

'Even if it's true,' Leah says, 'it still doesn't explain why Victor murdered my mother.'

'No,' Linden agrees.

'I want to know, though,' she says. 'I've got to know.'

'So we ask your father,' he suggests. Linden doesn't want to see the man again, no way, but he wants the answers for Leah.

'I told you, he's gone. He left me a note.' She pulls a

folded piece of paper out of the pocket of her jeans and passes it to Linden. He takes it, but before he looks at it, he says, 'What's the matter?'

'Read it,' she says, 'you'll see.'

'Okay,' Linden says, but still he glances at her face, worried, before he unfolds the piece of paper and starts to read. The words are scrawled in biro.

> Sorry, Leah love, I've got to get out of here. A reporter, Stella Crosby, has blown my cover and there's all sorts out to get me. Every lowlife I've ever been in contact with now knows I'm a cop. It's not safe for me to stay. There's cash, you know where. They may come looking for you too, but I know you can look after yourself. Whatever you do, stay away from Linden James. I told you I've warned him off but he'll be back. Scum like him don't give up. Don't come looking for me.

Linden shakes his head.

He raises his eyes to Leah but he doesn't know what to say. *Sorry, Leah, but your dad's a total jerk.*

She reaches out and takes the piece of paper from his hand. She folds it again and then she tears it slowly into tiny pieces that flutter to the floor.

Linden looks away.

'You know why I'm doing this, right?' Leah asks.

'Your dad says maybe you're in danger but he's going to run in the other direction. He's saving his own skin.'

'Yes,' Leah echoes, as though she's glad to have it put into words. 'He's saving his own skin.'

'He's running away from you too,' Linden says.

Leah blinks. 'What do you mean?' she says.

Linden shrugs. 'Don't come looking for me, that's what he says. He doesn't want you with him, doesn't want to have to answer your questions.

Leah stands staring at the floor but Linden's pretty sure that she's not noticing the floor, or the scraps of paper scattered there, or anything else that's in front of her eyes. Her mind is somewhere else.

'Oh, he's going to answer my questions,' she says. Her voice is so calm but so steeled and unyielding that what Linden remembers is her kick in the gym. 'I think I know where he is and I'm going to find him.'

Linden stares at her.

'I know what you're going to say,' she says. 'That we shouldn't follow him, that he's trouble. But if we're right about Victor he'll hunt me down wherever I am – and look what happened to Cheever. My dad's the only one who can tell me what's going on. You can get me a car, right?'

Her tone of voice is not one you want to say no to and Linden doesn't want to disappoint her. Not now. Not when she's still talking to him after he's messed up so badly. He wants to please her. And he can see the logic but he wants her to calm down. She's beginning to scare him. She doesn't understand what she's saying. He doesn't answer for a long time, let's a silence open up.

Eventually he says, 'I'm not going to steal us a car. I'm not going back to Feltham. Not even for you.'

She makes an exasperated sound, and starts to say, 'But—'

'You've got money, right? Your dad said he was leaving you money.'

She nods.

'So we catch a bus.'

'We catch a bus?' She can't believe her ears. 'But my dad said you—'

'I know. I *did* do all that stuff. But I'm not doing it now. We're catching a bus.'

It's funny. Linden never thought that deciding to catch a bus would feel like a big thing in his life, but it is. Like he never thought a job in a shoe repair shop would be a big deal. Or wanting a girl. One particular girl. But all these things make him feel like something's changed.

CHARLIE

33

'How much further it is? Are we nearly there?

Victor glances across at Charlie. The boy is looking green again. He had no idea kids puked so much.

'Do you have to keep asking that?' he says, with irritation.

'Yes,' Charlie says, 'I do. I feel ill, I want to stop.'

'Can't stop yet,' Victor says. 'Keep your eyes on the horizon, or close them or something, suck a sweet. Just keep your mouth shut so that nothing comes out. And I mean nothing.'

Charlie is silent. When Victor glances across at him again, he sees that he's crying silently, eyes screwed up, face contorted, fat tears rolling down his sallow cheeks.

'For Christ's sake!' Victor shouts at him. 'What's wrong with you?'

Charlie takes a huge breath, and howls, 'I want to go home.'

Victor opens his mouth to yell back, then shuts it again. Getting the stupid kid even more upset isn't going to help with his plan. He needs to keep his cool.

Up ahead, there's a sign for a service station and, when they reach it, Victor turns off into the car park and pulls into a parking space. Charlie is still crying, head curled into his arms. But when he feels the car stop he opens his eyes and looks around them.

'Sorry, kid,' Victor says. 'I'm a bit stressed. Why don't you go and throw up in the toilets here and get yourself something to eat.'

He reaches into his pocket, pulls out the handgun and places it on the dashboard, then pulls out some crumpled notes and hands them to Charlie. He picks up the gun and puts it back in his pocket.

Charlie stares at him.

'Okay,' Charlie says. Quickly, he turns and opens the passenger door and gets out. Turning, he realises Victor has got out the other side and his face falls.

'I can go on my own,' he says.

'No you can't,' Victor says. 'All sorts use these service stations, I'm going to keep an eye on you.'

Charlie walks towards the service station. He can feel Victor, two paces behind him. He looks at the people walking in and out of the glass doors. What would they do if he, Charlie, started to scream that he was being kidnapped? What would Victor do? Would he grab Charlie and bundle him back into the car, or would he just run, on his own, leaving Charlie? That's such an attractive thought that Charlie gets ready to scream. Then Victor calls his name and Charlie turns around to see Victor pat the pocket where the gun is. He only has to look at Victor's face to see it's meant as a warning. *Step out of line, and you're dead.* And anyone who comes to Charlie's aid? Dead too. He doesn't actually know if the gun's got any bullets in it but he can't take the risk.

Inside the service station, Charlie is surrounded by people but he feels more alone than ever. He follows the signs to the toilets but once he's there in a cubicle he can't do anything, everything just keeps on boiling up inside him. He doesn't know why he's so ill. He's hardly eaten, so it can't be food poisoning. He's just been drinking and smoking. Victor gave him something else to smoke this morning, said it would cure his hangover, but it just made him more scared than he's ever been in his life. Victor's waiting outside the cubicle, so he hasn't got long. Charlie thinks Victor would have come into the cubicle with him if he could.

He sits there on the toilet seat and thinks about his options. If only someone would spot the gun and call the police, or if someone would realise that Charlie was being held against his will. He thinks about making notes and scattering them around him. *Iv bin kidnapt, sayv me!* But he hasn't got a pen and paper, and anyway, Victor would see him throwing confetti everywhere and they'd be gone in the blink of an eye, and Charlie's body would be found in a ditch.

'Hey,' Victor bangs on the door. 'Charlie! You still in there?'

'Yeah,' Charlie says, trying not to cry. 'I'll be just a minute.'

Eventually, there's nothing to do but to leave the cubicle. Victor's waiting outside.

'Wash your hands,' he barks, so Charlie washes his one good hand, although he hasn't used them for much.

'Are you feeling better?' Victor asks.

Charlie shakes his head. He doesn't see any point in pretending.

'For Christ's sake,' Victor says. 'All you had to do was take a shit.'

Charlie notices that there's a man waiting for a toilet with two young sons, and that the man is watching Charlie closely, with a worried look on his face.

Charlie allows himself to start crying again. Surely Victor can't shoot him for crying. And maybe it will make someone think.

'You all right, kid?' the man says to him.

'Get lost, pervert, or I'll call the police,' Victor snarls.

The word pervert acts like a magic spell and the man turns quickly away, shepherding his boys out of the toilets, never looking back.

Victor puts his hand firmly on Charlie's shoulder and pushes until Charlie walks, like a robot, out of the toilets and back out into the mall. People are looking at them, knowing something isn't quite right. But they don't approach, they turn away, as if they don't want to get involved. They must be able to see from his eyes that he's been crying. How many of them are noticing the bandage on his hand and wondering what's wrong with him? Christmas music swirls around them. *Jingle Bells, Jingle Bells, Jingle all the way . . .*

Charlie sees the entrance to a newsagent's and says, 'I want to buy some sweets. You said I could buy what I wanted.'

Victor hesitates, then jerks his head as if to say, *Hurry up and get this over with.*

Charlie spots CCTV cameras on the ceiling.

If he steals something, they'll have to come after him, and then the police will ask him questions. They'll find out he doesn't want to be with Victor, that he wants to go home . . .

Victor has stepped a few paces away from him. He's looking at the newspaper headlines.

Charlie reaches out for a packet of Haribo. He doesn't do it quickly and cleverly, like he would normally. He does it like it's the first time he's ever shoplifted. He picks them up and he drops them on the floor and he picks them up again and then he shoves them in his pocket, with the top of the packet sticking out so it's obvious.

'Hey!' One of the shop assistants is approaching him. 'I saw you put that in your pocket.'

Victor swings around quickly. He's back at Charlie's side in an instant.

'Charlie!' he roars. 'What have I told you about nicking stuff?'

He snatches the bag from Charlie's pocket and thrusts it at the shop assistant, who looks uncertainly from Charlie to Victor.

'Are you his dad?' he asks.

He's too young, Charlie thinks. He's not sure what to do. If only it was an older store manager, a no-nonsense man fed up to the back teeth with shoplifters. But instead he's not much older than Charlie, easy for Victor to intimidate.

'I am,' Victor says, 'and I can only apologise – he's got a very low IQ, almost zero. He's seeing a shrink about his stealing. We'll be on our way.'

'I should call the police,' the shop assistant says, and Charlie tries to plead with his eyes: *Yes, call the police. Please call the police.*

'Nah, you don't need to do that,' Victor says. 'Give the kid a break. We sorted it out, that's all over and done with, yeah?' He reaches out and shakes the young shop assistant by the hand, squeezing so tight that Charlie sees the young man wince. Then he grins. 'I'm going to get this young scallywag out of your way.'

Victor puts his hand in the middle of Charlie's back and pushes him out the shop. As they pass the newspapers, Charlie catches sight of his own picture and he realises that he's the news now. Him running away is news. How can that be? He's no one. He thinks maybe some of those people who seemed to take notice of him inside the service station might have seen his face in the newspaper. Maybe the man in the toilet, who asked if he was all right, had seen his face and half recognised him. Well, it's too late now.

Outside, Victor takes Charlie's arm and drags him back to the car.

'My picture was in the newspapers,' Charlie manages to say, as Victor hauls him across the car park. 'Why was my picture in the newspapers?'

'Why do you think?' Victor hisses as he pulls open the car door and shoves Charlie back inside the car. 'You're on the run, the police think you killed your dad. There's a price on your head now.'

Once they're both sitting in the car, Victor yells, 'What did you think you were doing?

'Nothing,' Charlie says.

'Yeah and I'm Father Christmas, am I?'

Charlie starts to cry again.

Victor lets him sob for a while and then he says, 'Charlie,

come on man, grow up will you? What you've got to remember is that we're on the same side.'

He pulls the gun out of his pocket and puts it on Charlie's lap.

Charlie recoils. He stares down at it, snot hanging from his nose, the heavy black metal of the gun lying on his denim jeans. There is a raised star set in a circle on the handle. Charlie's lips move as they spell out the words engraved on it. *Made in Russia.*

'It's a Baikal,' Victor says proudly, 'modified to take nine millimetre bullets. See the big trigger guard? That's so Russian troops could use it with their gloves on. Useful in this chilly weather, eh, Charlie? Don't even need to take your gloves off.'

Charlie prods the gun with his finger, both fascinated and repelled.

'See? See how much I trust you?' Victor says. 'You look so cool like that.'

Suddenly, he has his phone in his hand and he's taking a picture. He shows it to Charlie, but Charlie doesn't even recognise the scared boy whose large eyes stare down at the thing in his lap.

'See?' he says, 'you look like a natural.'

Charlie looks desperately at Victor. 'Take it off me!' he says.

'Come on, think about that gun,' Victor says. 'Who would you shoot with that gun if you had a chance?'

He picks up the gun and places it in Charlie's right hand, squeezing his own hand over Charlie's so he can't let go and let the gun fall.

'See how good it feels? I bet you feel like a man now.'

Charlie's lip wobbles.

'See this on the side? That's the safety catch, got to remember to release that before you shoot. And this, at the end of the barrel, that's your sight. That's what you line up with your target.'

Charlie thinks the gun feels like it's killed people before. It feels cold and hard.

'Who would you shoot?' Victor asks again.

Charlie's eyes look wildly around the car and Victor laughs.

'You'd shoot me, would you? I don't think so. I'm on your side. I tell you who I'd shoot. I'd shoot that girl, Leah. Or I'd shoot her dad, because I reckon he's the one killed your dad.'

Charlie gulps.

'Wouldn't you like to avenge your dad?'

Charlie nods. He doesn't know if he really would, but he doesn't want to upset Victor any more.

Victor squeezes Charlie's finger on the trigger of the gun. There's a tiny click and Charlie jumps as though it was a cannon.

'Aww,' says Victor. 'No bullets!'

He opens the glove compartment again and reaches inside. When his hand emerges, it's holding something tight. He opens his fist to show Charlie.

Half a dozen dull metal bullets lie in his palm.

'We'll have to do better next time.'

LINDEN

34

Linden and Leah sit side by side on the coach as it makes its way along the frozen roads towards the north. He's holding one of her hands between his.

Leah turns to Linden and says, 'Tell me about getting arrested and Feltham and everything. Tell me everything.'

Linden got the window seat, and he's looking out at the fields and the cows, and he's thinking that what he'd really like to do is to close his eyes and sleep with her hand in his hands. It's warm on the coach and all the warmer for seeing the frost and the ice outside. His bruises still ache from her father's beating. He turns towards her, though, and he starts to talk, because he should have said it all long ago.

'I was thirteen.' He stops, not knowing how to go on. He tries again. 'I was thirteen and I was going to school, except, not as much as I should have been.' He stops again, clears his throat, and has another go. 'I was thirteen and instead of going to school, I was mostly doing jobs for Victor.'

'What kind of jobs?' She keeps her voice low, like he does. Neither of them wants to be overheard. He turns his head so his mouth is close to her ear. He likes the smell of her hair but he's trying to concentrate on what he's saying.

'Depends what was going on. Victor would do a deal, like the negotiations, and I'd be the one doing the trade. I'd take the money, I'd hand over the stuff.'

'Stuff?' she asks.

'Weed, crack, MDA.'

'So he negotiated and you took the risk?'

Linden thinks about it. Leah says it straight out, but even now, even when he thinks Victor's capable of much worse, it hurts every time he thinks his brother might have betrayed him.

'I was younger,' he explains. 'It made sense because if I got caught I wouldn't do so long inside.'

'He said that? Victor told you that?'

Linden sighs.

'I'm not stupid. I just thought the reason was, like, logical, good sense. Whatever Victor said was okay by me. He's my brother. He raised me, took care of me, I knew he would protect me . . .'

Linden's voice trails off. Leah shakes her head angrily, and after a moment Linden carries on talking.

'He taught me house-breaking, too. That's what we did together. It was like our – our game . . . Victor taught me to break in and go straight for the car keys. People always keep them in a bowl on the kitchen counter or on a rack in the hall or in a coat pocket, or somewhere just as obvious. I was really good at it. And so I'd get the keys and I'd drive the car away.'

'And I suppose Victor just planned it all? That's it? You were the one to get your hands dirty every time?'

Linden nods. He feels like a fool but there's nothing new about that.

'Then, one day Victor says he's sorted a big deal. A crack house we're going to supply, it's going to mean big money. So him and Tony and Sameer – those are his mates, he called them his "business partners" – they're all going in together, and he asks me to drive.'

'You were thirteen,' Leah reminds him.

'Yeah . . . Victor had taught me how to drive, and—'

'Why didn't you say no?'

Linden sighs heavily. 'You don't say no to Victor – I didn't even think about doing that . . . I'm not really thinking, you know? It's not like I'm taking my own decisions, he's brought me up, he's fed me, and I do what he says. Anyway, I'm just pretending it's not happening, like it's still just a game between me and Victor. He brings home this car – an SUV, not like a rust bucket or a bling thing, like a family car, so no one will think about it when they see it – I don't know where Victor got it. Anyway, I get in the car and I drive where he tells me to go. Victor's next to me and the rest of them are in the back, all laughing and joking.'

As Linden tells Leah how it unfolded, he's living it again in his head . . .

'Take it away, bro,' his brother says, grinning at him. 'It's good to have you at my side. This is going to be big for us.'

Linden turns the key in the engine, puts the car in gear and pulls away. He makes his mind go blank. He follows Victor's instructions, driving through the darkened streets. He doesn't even know where they are, this isn't somewhere he's familiar with. They drive south, he knows that much, deep into the suburbs. And when Victor tells him to stop, it's outside a house that goes with this car – Victor has planned it all. No police officer would look twice at this family car parked outside this family house. It looks like if you open the door to the house then children will come pouring out, jumping and running. But if you look closely, there are blinds over every window, nowhere to peek in.

Linden's skin crawls. He's only been inside a couple of crack dens and they're hell on earth. Men and woman, strung out, not fit for anything, the smell of bodies and unwashed hair, and sweat. People sitting talking with foul breath about nothing but crack, like crack's the only thing in the world and wondering when it's going to walk through the door and throw itself into their hands. Nothing like a home, nothing like this house looks like it should be. He's glad not to be going in.

Victor's antsy now, his knee jiggling up and down, and talking fast and low to the boys in the back.

'Only way out's through the front door,' he tells them. 'Back door's welded shut and so's the windows. So we go straight in and straight out, all through the front door. Sameer, you take the stuff, I'll deal with the cash. Tony, you're there as eyes. Anything you don't like the look of, you give me a prod like this . . . He reaches back and digs Tony in the ribs and Tony squeals. 'That way we all get out. Remember, through the front door. Linden, no need to say it, don't bugger off for a McDonald's, just sit tight, right?'

That last bit almost makes Linden laugh and he grins at his big brother.

The three from the back scramble out the car and Linden watches as they approach the house across the gravel. Sameer's carrying a back pack. When they get to the door, it opens almost immediately, as though someone's been watching, which of course they have, and they vanish inside quickly. After that, Linden waits. He doesn't like the waiting. It's only been a few seconds when he starts to get anxious. His heart is pounding and he's sweating like a pig. He's tapping the steering wheel but it doesn't make the waiting go faster, it just makes it noisier.

Then there's a tapping on the passenger door and he's turning to see what the hell is going on, and there's a man in all sorts of protective gear, and Linden's heart lurches to his stomach. After that, everything moves so fast, Linden can't keep up.

There's a crashing noise and when Linden twists back towards his door, it's shattering, and a gloved hand is reaching inside and unlocking the door, and the door is opening, and Linden's grabbed and pulled down on to the gravel outside.

Face down, spitting gravel out of his mouth, he twists his head so that he can see the front door of the house, where police are breaking the door down and shattering the window and climbing through. He's never seen anything like it. Never in all his years with Victor. It's like a military assault. Body armour and everything, like riot police.

There's shouting, screaming even, from inside the house, and then the police bring them out, the crackheads – but no dealers. No Victor, no Tony, no Sameer.

'So what happened to them? Where were they?' Leah wants to know.

'Victor said there was no way out,' Linden says. 'He said everything was welded shut except the front door – but it wasn't true. There was a back door – they used that, got over the wall at the back.'

'They got away.'

'Yeah,' Linden agrees. 'They got away.'

'Did you tell the police?'

Linden remembers how that conversation went.

'You were the driver?' the officer asks.

'I was drivin' a car,' Linden agrees, 'but I wasn't committing a crime. Not myself. Not personally.'

'You were transporting drugs in that vehicle,' the officer says.

'Not me personally.' Linden says what Victor's coached him to say, in case this day ever came. 'Some people I didn't know, I gave them a lift. The gear was theirs. I didn't even know they had it. I mean I'm hearing about that from you, I didn't know.'

'Why did you lie for them? They left you to take the blame and you didn't do anything, not really,' Leah pushes him.

'Didn't seem any point to have all of us in jail. I kept saying I didn't know who I was driving for and in the end they chucked me into Feltham and gave up.'

Leah doesn't say anything, she turns her head away from him and looks out the window at the landscape on the other side of the bus. Linden turns back to his window. He thought he'd feel better now he's told her but it feels worse. It feels like he's taken all the bad stuff from inside him and put it on her too. Somewhere along the line, her hand has slipped from his and he doesn't dare touch her again because she feels so separate from him. Maybe now she's heard all the things he did, she doesn't want to be with him any more. It's a lot for someone to think about – crack houses, stealing cars, Feltham . . . everything. He glances across at her but she's looking straight ahead, down the aisle of the coach. She's got her eyes on the road in front. It's like she's not thinking about him at all. The worst of it is he still didn't tell her the thing he suspects. Doesn't want to say it even to himself.

The thing is – he's starting to wonder whether Victor set him up that night and the thought is killing him.

CHARLIE

35

The storm terrifies Charlie. As if he were not sufficiently alone, sufficiently terrorised by Victor, the storm – with its noise and thunder and its crashing – fills his head with fear. He curls into the passenger seat, trying not to look outside at the lightning and the thrashing, furious rain. He holds his left hand, bloated and boiling, against his belly.

Curled on his seat, Charlie is almost beyond thought. All he knows is that since running away to join Victor, disaster has come upon him and catastrophe. His past, his pre-Victor life, is like a distant memory that haunts him, but wisps of knowledge reach his chemically-soaked, starved brain. He knew, then, who he was. He knew, or half knew, what he was doing. Now he has dissolved. He's hungry and tired and his blood runs with alcohol that Victor keeps giving him instead of food. He is terrified with drugs that Victor says will make him feel better but only do the opposite. He's had nightmares like horror films, dreams in which he's pulled the trigger . . . He can't remember when he wasn't in this car.

'You're scared,' Victor observes. 'How did I tell you to stop being scared?'

Charlie shakes his head, which is buried in his arms.

'The gun,' Victor intones. 'Nobody can do anything to you if you've got a gun in your hand. Come on, take it out, hold it in your hand, it will make you feel better.'

But Charlie doesn't move.

'Okay,' Victor says, 'have it your way.'

'Where are we going?' Charlie asks in a small voice. All these miles and miles of driving and this is the first time he's asked. The storm makes him desperate to be inside, not out in a car on the open road. Surely they have to arrive somewhere. Surely things will be better when they arrive.

'Where do you *think* we're going?' Victor asks, as if the boy's stupid.

But Charlie shakes his head.

'We've got the gun, Charlie, we're going after the girl and her dad. I thought that was obvious. I thought you were up for it.'

'But where are they?' Charlie asks, and for a moment he feels as though he's found about a teaspoonful of courage. 'How do you know where they are?'

'How do I know? I know because Martens is the worst undercover cop in the world, he's always running back to the same place any time he's in trouble. He's got no imagination. He thinks it's a secret, but I *know* all his secrets. I know where to find him and I know how to finish him, eh?'

Victor pats the glove compartment where the gun and the bullets are stored.

'It's quite a big responsibility, shooting a police officer,' Victor says seriously. 'But I think you can do it, Charlie.'

'Why do you hate him?' Charlie asks, because in his

strangely dislocated mental state he has seen with sudden clarity that Victor is always telling him why he, Charlie, should hate Leah Martens and her father. But why should Victor hate them? Why does Victor know everything about Martens? Charlie struggles through his clogged-up brain to remember how he met Victor, and when he thinks of the dark figure in the garden opposite his dad's house on the night his dad was killed, and how he trusted him and followed him, he wants to cry and scream to the heavens about the terrible mistake he has made.

'Martens is nothing to me,' says Victor, but Charlie knows, quite suddenly and certainly, that Victor is lying.

'Why do you hate him?' Charlie manages to say agian.

There's a long silence. Charlie's lost all sense of time. The silence might have lasted twenty seconds or twenty minutes. At last, Victor says quietly, 'I hate anyone who crosses me. You remember that, Charlie.'

But Charlie is lapsing once more into starved, exhausted lassitude. Victor's talk of hatred is like a mantra that sounds constantly in his head. Dimly, Charlie is aware that he hates Victor, hates this drive from which there's no escape, hates the gun. But all the hating melts and moulds itself into one giant, formless hate. The girl – because it's like Victor keeps saying so he can hear it chanted in his head – all of this began with her . . . All of this began with her . . . All of this began . . . Charlie resists taking the gun out of the glove department, resists weighing it in his hand. Because he is afraid that when he does he will need to pull the trigger.

LINDEN

36

The day ends ridiculously early. It's three-thirty when the sky begins to darken and it gets cold inside the coach. They're arriving on the edge of Morecambe and Leah's reading road signs anxiously. The wind is getting up, tossing the trees at the side of the road. Inside the coach they can feel the wind catching at the vehicle, pushing it.

'What are we going to do?' Linden says. Later, when he thinks back, it seems funny that he looked to Leah to make the decisions that night. He doesn't want to suggest anything, like getting a room in a hotel, because he doesn't know how much money there is. He's not sure of her mood, either, after he told her all about his past. He's not sure if she wants any more to do with him. If he suggests getting a room it might not go down too well.

'I don't know how to get to my dad's place in the dark,' she says. 'We'll go tomorrow. We'll find a place to sleep. We'll be fine.'

'Yeah,' he agrees, 'We'll be fine.' But inside he's thinking, *We'll freeze to death. They're going to find our frozen corpses in the morning, all rigor mortis and staring eyes.*

When the coach stops, they wait in the cold wind while

all the other passengers collect their luggage and hurry off home.

Leah says, 'I want to show you something.'

They follow the signs to the waterfront. It's deserted because of the storm. Waves are crashing against the shore and the sky is as inky black as the sea.

They stop by the sea wall and they're buffeted by the salty, freezing wind.

'I've never seen the sea before!' Linden has to yell over the wind.

'We used to come here for a week every year. My nan lived here and my dad's got a place he keeps. He says being here is like going back to the womb.'

A bloody vicious womb, with quicksand and killer tides . . . Linden thinks, but he keeps it to himself.

They stand there silent for a minute, frozen rain biting into their faces and soaking their clothes.

'What do you think?' Leah shouts.

Linden shakes his head. 'I don't like it,' he yells. 'It's too . . . too big!'

He sees her smile at that but he's not joking and her smiling irritates him. This isn't funny and he needs her to know that. He shouts over the wind.

'Someone like me . . . if I end up swimming out there,' he nods towards the horizon, where the angry sea meets the dark sky. 'I don't know which way's up and which way's down. I don't know how to make it to land. I'm lost. I sink. Do you get it? I drown. That's me. You swim, I drown.'

He can feel tears spring from his eyes and run together with the rain on his face. He's glad it's raining so she can't see how weak he is.

Leah grabs his frozen hand in hers. She pulls his face down towards hers and kisses him, his eyes and his mouth, and he kisses her back, and they stand there with their backs turned against the elements and their bodies pressed up against each other.

They find a fast-food restaurant to get out of the cold for a bit. They're the only customers and they eat burgers as their clothes soak the plastic chairs.

'Tell me more about your dad,' Linden says.

'You know enough about him already,' she replies. 'You've got the bruises to prove it.'

He shakes his head. 'Everyone loves their dad. You must have something good to say about him.'

She doesn't answer for a long time, just concentrates on eating. Then she says, 'He tries to be a good dad, he's nice to me when he's around. But what Stella Crosby wrote, about him being an undercover policeman? It makes sense. He disappears for days on end, sometimes weeks. And when he comes back, he's not himself, it's like he's someone else. Like he's that minute come off a stage and he's stuck in character. Every time he goes away a little piece of him gets left behind and now it's like I don't know him. He's a stranger. He's always thinking about himself and his job, not about me.'

'When he goes away, who looks after you?'

'No one. I don't need anyone. He taught me how to cook for myself, how to lock the door a million times, how to be safe. It was Dad who signed me up for martial arts training. He said if ever anyone threatened me, I should run as fast as I could. Run and scream, get attention. You can't compete with a gun or a knife, he says, no matter how good you are. But if anyone ever grabbed me, then the martial arts mean I would at least know how to fight.' She shrugs. 'So I learned how to fight.'

She stops talking for a while, and then she says, 'When I'm older, it's not what I want for my family. It's going to be different. No secrets. No lies.'

'Yeah, but it's not that easy, is it?' Linden says. 'You can't choose your family, you've just got them how they are.'

'Parents choose each other,' she replies. 'They get to start again. If they had hopeless parents, they can be better for their kids. You'd think they'd get it right second time round. You'd think the world would be getting better bit by bit, everyone learning from their own parents' mistakes – but it doesn't work like that. It's like everyone always experiments with their kids and when they get it wrong they shrug and forget about it.'

She turns to look at Linden and her eyes are angry and disappointed.

'I never expected nothing,' he says. 'I never thought things would get better. You get what you get. The way it seems to me, best time is when you're a kid. You're happy, you can mess around playing all day. And everyone thinks you're cute, and then as you get older and you understand what's going on, well, you just know it's not going to end well.'

There's a long silence and then Leah starts to laugh.

'What?' Linden says, grinning although he doesn't know what he's grinning at. 'What's so funny?'

'Us, we're so funny. Like we're so worldly wise.' She imitates his voice. 'You just know it's not going to end well.'

He stops smiling. 'You think it's funny but it's not,' he

says. 'When I got out of Feltham I tried to get a job. Victor wanted me to go back to all the things I used to do for him, the stealing and the driving, and I didn't want to do any of it. I was thinking I could do something better, make something of my life. But no one wanted to give me a job once they knew about my past. The only thing I could get was in a shoe repair kiosk in the arcade and even they got shot of me as soon as they could. So I know you say people should think about their life, and it will change, but thinking's not enough. Even if you really want it, you don't always get it. You're stuck with what you got given. And I got given Victor. So . . . well . . . I'm stuck with him.'

The mention of Victor makes them fall silent again and the piped music leeches into the vacuum. But they're both thinking about him.

After a few minutes, Linden reaches out and gently touches Leah's scar.

'If my brother did this to you,' he says quietly, 'that means he killed your mum and another woman, and I'm guessing he killed Cheever too, since stabbing seems to be his thing.'

Leah nods slowly, her eyes on his.

'So he did all that and I'm his brother. I've got his genes, you know? I know I said I'm not my brother. But we've got the same mum and dad. Whatever badness is in him, it must be in me too.' He hesitates, because he doesn't want to say it, but he has to say it. 'You shouldn't be anywhere near me. I'm no good.'

Leah looks at him.

'My dad attacked you, he could've killed you,' she says.

'And I've got his genes, but I could never do what he did. Genes are bullshit.'

Linden nods. He's grateful for what she said but he's still afraid she'll decide he's no good. Because even if her dad's bad, Leah hasn't done anything bad herself. She's done the right things, made the right decisions. Unlike him. If she decides she doesn't want anything to do with him after all this, he won't blame her. He'll blame himself. No point in blaming his genes, she's right about that. He'll blame the choices that he's made.

Outside again, in the howling gale, they look at each other, screwing up their faces against the rain, which hurls itself into their eyes and mouths. A night on the street is not an option. The bus station offers no shelter and, even if Leah's money would stretch to a hotel, they can't see one.

Linden looks up and down the street, looks for a parked car as far as possible from a CCTV camera.

'Come on,' he says. 'Let's get a room. I'm not stealing, but we'll do a bit of borrowing for a few hours.'

He picks the lock of the Nissan, glad of the dark to hide his shame, and they clamber into the small dry space. They sleep, uncomfortably crushed in each other's arms, wet clothing steaming into damp air, flesh rammed against plastic and steel, rain hammering on the roof.

Before dawn, they wake up and let themselves out of the car, stepping on to a street that glistens with the night's rain as the first glimmer of daylight cuts through the dark.

CHARLIE

37

The rain becomes so heavy that they can see through the windscreen only in between the gusts of wind that hurl rain against the glass. The wind is so powerful that it seems to threaten to whisk the car off into hyperspace.

'Look,' Victor says, 'I saw the sea.'

Charlie, who's never seen the sea, raises an eye from the safety of his arms.

The windows are streaming with rain and at first he can't see it at all. When at last he does catch sight of the white-tipped waves, he sinks back in horror. The sea looks like a black hole you would get sucked into. The raging waves would swallow you up and smash your bones into smithereens.

Victor is pulling the car off the road and he brings the car to a stop. Charlie can see blurry lights through the water, but he can't make out what anything means. His brain is becoming used, now, to this state of incomprehension where the world blurs around him and fails to make sense. If he's aware of anything, he's aware of the hot pain in his hand. It's getting worse, making his whole arm hurt.

'Come on,' Victor says, and Charlie realises that Victor is gathering things together – the gun, his jacket – and opening the door on his side, getting ready to step out into the rain. Charlie doesn't want to get out the car, doesn't want to step out into the raging weather. Why is the world so furious?

He whimpers.

'Oh, for Christ's sake, grow up,' Victor says. 'We're here.'

'Here' turns out to be a pub, with rooms above. Shown upstairs, Charlie blinks in the light, his eyes taking in two single beds, a sink in the corner of the room, peeling wallpaper, a patch of damp on the ceiling. After hours in the car it looks like a palace. He doesn't care what Victor does. Charlie lies straight down on a bed without taking his shoes off, and closes his eyes, and is asleep.

In the middle of the night, Charlie is awoken by a noise. The moment that he's conscious, he knows he mustn't move and that he mustn't show that he's awake. He's gone to sleep on his side, curled in a ball, and he opens his eyes just enough to see. The overhead light in the room has been turned off, but Victor hasn't closed the curtains, so there's light pouring into the room from a streetlamp outside. Charlie can see Victor, sitting on the bed opposite. He's stripped down to his boxers and a T shirt. He's holding the gun and his head is bent over it. Charlie sees him remove the magazine, take a handful of bullets from a pile that lies on the bed, and insert them, one by one, before sliding the magazine back into the gun. Charlie sees Victor raise the gun and then he does something which makes a loud clicking noise, and Charlie understands that this somehow makes the gun ready to fire.

Victor raises the gun, pointing it at Charlie's forehead.

Charlie closes his eyes tight.

He waits, hearing only the beat of his heart.

After what seems like forever, he hears movement again, a sound as though something is being placed on the bedside table, the rustle of the bed, and the creak of the springs.

Charlie opens his eyes and stares across at the opposite bed.

Victor is lying with his back to him, his body rising and falling as he breathes. Charlie thinks he is probably asleep.

Charlie can see the gun on the bedside table.

He imagines himself sitting up, getting out of his bed, going to the table and picking up the gun. He imagines himself putting the barrel of the gun up close to Victor's head, and pulling the trigger. He imagines blowing Victor's brains out.

But he feels sick at the thought. Sick and weak. What if Victor is not asleep? What if he is lying there with his eyes wide open, waiting for Charlie to do just what he has imagined? What if he is waiting to turn the gun on Charlie? Is this a test?

Charlie closes his eyes but he does not sleep.

He dreads the dawn and he is terrified of what it will bring.

LINDEN

38

Leah has never approached her father's place from the centre of town before, and their entire morning is spent on false starts. Still damp and cold from the storm the night before, they walk and bus their way around the bay, buying a sandwich for lunch when they get hungry. After thirty minutes walking down a street that Leah declares to be the right street, only to find that it is entirely the wrong street, Linden begins to lose his cool.

'I thought you came here all the time when you were small and you don't know, like, the name of the street? "On the bay" isn't really an address, is it?'

To illustrate his point, he jerks his head towards the bay. He's never seen anything like it before. With the tide way, way out, the flat sand lies gleaming for miles. Now that the rain has stopped lashing down, he's never seen anything as beautiful. Never seen anything as empty or as natural, without a manmade object sticking out of it. He wishes he could think, *Well, this is a lovely holiday, out here in the country-side, let's sit on the grass and look at the sky.* But he can't. All he can think about is the menace of the quicksand and the killer tide, and Victor. Because Linden fears, wherever he is, Victor will not be far behind.

Leah, fraught and embarrassed, glares into the distance. She frowns.

She turns to him.

'I think I can see it,' she says, her voice full of relief.

And the miracle is that she can.

It's a mobile home, in the middle of a field. Linden hadn't expected something that looks like a big caravan, he'd thought it would be a quaint cottage, or a little bungalow. Not so strange, then, that Leah doesn't know a street address, she just knows what the field looks like. It slopes down steeply, a gravel path leading to the edge of the bay. Beyond that is sand, for miles. More sand than you see on a travel agent's brochure. More sand, Linden thinks, than in Hawaii and Barbados all put together. Not that he's ever been to either but he's seen the pictures. They approach the door and Linden gets ready to leg it. He's still bruised from his beating at the hands of Leah's dad. He's trusting that Martens isn't going to dismember him in front of his daughter but you can never be sure.

Leah's hammering on the door and calling out to let him know it's her.

So when Martens opens the door and sees Linden there, he swears, and yells at Leah, 'What in Christ's name is he doing here?'

He steps out of the caravan, swinging his fists, ready to lay into Linden again, but Leah blocks him, catching his arm and pinning it down so he can't move. Linden enjoys the look on Martens's face. He can see the man thinking he should never have sent his daughter to martial arts classes. Linden would have liked to see Leah deck her dad with a quick jab, but instead, when her dad stops yelling, she says, 'Linden says his brother's going to try to kill me.'

A strange change comes across Leah's dad's face. Not surprise, just resignation. It's almost like he knew Victor would come, or feared it.

Martens shakes his arm free from his daughter's grasp, and turns without a word, disappearing into the mobile home. He leaves the door wide open so that they can follow him inside.

Leah's dad is sitting, hunched up, on a small sofa, his head in his hands.

Leah sits next to him and pulls his hands away from his head, so that he's forced to raise his head and look at her. 'What's going on, Dad?'

He shakes his head and looks away.

'Linden says his brother wants to kill me,' Leah says again. 'You've got to talk to me.'

Martens starts to sob and Leah looks in desperation at Linden.

'I've never seen him like this,' she murmurs.

Linden watches, not knowing what to do. After a few minutes of the sobbing he decides he's got to put an end to it, because crying never got anyone anywhere. Outside, the sky is already darkening. Black clouds are rolling in, and in any case they've wasted so much of the day getting lost that it won't be long before the sun sets.

He crouches down in front of Leah's father so he's looking into his face.

'Mr Martens, you've got to pull yourself together,' he says. 'If we could find you, so can Victor – and I don't think he's fussy whether he kills you or Leah. If you tell us what's going on, maybe we can stop him.'

Suddenly Leah's dad kicks out at Linden, his foot making contact with Linden's knee and Linden is thrown off balance, staggering backwards.

'What's the matter with you?' Linden shouts, scrabbling to his feet. 'Your daughter needs you and all you can do is cry and kick people? Come on, Leah, let's get out of here.'

Leah glances at Linden, then looks back at her father.

'He's right, you know?' she says angrily to her dad. 'You always said you should have protected Mum. You always said you should have saved her. Well now I know it's all talk. You're nothing but a coward.'

Martens roars and lunges at Linden, who grabs Leah by the wrist and pulls her out through the door, back the way they came.

They're halfway across the field when they hear footsteps behind them. Linden spins around with his fists raised, expecting Martens to start hitting him again. But Leah's father is standing there with slumped shoulders and head bowed.

'I'll tell you what you need to know,' he says miserably. 'Just give me a minute. It's not something I'm proud of.'

Leah glances at Linden and he shrugs – this is her decision, not his. A moment later the three of them are making their way back across the field towards the caravan.

Inside, Leah moves towards the sink and kettle to make a cup of tea. She runs the water, puts the teabags in the mugs. All the while she's watching out the window, making sure they're still on their own.

When he's got his cup of tea, Martens begins to talk.

'You'll have read Stella Crosby's story by now,' he says, his voice low. Leah nods. 'So you know that I was working undercover when you were attacked in the park, she got that right.' He looks quickly up at Leah. 'From the day you were born, and long before, I was working undercover. I loved it. It was everything to me. I loved your mum and you but having a family was a problem for me. I didn't want to spend my time with you – it wasn't me. It felt like time wasted: baby-sitting, changing nappies, bath time – it wasn't enough for me. Your mother understood and she looked after you. She woke up in the night and fed you, and she changed you, and she played with you. I was hardly ever home. I would go undercover for days and sometimes weeks on end and your mother wouldn't know where I was. Look – I don't want to have to tell you this, but I have to, because it's part of what came next and there's no point in me lying to you about how it was.'

Linden's watching Leah's face. She looks so pale.

'The job – it was like acting. Like getting in character. If they didn't wash, I didn't wash. They didn't shave, I didn't shave. They smoked and drank, I smoked and drank. When I did come back home, your mother hardly knew me . . . Most of the jobs were quick, in and out. Get accepted, gather some information, get right out again. Sit back and wait for the arrests. Most of the time, the people I was involved with didn't know I had anything to do with it. And even when they did, they wouldn't have recognised me if they passed me in the street. You know what, Leah? Your mum and you did pass me one day in the street and you didn't know me. Your mum hardly even looked in my direction. That was the day I realised I was in too far.'

'What was Operation Gold Medal?' Linden asks. He wants to hurry things up here, wants to put Leah out of her suffering. He thinks Martens is a jerk. Even if he didn't like his baby daughter much, what's the point in telling her that? It's rubbing salt in the wound.

'You give gold medals to winners—' but Martens is cut off by Leah.

'Victors,' she says. 'Linden worked it out.'

Martens glances at Linden, but he's beyond caring. 'It was all about your brother,' he confirms, talking to Linden. 'We didn't think it would be because he was so young. So it started out as Operation Magpie. Then, when we realised the whole thing was masterminded by Victor, we changed the name.'

Linden nods. He's glad to get it right, but the more he hears, the more he realises that his worst fears are about to be confirmed. He would have preferred it if Martens had never heard of Victor, if the whole Operation Gold Medal thing turned out to be a misunderstanding.

'We thought cracking Victor would be easy because he was young, not much older than you are now. He looked like nothing, like an amateur, a kid, but once I got close to him I could see he wasn't any of those. He knew exactly what he was doing and probably had since the day he was born. He kept very few people close and he always had a plan. There was us thinking he'd had a streak of good luck – but, once I was in, I could see it wasn't good luck, it was good planning. I realised quickly that I was in trouble. As soon as Victor took me under his wing, he wanted total devotion. But he was smart too. There I was, getting in close to get a hold of information, but he kept everything to himself, so I wasn't getting anything. Which meant I couldn't get in and get out, I was stuck there, week after week. I couldn't work out what the problem was, whether he didn't trust me, or whether he was paranoid about trusting anyone. To be honest, I was scared. He'd get me involved in his dealing activities but always in a way that left him deniability.'

'Why didn't you walk away?' Leah says.

Linden's dad shrugs.

'A job's a job, you don't get to pick and choose when you leave. Besides, I was fascinated by him. I'd never met anyone like him. I wanted his scalp. You're only ever as good as your last job. And I needed to be the best.'

'What happened?' Linden's frustrated by all the talk of the past. Outside the window, anything could happen – right here and now. He doesn't like it when he can't see Victor, when he doesn't know where he is. Times like that, Victor can be right behind you. He thinks of how Victor sent him into the empty house to look for Sameer. That was Victor's idea of a joke, hiding in the shadows, behind Linden all the time. He remembers how Victor slammed him up against the wall. He feels like that now, as though any minute now he's going to find out that this whole thing, this whole journey with Leah, was Victor's plan, not his, and Victor's going to grab him and slam him against the wall.

Martens is shaking his head, like he's changed his mind, he doesn't want to talk about it any more.

'Come on.' Linden says it like an order, never mind that this man is Leah's dad or a policeman, right now he just wants answers and quickly.

'He found out I was a police officer,' Martens says.

'How?'

Martens shrugs. 'Must've been a tip-off from someone inside the operation.'

Linden frowns at Martens. He doesn't think Martens is telling the truth.

'You did something to piss him off,' he says.

Martens shakes his head, but Linden knows he's on to something.

'You did, didn't you?' he says. 'You did something. What did you do?'

Martens looks down at the floor.

'Tell me,' Leah pleads. 'You owe it to me. He's after me, because of you.'

'Really, I owe it to you?' Her dad laughs bitterly. 'This is a debt you don't want paid.'

He shakes his head again, then takes a deep breath.

'I panicked,' he says. 'I wasn't getting any information from him and I knew I was going to be pulled out or reassigned. The job before Operation Gold Medal didn't go so well either, so my reputation was in the can. I thought I might be out of a job and I blamed Victor for that, for being too bloody clever. I was in debt – having a kid is expensive, and your mother wanted everything perfect for you, she didn't understand I didn't make enough money . . . Meanwhile, Victor's raking it in, he's got money to buy whatever he wants, he's never short of anything. Victor who thought I was great, who was beginning to trust me. The problem was, a couple of the losers who worked with him were starting to look at me funny. Maybe they were jealous that Victor seemed to be trusting me more than them, or maybe they were just worried about being left out in the cold, but I thought it couldn't last. I thought they were going to find out who I was, and then I'd be finished. So I decided to cash in while I could.'

'Cash in,' Leah echoes, uncomprehending.

'You *stole* from Victor?' Linden's amazed. He can't believe anyone would think of stealing from his brother. It's suicidal.

'What did you take?' Leah's voice is cold.

'Cash,' Martens says. 'Seriously. A stack of cash. Thirty thousand pounds. I knew where he stashed cash after a big deal, in a cupboard in his flat – and I just took it, walked out with it in a Tesco's bag . . . And then I ran . . .'

'You came here,' Leah says. She knows there's only this place, nowhere else.

Martens nods.

'As soon as I'd done it, I knew it was a stupid mistake. Victor couldn't report a crime, because the cash was drug money, but he knew that I had to have taken the money. It was only a matter of time before he did some digging and found out I was police. As if stealing wasn't bad enough, I'd been fooling him, trying to get him arrested. It was obvious that he'd come after me. He thought I was his friend . . . I couldn't imagine what he'd do to me.'

Leah stares at her father.

'But he didn't go after you, did he?' she says.

He shakes his head.

'He found another way to hurt me,' he whispers.

'You left us behind.'

Martens nods.

'Did you warn my mother?'

'It would only have worried her.'

Leah can't bear to look at him. She turns away from him, closing her eyes, running her hands through her hair. A sound like a strangled cry escapes from her. Then she turns back towards him angrily.

'When did all this happen? What date did you take the cash?'

'May the twenty-sixth. Twelve years ago.'

Linden looks from Leah to her father. They're staring at each other. There's something momentous about the date, something he doesn't understand.

'May the thirtieth,' Leah says softly 'May the thirtieth, twelve years ago.'

She's staring at her father with horror in her eyes and he's started sobbing again.

'Victor couldn't find you, could he? Leah says. 'You'd done a runner, and you'd left us behind, and you hadn't even warned my mother of the danger! He came to the park looking for us because he couldn't find you. He didn't know about this place back then. What did he do? Did he follow us, planning it? He waits in the trees because he knows that's the way we go home. Only he botches it. He sees Erica Brigson from the back and thinks it's Mum. He sees me running towards her with a stuffed toy, and she's holding her arms out . . . and he grabs her from the back and kills her . . . and then he sees Mum, and he realises what he's done, and he goes after us too.'

Martens has his head bowed.

'Look at me!' Leah screams at her father, but when he looks up, she slaps him hard across the face. 'You knew

Cheever didn't do it!' she cries. 'You must have known all along that the wrong man was in prison.'

He shakes his head furiously. His face is red from the slap, his eyes are watering.

'I didn't know,' he insists. 'Not for sure. I had my suspicions but everyone thought it was Cheever and—'

'And you wanted to believe it,' Linden interrupts, 'because you felt guilty, you didn't want to think it had happened because of you. And on top of that, if you told the police what you suspected about Victor, it would all come out about you stealing from him and you'd have lost your job right away.'

Martens runs his tongue over his lips. He looks like he's aged twenty years since they arrived. He's a yellow-grey colour, like a waxwork. Grey, with an angry red patch on his cheek where Leah hit him.

'When you came back to London, did you coach me to choose Cheever from the line-up?' Leah asks, hissing. She's frowning, like she still can't process the enormity of what her father's done.

Martens blinks. He looks pleadingly at his daughter.

'I'd already been persuaded by the other police officers that it must have been Cheever. I went with you when you looked at the photos. I asked you if it was him and after a while you said it was, and I . . . I chose to believe you . . .Then afterwards, after you'd identified him, you were at home and you told me one day about how the man who'd attacked you had cut himself and his face was bleeding – and I wondered . . . I asked the arresting officer whether Cheever had a cut on his face when he was arrested and they said no. I didn't know what to do. The case against

Cheever was strong . . . It was easier – I persuaded myself you'd got it wrong. I thought . . . I thought maybe you'd been so scared that you'd imagined it . . .I don't know what I thought. But . . . I went with it. Cheever was convicted. He went down.'

Leah glances at Linden, frowning.

'So what I remembered, about him slipping and cutting himself, I must have known it at the time and then forgotten it.'

'You told me about it when you came home from the hospital,' Martens says quietly. 'I asked if you'd told the police and you said no. You were so small, you didn't realise it was important. After that, we never spoke about what had happened that day. Perhaps you forgot.'

'I forgot a lot,' Leah says. 'Or at least, I pushed it to the back of my mind. Maybe I pushed it into my dreams.'

'Did you see Victor after that?' Linden asks. He's got to know, now, no half measures – even if he doesn't want to hear the answers.

'I didn't go anywhere near Victor for years, kept well out his way and he seemed to keep out of mine . . .'

'You still had his money,' Linden says. He doesn't think his brother gives up that easily. 'And after Cheever was jailed, Victor must have thought he'd got off scot free. No one suspected him except you, and you weren't telling. So why didn't he go after you?'

Martens ducks his head as though he doesn't want to answer, but Linden waits . . . and waits . . .

'I gave the cash back to him,' Cheever mutters eventually.

'You what?' Leah asks.

Martens shakes his head.

'I didn't know if it was Cheever or Victor who killed your mum,' he says to Leah, 'but I was frightened of Victor either way. I knew I'd never feel safe with his cash in my hands. I knew you'd never be safe . . . And if anyone in the police found out my career was finished. So I got it back to him through a third party. Then he never had a reason to come after me.'

'But he has a reason to come after you now,' Leah says. 'And that reason is me. He thinks I remember him. He thinks I can put him in jail. Does he know about this place now?'

Martens sighs.

'I think maybe he's been watching me over the years,' he says. 'I think he knows where I go now.'

Linden and Leah glance at each other and their eyes go to the window, but the field outside is as empty as it was when they arrived.

Martens is still talking and they turn back to him to listen.

'One day five years ago, I was on a job and I saw him in a crack house, and I saw the scar under his eye . . . That's when I knew.'

'And you didn't kill him, did you?' Leah's voice is like ice. 'You just carried on as if nothing had happened.' Leah is trying to control herself, Linden can see that, but he doesn't know how much more she can take. Every word her father utters paints him in a worse light.

'I wanted to kill him, make no mistake,' Martens voice sounds tired now. 'But there was nothing I could do. I couldn't tell anyone why I thought he might have wanted to hurt me or my family. And I thought about you, Leah, and your safety. I thought if I went after him, either I had to put him completely out of action, which I couldn't guarantee unless I killed him, or I thought he might come after you.'

'Thank you for your concern,' Leah spits at him. 'Don't you think it was a bit late to think like that? Shouldn't you have been thinking about me from the beginning, protecting your family, not putting us in danger?'

'I should,' Martens sobs, shoulders heaving, 'I'm so sorry.'

'So you did nothing?' Linden knows he can't keep asking questions, but he really needs to know the answer to this.

'No, I did something.' Martens wipes his nose on the back of his sleeve. 'I went undercover again. I got as close as I dared, so I heard the talk about who Victor was meeting, what was being negotiated. I watched and waited until I knew a big deal was planned, and I knew when and where, and then I informed the drug squad. I thought I'd got him then, I thought he was going down for years. So there I was, waiting in the station, thinking I was going to see Victor dragged in in handcuffs, and the only one they brought in was you . . .' He nods to Linden. 'Do you remember me? I was there when they questioned you . . . you were a cocky little bastard.'

Linden doesn't say anything. He remembers. There he is, in the police station, sitting at a table in a bare room, two men opposite him, sneering at him, asking him all those questions about what was in the car and who was in the car, and everything. One of them Martens.

'Afterwards, I asked the drug squad who carried out the

raid what went wrong, why they didn't get Victor. They said it looked like your brother set you up, like your brother got wind of the raid and he thought if the drug squad got one arrest out of it they'd get off his back, so he sacrificed you. There were drugs in the car to incriminate you, and a knife, which made it worse. No sign of your brother in the house by the time they went in. None of your brothers' fingerprints anywhere, or his mates'. They went in the front door and straight out the back door, leaving you sitting out front. You knew that, right? You must have known your brother set you up.'

Linden doesn't know what to do with himself. He can feel Leah's eyes on him, full of concern. He doesn't know why he asked, why he insisted on knowing. He feels as though he's left his body, as though he's floating on the ceiling of the caravan, looking down at Leah and his dad and himself, and they all look like dead bodies, like the life's been wrung out of every one of them. There's no movement, not a breath to stir the air.

Suddenly, into the silence, comes the creak of the door.

CHARLIE

39

Charlie is dozing, lulled by the warmth of the sun through the car window. That morning, when he awoke, his terror of the night before had receded slightly, but he'd started to feel feverish, hot and cold by turns, sweating one minute and shivery the next. He hadn't mentioned it to Victor, he knew enough to know that his wellbeing was of no interest to his abductor. He'd got very little sleep after Victor pointed the gun at him. Now, in the daylight, although Victor and the gun are still close by, he relaxes enough to sleep. He opens his eyes blearily to see sand stretching for miles, and he assumes that it's a dream, or that he has died and gone to heaven, and both are fine by him, so he closes his eyes again. Dimly, he hears Victor muttering to himself: *Which way was it? Left or right here? That looks familiar.*

Now the car is pulling in on a bumpy surface and Victor kills the engine.

'Stay here,' Victor instructs, and gets out of the car.

Charlie watches him walk over to the mobile home at the edge of the field. Charlie has the sudden thought that he could run. There's nothing to stop him opening the door and sprinting across the grass and out through the gate he can see in the wing mirror. But he feels heavy, anchored by a sudden weakness that has come over him. Besides there's no one around, so if he runs Victor could easily rev up the engine and chase him down the country lanes, and he would be kidnapped again, or mown down.

He can see Victor peering in the window of the mobile home, peeking around the window frame, making sure he's not seen. Then listening at the door. Something he hears makes him smile and Charlie's heart contracts in fear.

Victor strides back across the field. He gets back in the car and says, 'We're in business, Charlie, my boy.'

'I'm not your boy,' says Charlie. He doesn't know where it's come from, this sudden rebellion. A moment ago he was asleep and now it seems he's waging war.

Victor looks surprised but he turns and grins at Charlie with a smile that does not reach his eyes. Charlie hates his good mood.

'You are, for the purposes of our little project,' Victor says.

'What project? What are you talking about?'

'We've been through this,' Victor says. 'There are two people to blame for everything that's happened to you and that's Leah Martens and probably her dad. You could say she killed your dad. Because either someone heard her accusing your dad that day, outside the courthouse, and that someone took it into their own hands to kill him because of it. Or else, it was her dad that killed your dad in revenge. I can't tell you, in all honesty, which one it is but it's the same people to blame for both.'

Charlie remembers that day in the court, seeing

Leah Martens sitting in front of him, clutching the seat with her white knuckles, and turning her face and seeing the scar, and later, screaming at his dad, blaming him even though he was innocent. Charlie is prepared to agree that he hates Leah Martens and he's never met her dad but he's prepared to believe he's as bad as his daughter. He nods. He feels so hot, and he's bathed in sweat.

'Well your girl, Leah, is in there,' Victor says, nodding towards the mobile home. 'And she's with her dad. Two birds with one stone.'

Charlie's jaw drops.

Victor reaches forward and opens up the glove compartment and pulls out the gun.

'Here's the stone.'

Charlie blinks. His progress towards catastrophe has suddenly accelerated. He was asleep, just minutes ago . . . Beyond this field he can see the stretch of blue again. Heaven seems so close at hand . . .

He shakes his head. 'No thank you,' he says.

Playfully, Victor points the gun in his direction. 'Bang bang, you're dead,' he says.

'No thank you,' Charlie says again. He can feel the sweat under his arms, drenching his clothes and dribbling down his forehead.

'No,' Victor says. 'Bang bang, you're really dead. After all I've done for you, you have to do this for me – I'm not asking you, I'm telling you. Go in there, get it over and done with. Once I've seen it's done, we'll get back in the car and I'll drive you wherever you want to go, and we'll go our separate ways.'

Charlie is gazing at him.

'It's loaded.' Victor slides out the magazine, shows him the bullets Charlie had watched him insert. 'Remember what I told you – here's your safety. Once that's off, here's the trigger, line up your sights . . .' Victor holds out the gun to Charlie, but Charlie won't take it.

'You'll never see me again,' Victor says. He leans across Charlie and opens the car door. Then he presses the gun into the palm of Charlie's right hand – and this time Charlie's hand closes around it.

Without speaking, Charlie gets out of the car into the gloomy chill of approaching night.

He starts walking across the grass, one foot in front of the other, towards the mobile home. He hardly has the strength to lift his feet. At any step, he could turn and fire the gun through the windscreen at Victor's head. The glass would shatter, like it does in films, and Victor would have a neat red hole in the middle of his forehead and his eyes would be open and staring at the sky. Charlie's imagining all this but he carries on walking. Because the moment he turns around and threatens Victor he knows he's dead. He doesn't want to look but he thinks maybe Victor's got a gun trained on him. Perhaps a huge machine gun, like an AK47 or something. Victor's not going to let a boy get the better of him. And the other problem is, the moment Charlie decides to turn around and shoot Victor in the head, he leaves Leah Martens in the mobile home, untouched. And while he doesn't really want to shoot her dead, he doesn't want her to carry on living without knowing what she did to him. He's got to tell her, at least. And maybe, with a gun in his hand, if he gets angry, he'll kill her.

He reaches the mobile home and stands at the door, waiting. At this angle, from the corner of his eye, he can see Victor gesticulating, telling him to get into the mobile home at once. Charlie lifts the gun, how he's seen police doing it on television, holding the gun high, straight-armed, looking down the barrel at the sights. His left hand is burning and swollen and red, with red streaks that run up his arm, and it hurts to lift it and hold the gun, but he tells himself this will all be over soon. He swivels around on to the steps into the mobile home and moves inside.

Inside, he blinks, trying to process what he sees in front of him. The girl is there, staring at him. He expected her and her father, but there are three of them, all turned to face him, astonished. There's the girl, Leah Martens, and there's a teenage boy, a few years older than Charlie, and there's an old man who must be about fifty.

He waves the gun from side to side, to make sure they're all covered. But he's beginning to panic. What's he supposed to do? Shoot them all? It's going to be a bloodbath.

'Who are you?' the older man says.

Charlie's surprised that the man cares who he is, when what's important is that he's got a gun in his hand. Maybe the man is used to having a gun waved at him. In which case, Charlie doesn't know what else to do to scare him.

The teenage boy is frowning. They all seem more surprised by who he is than by what he's carrying. He thinks maybe he should shoot it at something to make them realise it's real. He's not playing. This is a real gun.

He points the gun at the girl because he thinks she'll be more easily scared than the others. He holds the gun so it points at the middle of her forehead.

'Come on, lad, you don't want to be doing that,' the old man says, but Charlie can hear the fear in his voice now, and the fact that he can make a grown-up so frightened makes Charlie glow with pride.

'She deserves it,' he says.

Leah Martens isn't crying. He wishes she would cry and beg. If she doesn't beg, he'll have to shoot her, or they won't believe him.

'Lad, you'll regret this for the rest of your life,' the old man says. 'This isn't the way to solve anything.'

'Shut up!' Charlie snaps, waving the gun briefly at the old man. Charlie's feeling nervous now. He feels like the two men are crowding him, although they're still sitting where they were when he walked into the mobile home. They're not moving a muscle but they're forcing him into a corner. And the girl won't cry. She won't show any emotion. He'd thought she'd be scared but she's watching him so calmly, it's like she doesn't believe he'll do this either. He waves the gun around. His arm is getting shaky, and his fingers. His hand is sweating, losing its grip. He's afraid that he might fire the gun by mistake.

'Did Victor put you up to this?' It's the teenage boy speaking. The boy is standing up, slowly, and he's walking over so he's standing between Charlie and Leah Martens, so the gun's pointing right at him – if you can say the gun's pointing anywhere, because it's wobbling around so much. 'My name's Linden and I'm Victor's brother.'

Charlie stares at Linden.

'Victor hasn't got a brother,' Charlie says.

'Victor's a liar and a bully,' Linden says. 'I know what it's like because he bullied me into doing things I didn't want to do. He bullied me into selling drugs and stealing cars . . .'

'Really?' Charlie says, despite himself. He doesn't want to have a conversation now, just wants to do what he has to do and run. But hearing those words from someone who knows Victor, who's been through what he's been through in the last few days, makes him think he's going to burst into tears.

'I went to prison for Victor,' Linden says. 'For three years. They locked me up every day. Crap food. Crap everything.'

Charlie feels gravity weighing on his gun arm. It's so tiring, having to point a gun like this. He thinks he might pass out. His vision is growing dim. He's finding it hard even to stand upright.

'You'll go to prison too, if Victor gets his way,' Linden says softly. And while he's talking, he's reaching out. His fingers are touching the barrel of the gun. 'If you let Victor bully you into this, you're killing yourself at the same time. Same as if you put the gun to your own head.'

Charlie whimpers. His arm drops suddenly and the gun slips from Linden's fingers. The boy drops to his haunches, still holding the gun, squatting on the floor, head bent, sobbing. Linden squats down next to him. He doesn't want to grab the gun, doesn't want to cause the boy sudden alarm. He touches the boy's arm – he can feel the burning heat of it.

Linden hears a moan of fear from Leah and when he raises his head he sees another figure silhouetted against the doorway.

'Charlie,' Victor says. 'Did things not go quite to plan?

Leah, we meet again. You, Martens, you traitorous coward, long time no see.'

Victor steps into the caravan and takes another step towards the boy. But at the sound of Victor's voice, Charlie leaps to his feet and brandishes the gun and this time he points it at Victor's head.

'Hey, Charlie boy,' Victor says calmly, 'are you getting a bit hot under the collar? You've got to understand. You're such a loser. If you can't shoot them, you can't shoot me. Might as well give me the gun. Come on, give it here.'

Charlie shakes his head.

'You're a bully,' he says to Victor. 'Even your own brother says you're a bully.'

Victor glances at Linden.

'That's the kind of thanks I get, is it?' His voice rises. 'Don't pull this shit with me, kid, okay?'

Charlie wilts, visibly, and Victor walks straight up to him and removes the gun from his hand as if he's taking a lollipop from the hand of a child.

Charlie staggers backwards and falls on to a couch, where he curls into a foetal position, sobbing.

'So,' says Victor. He's not pointing the gun at anyone in particular, but he doesn't have to. He's the only one with a gun in his hand, which gives him an advantage. He sits down next to Charlie.

'You tried to get him to kill me?' Leah says angrily to Victor. 'You can't even do your own dirty work?'

Linden wishes she would shut up. He wishes she could read his mind. Wishes she would glance at his face and he could warn her. The way she is now, it reminds him of seeing her outside the court, unable to contain herself, so furious that she yelled in front of anyone who wanted to hear. It's the same now, she can't contain her anger, only this time she's not shouting at a camera lens, she's shouting at a man with a gun.

'Why do you even care?' Leah hisses at Victor. 'I couldn't have identified you to the police. It was twelve years ago. Who remembers a face that long?'

Linden, watching his brother, sees irritation and doubt cloud his face.

'Leah,' her father's saying quietly, 'be quiet. This isn't the time.'

'You said—' Victor starts to speak.

'I know who you are. But if I told the police I've got this hunch that it was your face I saw when I was four, are they going to arrest you? If I go to them and I say it must be you, because you creep me out? Even if I tell them you've got a scar under your eye? Is that a basis for an arrest? After all this time? After I accused someone else and swore blind it was him? You're such an idiot.'

Linden and Martens both grab her to try to stop her. Her dad puts his hand over her mouth, but she tears if off.

'All of this,' she screams at him, 'all of this for nothing, you idiot!'

Victor is staring at her, bemused. Linden still has his arms around her, trying to restrain her, so she doesn't throw herself at Victor and get shot. Martens has given up trying to shut her up. He stands there staring, appalled, at his daughter.

'Idiot?' Victor echoes the word as though he's never heard it before.

'And if you killed Cheever you had no reason to because

he couldn't have identified you either,' Leah shouts. 'Even if he saw you, there's no way the police would arrest you now just because of what he said. Especially with his alibi in trouble. They'd have thought he was covering his own back. And you killed him for that? Are you crazy?'

'Crazy?' Again Victor echoes the word, as though he's never heard it before.

What happens in the next few moments happens too fast for anyone to follow.

Victor raises the gun from his side and swipes it hard down the side of Leah's cheek, cutting into her flesh. Leah screams, clutching at her face, her hands instantly covered in blood.

Charlie grabs Victor's arm from behind, forcing it down.

The gun goes off and Charlie screams in agony. In the confined space, the two sounds are deafening.

Linden launches himself at his brother.

The gun goes off again and this time Martens gives a single shout of pain and falls to the floor, and Leah cries out, throwing herself down on to the floor to cradle her father.

Victor extricates himself from the scrum, holding Charlie around the neck with his left arm. Blood is pouring from the boy's knee, and he's screaming and holding his leg. Victor hits him hard and the boy's head jerks backwards and he falls to the floor.

Into the shocked silence that follows there comes an unexpected sound. A voice through a loudhailer . . .

'This is the police. We are armed. We have reason to believe Charlie Brigson is being held here against his will. Release the boy now and come out with your hands up.'

Victor strides over to the doorway and peers out around the doorframe, his gun arm held at his side. He begins to swear.

Linden glances out of the window. The light has all but gone now but he can see that there are two police cars parked alongside one another, twenty metres from the mobile home. A dozen police officers in body armour are standing watching, one of them with the loudhailer to his mouth. As Linden watches a third car arrives, struggling over the boggy ground. It parks alongside the other two cars, more men get out. In the road he can see a flashing light and as it gets closer he sees it is an ambulance.

Linden's eyes go back to Leah. She's staring blankly at her father, who lies motionless. There is no rise and fall of the chest. His eyes stare, unblinking, at the ceiling. The boy lying unconscious next to him is showing more signs of life, his diaphragm slowly rising and falling. Linden crouches down by him. He doesn't know what to do for him. He's worried that even if the boy's alive now, he soon won't be if he carries on bleeding so badly from his knee.

'Release Charlie Brigson,' the voice instructs. 'Come out with your hands up.'

Victor swears again.

'They want the kid, they can have him,' he mutters. He gestures to Linden to pick the boy up. Linden crouches down. He doesn't want to hurt the boy more but he can't see any way round it. He picks him up, one arm under his legs, one under his shoulders, and the heat of the boy's body is like a furnace. In his arms, the boy moans in pain and begins to come round, opening his eyes.

Linden steps into the doorway with Charlie in his arms.

Slowly, so as not to alarm anyone with a gun – either Victor behind him or the officers in front – he carries the boy down the two steps on to the field, where he stands, waiting under the darkening sky. Two paramedics come forward, and as Linden places the boy on the stretcher they're carrying, he mutters in a low voice, 'It's not just the gunshot wound – he's burning hot.'

He watches as they hurry to the ambulance.

'Someone else got shot,' Linden shouts to the officers, 'he needs a doctor.'

Behind him Linden hears Victor swear and call him back inside the caravan.

For a moment, Linden doesn't know what to do. He's standing there. Would Victor shoot him in the back if he walked away now? Then he thinks of Leah, bending over her father's body, dying or dead, and slowly, with his hands raised, he retreats back into the caravan.

Victor's inside the doorway and he's got Leah with him, his arm around her neck, the pistol at her temple. She doesn't seem to notice the danger she's in. Her eyes are fixed on her father lying still and staring on the floor.

'Come out with your hands in the air.' The voice comes from outside again, filling the caravan. 'We know one of you needs medical attention.'

Linden and Victor both look at Martens on the floor, clearly beyond medical attention. Victor breathes deeply.

'We're out of here,' he says. 'And there's only one way out.'

Linden shakes his head.

'No way,' he says. 'The bay's a deathtrap, no one goes

out there – Leah told me, it's lethal. There's quicksand all over and the tide comes in so fast it can drown a man.'

'It's a fucking beach,' Victor says. 'What are you, my health and safety officer?'

Linden shakes his head.

'It's quicksand,' he says. 'You want to drown in sand?'

Victor gives a bark of laughter.

'You talk like any of us have got a choice,' he says.

Into the line of fire, Linden thinks. He doesn't dare look at Leah. Slowly, so as not to alarm or surprise the officers, he steps outside, with his arms raised. He can feel Victor close behind him with Leah clasped, unprotesting, to him. If they shoot, Victor will be the last to feel it.

Linden steps out into the cold, darkening night. The rain spits at him.

Ahead of him there are ten officers he thinks he can make out, but it's hard to see in the poor light. Most of them are in full protective clothing. He can see half a dozen firearms pointed at him.

There is silence, except for the sound of breathing and footsteps on the caravan steps and then on the wet grass. A spotlight swings across the field and finds them.

The officers must be able to see Victor now and his hostage. They must be able to see the gun held at Leah's temple.

'Release the girl,' the loudhailer voice instructs. 'Release the girl. Surrender your weapon.'

Linden keeps moving, does as Victor has instructed him, edging slowly around the perimeter of the mobile home. Behind him, so close that they are almost touching,

Victor moves, with Leah. The police keep their distance, but they keep the light shining on them, and Linden is afraid that their patience will wear thin and that a bullet will fly in their direction.

When they've reached the path, they edge, sideways, towards the gap in the enclosing wall.

'Stay back. You start to follow us, she gets it in the head!' Victor yells to the police.

Linden risks a glance at Leah. Her face, blood-smeared, is paler than anything he has ever seen in the glare of spotlight. All three of them look like ghosts. He cannot read her face, cannot tell whether she is paralysed from fear, or beyond it.

The three of them edge further down the path, passing through the gap in the wall. They progress sideways, like crabs, so that Victor can make sure the path behind is clear, as well as the path ahead. As they move, the spot-light falls away from them and for a moment the darkness seems complete. The bay looms like a black hole. It is impossible to see what awaits them.

The only way that Linden knows that they have reached the shore is that the land flattens out – and then, moving tentatively forward, they reach a drop, which must, he thinks, take them straight down on to the sands.

'We can't go any further, we'll be killed,' Linden says, trying to speak to Victor in a reasonable way. Like brothers.

'That's why the sands are the only place they won't follow us,' Victor retorts.

'Because they'll die, Victor! This is crazy—' Linden begins to lose his temper, but Victor cuts him off.

'You think I care?' Victor explodes. 'I'm finished –

there's a man dead back there. They've got the boy, they know that I took him. It's over for me.'

'Vic—' Linden begins to speak, to plead, to beg, but Victor takes the gun from Leah's head for an instant and fires it into the sky.

'Next time it's her!' he yells at Linden. 'Now move!'

Linden thinks if he runs now, he might be able to make it. Visibility is down to almost nothing. Even if Victor shoots at him as he runs, he's likely to miss.

'You run, she gets it,' Victor reminds him, still able to read his baby brother's mind.

The clouds part above their heads and, in sudden moonlight, Linden can see Leah's face, lifted by Victor's arm, which is wedged under her chin. She's having difficulty breathing. Her jagged scar, the bloody cut, are stark and vicious.

Her eyes seek his face.

Linden clambers down on to the sand. His feet land on what feels like solid ground. Like a beach with the tide out. He reaches up to help Leah down, and as she descends, her body presses against his and he draws comfort from it. They can scarcely see Victor above them, are only aware that the gun is somewhere, pointing down at them, or away from them, it makes no difference at this moment. There is nowhere to run to, even if Leah were in a fit state to try. A moment later, Victor's down next to them and grabs Leah again, forces the gun once more against her head, stamps his feet, tentatively, on the sand, then laughs in a forced way.

'Lin, lead the way,' he orders his brother.

Linden inches across the sand. The temptation, where the sand is firm, is to assume the sand will be firm ahead, that the quicksand is the exception, not the rule. That way is death. He knows that. But it's a struggle not to run – to get this over with. Behind him he can hear Victor's breathing and Leah's. He slows down. What does it matter if they take forever? Linden's left foot disappears from under him . . . He twists away, returning his weight to his right foot, which is on solid ground. The quicksand releases his left foot with a loud belch.

He stands still, breathing heavily. They're finished. There's nothing to guide him. He could be in the middle of a universe. He could be in the middle of a sea, or a vacuum. He can hear himself breathing . . . He can hear Victor and Leah breathing . . . He can hear the sand breathing underneath him and the land breathing around him. He has lived contained in a cell, desperate for open air and wide spaces and now he will die out here, no wall in sight. No bars. Nothing in sight. He wishes he could feel better that he is to die so close to the world, but all of this feels terrible.

He takes another step. The ground underneath him rocks slightly but it allows him to stand. Behind him, the fall of their feet on sand echo his. He takes another step.

Suddenly, there's a beating, pounding noise that grows louder. Linden raises his head. Above them in the dark skies is a light that dips and rises, curving towards them. Beneath it is a ray of light that races across the ground. Linden sees sand banks and creeping water. Now the searchlight sweeps towards them. He turns to find Leah and Victor right behind him, their faces raised towards the helicopter. For the first time since her father was shot,

Leah looks alive, as though her eyes are watching, and her ears are listening.

The wind from the rotors reaches them, stirring the cold air violently. Another voice through a loudhailer: 'Clear the sands. The tide is coming in. You'll drown if you stay where you are.'

Linden and Leah look at each other, eyes wide, illuminated in the searchlight. The pistol Victor's holding to Leah's head is illuminated too.

'Surrender your weapon and we'll lower a rope for you.'

Victor starts to yell, his words eaten up by the chop of the blades.

'Go on,' he yells at Linden, waving him forward. 'Move.'

'Give up,' Linden yells at his brother, 'or you'll kill us all.'

From the corner of his eye, Linden sees Leah adjust her stance and then, from nowhere, and with speed and power that astounds him, she kicks back with her foot, hard, to make contact with Victor's kneecap. At the same moment, she twists away from him and jabs her elbow into his chest. Victor fires the gun wildly, the report echoing sharply over the bay as the helicopter swings away, and Linden sees Leah fall. Above them, the helicopter is hovering close by, the light still on them. Linden cries out, but Victor is coming for him. To defend himself, Linden punches him, catching him under the chin. Victor staggers, Linden grabs the gun from his fist and flings it away from him, far across the sand.

Victor lunges after the gun, but he has taken no more than five or six steps when his legs plunge into the sand. He screams.

'Don't struggle,' the loudhailer voice instructs from above them in the sky. 'If you struggle, you'll sink.'

Linden sees his brother stretching out his arms to him, begging for help.

Linden turns, desperately, looking for Leah. She's scrambling to her feet and shouting, 'Leave him, Linden! It'll get you too!'

Slowly, carefully, Linden turns back to Victor and moves towards him. When he's close, Linden lowers himself on to his stomach on the sand. He grabs his brother's flailing hands, but at once he knows he's done the wrong thing – Victor is pulling him in,

'Stop moving,' Linden yells at him. 'Be still, or you won't get out.'

But Victor can't or won't stay still. His feet are cycling in the liquid sand and his hands tug at Linden. Linden stares into his brother's eyes and what he sees there frightens him as much as the knowledge that he will drown in sand . . .

'Lean into the sand.' The voice comes from above. 'Don't struggle! Stay still, it's the only way to get you out.'

'Stay still, Victor!' Linden screams at his older brother, and for the first time Victor stops thrashing his legs around and instead leans forward, on to his stomach, so that he is almost swimming on the sand. Linden pulls, digging his feet into the sand behind him and, inching backwards, pulling his brother forward on his stomach.

Victor's legs come free with a great groan, as though the sand has spat him out. He lies for a moment on the sand, exhausted, next to his brother. Then he staggers to his sodden, sand-drenched feet. He doesn't look back. He starts to run across the bay, his feet splashing heavily through the water-slipped sand.

'Come back!' Linden yells, but his voice is drowned out by the voice from the helicopter.

'Stay where you are!' The voice through the loudhailer orders. 'Stay where you are! You are in danger!'

The helicopter hovers, then it dips in the sky and speeds off in the wake of Victor, and as its light picks out the landscape of the bay, they can see a dark looming line approaching.

'The tide is coming in!' the voice booms, warning them. 'Clear the sands!'

CHARLIE

40

Charlie is lying in bed. He's immobilised by the dressing on his knee, but he couldn't care less. At last he feels safe. His auntie has been fussing over him no end. She arrived in the hospital with a face he'd never seen before, so frightened and worked up. He liked the fact that she was worried about him. It sounded like she'd gone crazy when she found him gone, harassing the police until they found him.

Turned out that he'd been recognised by the shop assistant in the service station where he did the fake shoplifting. The assistant had realised that Charlie was the same boy as the picture on the front of the newspapers on the shelf in front of him, and he'd run out into the car park to see what car they'd got into, and he'd taken down the number plate and rung the police. Charlie liked the fact that Victor had got that wrong. Victor had thought the shop assistant was nothing but he'd turned out to be brilliant.

When the ambulance took him to hospital, they discovered that not only was his kneecap smashed by Victor's bullet, but that his hand had got so infected that the poison had passed into the blood and he'd nearly died from that.

Since Charlie had got home, his auntie had fixed up his bedroom like a hotel suite. She'd moved the TV up to his room, and she kept climbing the stairs with good things for him to eat, like hot buttered toast and tomato soup from a tin. He existed, at first, in a haze of painkillers and warmth and again he had that strange feeling that he'd had in the car when he glimpsed the sands – that he might have died and gone to heaven. He never wanted to see the sand or the sea again. He hoped heaven was nowhere near the sea. This room at home was a much better heaven.

His auntie knew it all. She'd been there all the time the police officers had come and sat by his bed in the hospital and asked him question after question. The only thing he hadn't said was about the burning T-shirt at Leah's house. And he hadn't said it because he couldn't bear his auntie to hear it. But everything else – the running away, and the gun, and the threatening, he told them everything.

One day – he'd lost count how many days he'd been home – his auntie came in and perched on the side of his bed.

'You're feeling better, aren't you?' she said. 'I can see it in the colour of your cheeks.'

Charlie reluctantly agreed that he was. He was afraid that his recovery would open a new and disappointing chapter, which might involve getting out of bed, and going to school, and being required to do the washing up.

'Lots of people came round while you were gone,' she said. 'They were very good to me, they came to show moral support and tell me they were thinking of me and of you.'

'That's nice,' said Charlie.

'Some of your teachers came round.'

'Why did they do that?' Charlie said, appalled that people like that had been inside his house.

'They came to comfort me,' his auntie said, 'to say they were worried too.'

Charlie didn't say anything. He thought they must have been lying but he couldn't work out why they would bother.

'They told me that sometimes when they speak to me on the phone, I speak in an Irish accent,' she said, and raised her eyebrows at Charlie.

'Do you now?' he said, playing for time, but he could hear the Irish creeping into his voice even as he said it.

'No,' she said, 'I don't, do I?'

'No,' he said. 'You don't. I guess sometimes I do, though.'

'But why?' his auntie said. 'Why would you stop me talking to your teachers?'

'Why do you think?' said Charlie. 'They think I'm rubbish.'

'No one thinks you're rubbish, Charlie,' his auntie said. 'Your teachers have said that they think you need help with your reading and writing, that's all.'

'I'm stupid,' he said. 'I can't help it.'

'But Charlie,' his auntie wails, 'your teachers can help you. I spoke to Mrs Tepnall, they've got strategies and things to help with dyslexia. I can help you. Why are you stopping us?'

'They all want to tell me off,' said Charlie, 'and they want to laugh at me. Everyone knows everything goes wrong for me and now they'll laugh more than ever. I'm jinxed.'

'Charlie,' his auntie said, with tears running down her face, 'Charlie, how can you say that? It's not very nice to me who spends time and money looking after you.'

'You've got no choice, you had to take me in,' Charlie said. 'It wasn't because you wanted me.'

She cried more then and shook her head, and cried some more, and Charlie hoped this would soon be over.

'Charlie,' she said at last, heaving a shuddering sigh, 'I'm sorry. When you came to me, you were a tiny thing and I didn't know you were taking everything in. My husband had walked out on me and then my beautiful Erica was killed, and I got her little boy to look after. But I was so young and I had to work so hard to look after you and I had no experience, and I was so sad about all the things that had happened to me. And you were so angry with me that I wasn't your mother, so I stopped trying. I thought that cooking for you and making sure you were safe was enough. But if you don't think I love you now, then you are blind.'

Charlie stared at the duvet. He let himself be hugged.

'I should have kept a closer eye, like your mother would,' his auntie's mouth was close to his ear, 'and I should have seen through your tricks.'

Charlie shook his head. His own eyes had filled with tears and he was desperate to change the subject.

'No one can see through my tricks,' he said. 'You shouldn't beat yourself up.'

She looked at him and smiled in a weepy kind of way.

'All right,' she said, 'I won't beat myself up. But I'm putting the TV back downstairs tomorrow and you and I are going to start reading some books.'

'All right,' said Charlie, and he watched her go with a heavy heart. Just when he'd thought life was on the up.

That night, before he went to sleep, he thought about his half-brother who he'd glimpsed through the open door of his dad's home, the half-brother who looked like him and like his dad. Charlie thought it might be interesting to meet him one day.

But not just yet.

LINDEN

41

Linden knows this probably isn't going to work. He wants it too badly. He still thinks this could be his flow. And if not this, then what? But if there's one thing he knows, it's that life doesn't go according to plan. Too many people lose their flow, or never find it in the first place. A month ago he was standing in the middle of a bay, surrounded by quicksand and threatened by a racing tide that took his brother's life, sending him twisting and turning in the water, beating the air out of his lungs, struggling against his fate for the last time. So he feels as though he knows now about life and death. He knows that death, when it's the death of your brother, hurts even when your brother hurt you. As for life, it seems to him that life is made up of flow and love. Flow is about feeling at home, and feeling like you've found the place that you can work and be yourself, wherever this life takes you. And love is like that too, but it's a person, and also it makes you go weak at the knees. If he can't have love, then maybe at least he can have the flow. If he works at the shoe repair shop he knows it will never make him feel weak at the knees, but he will learn to live without that.

'Hey, Marky,' he says.

Marky looks up from the shoe he's reheeling, and turns and greets Linden.

'Hey,' he says. 'How's things? I heard about . . . I'm sorry, man. I didn't know all that stuff was going on with you.'

Linden shakes his head. He doesn't know what to say to anyone about Victor.

'Yeah,' he says, 'thanks.'

He hesitates. Marky's clearly embarrassed that Linden's there but Linden can't help that. That's Marky's problem, not his. You can't go through life not saying what you want to say because it's embarrassing.

'Marky,' Linden says, 'do you think there's any chance they'd take me back here?'

Marky scrunches up his face like he doesn't want to have this conversation.

'I don't know, man,' he says, but he's shaking his head while he's saying it.

He looks up and nods a greeting at someone behind Linden, and when Linden looks around he sees it's the manager who hired him. The same one who fired him.

'Hello,' Linden says, holding out his hand. At first the man looks at him like he doesn't remember him, and then he remembers, and then he looks embarrassed too and he shakes Linden's hand, but reluctantly.

'I came to ask if you might take me back,' Linden says. If he can stand in the middle of a quicksand and not sink, then he can do this.

'I don't know,' the manager says, and he's shaking his head too, like he does know and the answer's no.

'I really liked working here, sir,' Linden says. 'I know

you've heard a lot about my life and all the things I did wrong, and what a mess my life was, but if I didn't want to change I wouldn't come back here like this and humiliate myself.'

The boss looks at him. He doesn't say anything but Linden has the impression that he's listening, so he carries on talking.

'I like it here,' Linden goes on. He doesn't know where this verbal diarrhoea has come from. He wishes he could shut his mouth, but he can't. 'I like the arcade. I like seeing all the people, and the kids and the mothers with their pushchairs, and the old people. I like helping them with their shoes, and their heels and their laces and stuff. I just want to earn some money from doing something honest. I don't mind studying. It's no problem for me. I learned a lot about cashflow and that from my brother . . .'

Linden stops short. He's said too much. Way too much.

He shakes his head. He feels tears in his eyes again. Why would a shoe repair shop make him cry so much? Even people dying doesn't make him cry as much as this.

He turns away.

'Linden,' the manager says, and Linden turns around. 'We'll think about it. Seriously. We should probably do things properly, have a word with your social worker, and see your release papers from Feltham.'

Linden nods, but he's not getting excited. It sounds like a lot of paperwork. Like lots of pitfalls. And then he remembers.

'About the release papers,' he says. 'They gave me a recommendation for breaking up a fight. The week before I left. A group of them set into a young kid, and they wanted me to join in, and I got them off him. That's good, right?'

'That's good,' the boss says, and this time he looks less embarrassed, more interested in the proposal that Linden is putting to him. 'That should help. Linden, I've read the newspapers, I know you've been having a tough time. We'll see what we can do.'

Linden nods and thanks the manager. He knows this is all he will get for the moment. He doesn't want to hang around, best to leave while things are looking good. So he leaves his phone number again just to make sure, although they think they have it from last time, and then he checks to see the boss has entered it into his phone correctly. Then Linden says goodbye and he goes on his way. He's hoping hard. He thinks Marky and the boss could probably see how hard he was hoping.

His feet take him through the arcade. It's closing time, with staff chatting about their evening plans, and relieved to be going home, and pulling down the shutters and locking the doors. There's only three days to Christmas, and it's been a long day in retail. Linden can see Christmas spirit all around him but he can't really feel it. He hasn't got a single person to buy a Christmas present for. He walks out the door at the far end and into the alley where the plaque is on the wall for The Empire, and he pushes the door open and he runs up the stairs. On the second floor, Linden stops at the glass door to the gym and scans the room. Inside, Chris is there with a handful of people. With Christmas around the corner, only the most dedicated are there.

Leah's not one of them.

Linden pushes open the door and goes in. He pulls off his sweater so he's in a T-shirt and sweatpants, and he pulls off his shoes and socks so he's in bare feet. As the class gathers in front of Chris, Linden joins them. He doesn't really hear what Chris says – something about Christmas, and getting arses up off couches – all he can think about is Leah. Like a machine, hardly even hearing the instructions, he moves with the flow of the class, stretching and touching toes, and pushing up from the floor. Soon there is only the sound of bare feet on rubber mats and of breathing.

It was all they were aware of then . . .

in the middle of nothing, even over the roar of the helicopter as it chased Victor across the bay until he met the incoming tide and was lost. Just their breathing, and the soft belching of the sand around them as it readied itself to swallow them up, and the approaching hiss of the tide.

Leah tugged at his hand.

'We have to try,' she said.

They had lost all sense of direction, all sense of which way to go towards the land, which way to death. He let Leah choose the direction.

They ran, then, across the sand, away from the hiss of the tide, with the fear of death at every footstep, hand grasping hand, their feet touching the ground as lightly and as fast as it was possible to touch, almost like flying . . .

The door to the gym swings open. Linden's head snaps towards it. It's her. It's Leah. His heart fills and twists. She doesn't look at anyone. She walks in with the same confident stride, but her scarred face is swollen still, and bruised. Chris greets her, carefully not making a big deal of it, and she nods in his direction and retreats to a corner of the room to pull off her outer clothes. Everyone's eyes are on her. Some people wave or smile in greeting, and she acknowledges every one of them with a nod of the head and a small tight smile. When she turns, her eyes meet Linden's for an instant before she turns her back on him and sits and starts to stretch. She doesn't try to catch up with the class. She stands and stretches, sits and stretches, part of the class and yet apart from them – apart from him . . .

When they reached the shore, it seemed they had achieved the impossible, as though it was a mistake. They scrabbled their way up the earth onto the land, panting and disbelieving. They stood and shivered, looking out over the dark bay, hearing more than seeing as the tide hissed its way in relentlessly. So close behind them, it must have kissed their heels. Within minutes, they were surrounded. Police first, then paramedics, bundling them into an ambulance, racing them into the town. They sat, wrapped in blankets, staring at each other, unable to speak. At the hospital they had been separated. Questioned by the police, separately. Linden, questioned aggressively, suspected of working with Victor, knew his life was in the hands of Leah, and that when he was released it was because of the good things she had said about him.

Released to nothing – no brother to return to, not even the body of a brother to bury, lost forever in the rush of sea . . . No job . . .

He sought out the uncle he had stayed with and was turned away . . . He slept on Sameer's floor . . . He learned from the police that Leah's father died there on the caravan floor, with Victor's bullet inside him. Leah didn't return his calls. An anonymous, recorded operator reported that her number no longer existed.

The class has moved on and Linden moves on with it. Leah still sits apart, stretching, warming up. They put on their pads, get ready to spar. They watch the instructor – kick, jab, jab, kick . . . Linden loses sight of Leah as they all pair up and start sparring. Linden kicks and jabs but his heart isn't in it. He raises his gloves to protect his face but he hardly cares if someone knocks him out. What does it matter? Conscious or unconscious, without Leah it's the same thing. She's the only one who makes him feel like he's living a life. Partners are switched, the routine changes. He thinks that she's left. Maybe her courage has failed her . . . He can't blame her. Bravery has its limits. Even Leah's. Once scarred, swearing she'll never be afraid again, and then made afraid again, not once but twice, both times at the hands of his brother. Hands that share his flesh and blood.

Then she's there, in front of him. He blinks, thinking he's hallucinating the scars and the bruising. His eyes meet hers and she doesn't disappear. For a moment they stare at each other.

'I'm sorry about your dad,' he mumbles.

She thinks for what seems like an age.

'I'm sorry about your brother,' she says.

He nods.

'Genes are bullshit,' he says.

Softly, with her gloved hand, she swats him across the face. She smiles. He's not imagining it. She could have left. She could have partnered someone else but she's choosing him. His eyes fill with tears. He grins, to cover his emotion.

'Don't be scared,' she says, and smiles. 'I'll be gentle with you.'

They're like vultures, sitting on a branch, watching me with their beady eyes . . .